SHATTERED GLASS

MICHAELLA DIETER

SHATTERED GLASS

Copyright © 2022 by Michaella Dieter

All Rights Reserved.

First published in 2022 in the UK by Michaella Dieter.

ISBN: 9798355629830

No part of this publication may be reproduced, circulated, stored in a retrieval system or transmitted, in any form or in any means - by electronic, mechanical, photocopying, recording or otherwise - without prior written permission by the author, except for brief quotes used in a review.

This book is a work of fiction. Names and characters are the product of the author's imagination and any resemblance to any actual person, living or dead, is unintentional and entirely coincidental. Locations or products mentioned are either fictional, or used in a fictitious manner and the author fully respects the copyrights of said products.

This book is only available on Amazon. If you are reading it elsewhere, it is a stolen copy, and the author has not received payment. Please do not support piracy, only purchase legal copies.

Cover & Interior Design: Jay Aheer at Simply Defined Art

Proofreading: Dee's Notes: Proofreading Services

Editing: Michaella Dieter

Formatting: Michaella Dieter

Also by Michaella Dieter

DARK ROMANCE

Upon Blooded Lips
Retribution
Vengeance Mine

FAIRY-TALE RETELLINGS

Shattered Glass

HOLIDAY-THEMED NOVELS

When Snowflakes Fall

Author's Note

Shattered Glass is a paranormal fantasy fairy-tale retelling, featuring Snow White. It is written in the style of a fairy tale, and takes place in a fictional world. It is set in the equivalent of our Middle Ages (approximately the fifteenth century). Any intimate scenes between the main couple are 18+ and consensual. Although a fairy tale, it is not intended for under 18s, due to adult themes.

Some of the characters within were inspired from different fairy tales, stories, myths, and legends from around the world. From Greece to Ghana, Egypt to Scandinavia, (and, of course, from the marvelous Grimm Brothers themselves) ... I've hopefully managed to bring them to life to add richness to the story. Although I've done my best to keep these legendary figures as close to their origin stories as possible, some creative license has been used.

Darkness levels and triggering content is personal to each reader. Although I wouldn't class Shattered Glass as overly dark, it does contain some very dark themes which some readers may find upsetting. I have listed the main culprits below, but please be warned that this list is not conclusive.

Child abuse (all forms)
Mental health
Imprisonment
Forced miscarriage
Graphic murder, torture, and sex scenes
Poisoning
Revenge
Mind control / loss of free will
Non-consent (villain related)
Incest (villain related)
Cannibalism (villain)
Human sacrifice (villain)

Reaveton Continent

- The Oracle
- Forbidden Isles
- Black Valley
- Kingdom of Lokoma
- Morningstar Empire
- Caledonian Territory
- Dun Plains

To all those that still believe in magic.

Once upon a time, in the kingdom of Valderán, there lived King Silas and his queen, Elspeth. The kingdom was known throughout the lands for its lush valleys, jagged mountain peaks, and bountiful harvests of apples so delicious, they were described as having come from the gods themselves.

The king and queen were happy, their people content. They agreed amongst themselves, as they wandered the markets or enjoyed ale in the pubs, that they were lucky indeed; neighboring kingdoms did not fare so well as Valderán and were not ruled by such gracious and kind monarchs.

As the years passed, the prosperity continued, and talk began to turn of an heir for the king and queen. Whispers started to circulate that perhaps the queen was barren, for surely there would have been a child by now? Queen Elspeth, upon hearing the rumors, descended into a deep depression. The once bright airiness of her chambers became dark, the thick curtains drawn tight against the sun, the air stifling and stale as she sobbed to herself. The king, despairing for both the future of his kingdom and his wife, sent out his great hunters to roam the lands, searching for someone who could help them. Surely a powerful sorceress, or the Fae perhaps, could help his wife conceive

His love for her was all-consuming, and he missed her friendship, affection, and passion.

A month went by, then two, the queen's life force withering away from lack of nourishment. She would not eat, nor even leave her rooms, her anguish so great. Finally, the men returned with a beautiful woman riding in front of Alaric, the lead huntsman. The king, upon hearing the guards' shouts and the horses' mighty neighs as they galloped into the courtyard, hurried to throw the doors open and welcome them back.

King Silas was at once struck by the beauty of the woman his men had returned with, and she blushed prettily as she sank to her knees in a graceful curtsey. Descending the stairs in a hurry, he thrust out a hand, helping her to her feet. She introduced herself as Morana, a healer from a small family at the base of Clawback Mountain in the north, just south of the border of the kingdom of Granton. As the king led her into the castle, she explained she had an extra gift given to her by a distant Fae relation—a small amount of magic, just a smidgeon really—that allowed her to aid women like the queen, who found themselves desperately wanting a child but unable to conceive.

The king rejoiced upon hearing this and ushered her to the queen's chambers. Just in time too, for the queen lay on her bed, her breaths slow as the fight within her waned. Morana gasped at the sight, a tear falling gently down her downy cheek, and the king was moved at the evidence of her kind heart.

Morana rushed forward, withdrawing an apple from her skirt pocket. The king had never seen its kind; the deep red of a ruby, with flecks of pure gold decorating the peel. Morana dropped to her knees beside the bed and gently raised the queen's head, begging her to take a bite. She whispered promises of health and an heir, and a bit of life returned to Elspeth's eyes. Leaning forward, she took a bite, her hand shaking as she reached for it. One bite followed another until it was gone—seeds, core, and all.

Smiling brightly, Morana stood and threw back the curtains. The king and queen flinched against the golden glow of the sun flooding the room. Flurries of dust motes danced around the room before scattering when Morana tossed open the windows, allowing an autumn breeze to sweep through, carrying away the despair and heartbreak.

When the king turned back to his wife, he gasped with joy. Her hair, before greasy and tangled, now shone like ebony. Her ice-blue eyes, once devoid of life, now sparkled with hope. Her lips, downturned and pale, now smiled happily, their rosy hue returned. He rushed to her side and kissed her hand, his happiness at her miraculous recovery clear for all to see. Once he could tear himself from her side, he thanked Morana profusely, pressing a heavy bag of gold coins into her hands. As he led her to the courtyard, she stopped him, placing a hand on his arm. He shuddered when his eyes met hers; for a moment, he swore he could see something else looking back at him from within them. Just as quickly as it was there it was gone, replaced by the beauty standing beside him.

Alaric helped her into a carriage that had been prepared for her, and as it started away, the king caught a whispered phrase rising upon the wind. "Remember, Your Majesty, all magic comes with a price. A life for a life." But then he heard the queen call to him, and the strange words fled his mind, just as they were intended to do. It would be seven years before he remembered the saying of them.

And that is where our story begins . . .

Chapter 1

Morana

Dawn breaks, thin tendrils of oranges and golds painting the sky in a stunning mural. Birdsong erupts as the small creatures awaken, heading out to break their fast. Pulling my arms above my head, I stretch out my back, groaning as the chilly air in the room breaches the warmth of my blankets.

I'm about to close my eyes again when I remember the date. November first. The corner of my mouth ticks up as I throw the blankets off and ring the bell for a maid. November first. The last seven years have dragged past, taxing my patience dearly. But it is finally here, and my breath catches in my throat at the joy that bursts through my veins. Excitement is fast on its heels, and I leap from the bed in a rush. There is much to be done today, and no time to waste.

The heavy oak door to my room squeaks on its hinges, and Marison, my maid, pokes her head through, eyes downcast. The little fool is terrified of me—as she should be—but I don't have time to pander to her today. "Get in here, girl," I growl, and she scurries in, hands clasped tightly in front of her. "I will wear the purple gown today and the black overdress. Lay them out for me, and get my breakfast. And get someone up to fill my bath and stoke the fire. It's as cold as a witch's tit in here."

Marison executes a hastily sloppy curtsey, utters a "Yes, mistress," and then scampers into the adjoining room to find the clothes I demanded. An hour later finds me bathed, appropriately dressed, and fed. Catching sight of myself in the mirror, I quickly smooth back my waist-length brown hair. Jade-green eyes surrounded by thick lashes peer back at me, and I straighten my shoulders. Perfect, as usual.

Ensuring the maids have left, I pull a heavy key from its hiding place in a jar above the mantel. My fingertips slide across the left-hand wall, feeling for a concealed groove in the rough stone. Excitement flares as I unlock the hidden door, which swings open silently.

My black and purple skirts swish around my legs as I race up the stairs before me. Torches flare into existence at my presence, illuminating the twisted circular steps. Up and up, 'round and 'round I go, climbing up the tower to the room waiting for me at the top. I lean against the door frame to catch my breath, my heart thumping furiously from the climb before striding across the room.

Thick tapestries showing my family's history line the walls, covering the windows to keep out the chill. I move along each one, admiring the scenes stitched into the fabric before moving them aside to let the light in.

Two hundred years ago, my family was poor. Since mankind first appeared on this land, my family has made its home here, at the base of Clawback Mountain. Farmers and shepherds, we worked the land and survived by providing food for the nearby village. But that all changed one day, when my great-great-grandmother, Ravensly, was whisked away to the land of the Fae by one of the princes who had fallen madly in love with her beauty.

When he returned her, dumping her in her bedroom pregnant and alone, he left behind a mirror, instructing her to use it to contact him once the child was born. Ravensly was distraught, as she loved him deeply, and to lose him and her family—who had long since perished—at the same time was distressing. She wrapped the mirror with blankets and tucked it into a closet, promptly forgetting about it as she fell into mourning.

After the birth of her daughter, Ravensly remembered the gift and hauled out the large silver mirror. She ran her fingers around the frame, and as she did so, fairy runes shimmered on the surface before disappearing once more. Ravensly had been confused upon seeing this evidence of magic and quickly hung it on the wall, stepping away from it when the runes lit up again.

Legend says the mirror then spoke to Ravensly, imparting its secrets to her. And the family of farmers and shepherds became powerful sorcerers, the nearby villages quaking in fear of their power. The huts they had previously lived in were demolished, a dark gray castle rising in their place. With the might of the Clawback Mountain protecting their back, a moat filled with man-eating fish surrounding the front, and powerful magics the poor villagers could not hope to defeat, no one dared to go against them.

Since that time, my family has worked diligently to keep the news of our powers from the royal family. If there is one thing we have learned, it is to plan ahead, have patience, and pretend to be less than we are. Unfortunately, over the years, fewer and fewer children have been born, and now, it is just myself left.

The distant call of a raven stirs me from the past, and I stride over to the final tapestry. Whipping it aside, I catch my breath as the mirror is revealed. The sight of it always leaves me breathless, its power gently humming a melancholy tune. Sweeping my hand along the edges, I activate the runes which glow an electric blue as my fingers brush over them.

The mirror shivers, a dense fog clouding the pane. I step back, standing tall and proud in front of it. "Mirror, mirror, on the wall, who is the fairest of them all?" I chant. This monthly ritual must be fulfilled. My pride will not allow another to best me in any way. Especially some peasant girl—can you imagine the shame? Shuddering at the thought of some lowly peon being more beautiful than I, I await the mirror's pleasure.

You may call me vain; it wouldn't be the first time someone did. I may be. It was drilled into me from birth that perfection was the only allowable standard for members of our family, whether it be in magic wielding, beauty, or academia. Nothing but the best, and should it not be forthcoming, then we would be mercilessly beaten in the dungeons. My mother was relentless in her teachings, and my initial defiance quickly turned into submission, then determination. I would have done anything to stay out of the dungeons.

One day, I know, the mirror will no longer name me the fairest in the land. It is inevitable. Sacrifices and spells may have kept me looking younger than my years, but the time will come when another threatens my place. When it does, she shall find herself laid out upon my altar, sacrificed to both the mirror and the gods, as I tear her still-beating heart from her chest.

The fog dissipates from the mirror, and a deep booming voice answers my question. "In the kingdom of Valderán, you, Morana, are the most fair." Dark laughter bursts from me while I spin in a circle with delight. *Of course I am*, I tell myself, flicking my dark hair over my shoulder. The serfs are safe from me today.

"Mirror," I command, "show me the royal family." The glass once more fogs over before slowly revealing a field at the back of the palace. The king and queen sit upon a brightly colored blanket, hands clasped tightly together as they share sweet kisses, while their daughter, Snow White, dances amongst the wildflowers. A boy a few years older than her watches over her, while several of the huntsmen stand guard nearby.

Throwing my arms up, I begin chanting in the old language. The words spill from my lips and the runes on the mirror glow a dark red, the color of blood and death. As I speak, I watch intently as thousands of ravens descend from the sky, settling on the branches and around the palace. Snow White screams as they swoop around her, tearing at her clothes and hair.

Cackling wildly, I continue chanting, my voice growing louder and stronger. Black clouds cover the sky, lightning ripping through them while thunder booms. The horses bolt in terror, the guards shouting for the family to come with them.

The spell complete, I flick my wrist, conjuring up a throne. As I settle down to watch the chaos I've created, a satisfied smile settles on my face. Speaking the words I did once before, I send them through the mirror. "Magic always comes with a price. A life for a life."

Chapter 2

Snow White

Six Years Old

A giggle escapes me as I race through the tall grass, wildflowers whipping past me as I move. My long black hair flows around me like a dark curtain while I try to escape the boy at my back.

"You'll never catch me!" I shout behind me, Cassian hot on my heels. The son of Papa's lead hunter, Alaric, Cassian is four years older than me. We've been the best of friends since I was born, when Alaric declared him to be my personal protector. He mostly takes his duties seriously, but other times, I'll find a frog in my bed or snails in my soup. I shriek as he grabs the strings on my gown, but I manage to slip out of his grasp. "Slow poke!" I call out, taunting him.

"I'll catch you, Snow!" he shouts back, and I speed up, cursing my dress. It must be so much easier to run in breeches and a tunic. I brought the matter up to my nanny once, extolling the virtues of keeping my gowns clean and untorn, and got a slap over the head for my trouble. I didn't ask again.

Ducking behind a tree, I come to a stop, hands resting on my knees as I suck in greedy breaths. I blame my heart thundering like a herd of wild horses for not hearing the footsteps coming up behind me.

"Gotcha!" Cassian crows, wrapping his arms around my waist and lifting me into the air.

"Put me down, you-you cretin!" I shout, trying not to laugh when he starts tickling me.

"I'll always catch you, Snow," he promises as he sets me down. "Come on. If your parents stop kissing long enough to realize they can't see you, I'll get whipped for sure."

He takes my hand and leads me back toward where my parents are sitting. "They're so gross," I moan, seeing they are indeed still kissing. The forest around us suddenly goes quiet, and a shiver curls down my spine, turning my blood cold. Tilting my head, I whip around, letting go of Cassian.

"What is it?"

"I don't know. Something's wrong," I whisper. Taking a couple of steps, I come to a stop and glance around. The dread continues to grow, making my heart leap in fear. The sound of thousands of birds in flight reaches me, and I scream as they dive out of the sky. Little claws grasp at me, the talons sharp enough to cut. One gets caught in my hair, ripping me backward as it tries to free itself. Another screams in my face, slicing my cheek. Hot blood gushes from the site, dripping down my face and gown. Shrieking in terror, I start to rush toward my parents who are shouting my name. I'm tackled from the back, Cassian landing on top of me, shielding me with his body. He jerks as several ravens attack him, but he stays strong, keeping me safe.

The brilliant blue sky goes eerily dark as thick gray clouds blot out the sun. A freezing cold wind whips over our heads, the trees almost bending in half with the force of it. I manage to lift my head up enough to watch as the ravens lift from the trees, flying against the wind. Thunder booms so loudly I fear losing my hearing, and the birds all drop from the sky. One lands in front of my face, its beady eye glaring at me. Maggots cover its body, squirming and writhing as they feast on the rotting flesh. I scream again, the horror all around me too much. Cassian leaps up and scoops me into his arms, racing toward my parents who are once again calling my name, their voices filled with terror.

Cassian slips on one of the dead ravens, skidding in its blood. We crash to the ground, another loud crack of thunder booming across the heavens. "Stay down!" he orders, but I don't listen. I want my momma. She's the only one that can scare away the dread in my heart. A flash of light blinds me, and Cassian grabs my hand, pulling me into his chest.

"Don't look," he hisses, rocking me back and forth, his voice shaky. This alarms me more than anything else, for Cassian is the bravest person I know. Nothing scares him. My hands tremble as I push against him, desperately trying to free myself. He holds tight, refusing to let me go. "No, Snow. Stay with me. Don't turn around."

A terrible scream rips through the air. It is one of torment, of a grief so profound it can be felt down to the very soul. Ripping myself away from Cassian, I turn toward the sound, my feet moving of their own accord. My father is on his knees, tears streaming down his face. The scent of burning flesh assaults me, and I gag into my sleeve, my eyes roaming over the scene while my brain refuses to compute what my heart tells it is true.

My beautiful mother lies dead in my father's lap, half of her body scorched and smoking. A jagged line runs vertically down her face, separating the burned side from the whole. It's as if the lightning left its mark, claiming victory in her death. Her eyes stare blankly at the sky, the heaving clouds reflected in the unblinking orbs. "Momma?" I cry out pitifully, falling to my knees beside my father. I shiver as my body goes cold. I know she's gone, but I can't help but call for her anyway, hoping for some miracle to occur. Sorrow pierces my heart when she doesn't answer, and hot tears spill down my cheeks.

Papa lets out another cry, and I clap my hands over my ears, unable to listen to the soul-destroying sound again. A sob rips itself from me when Cassian comes up beside me, placing his hand on my shoulder. I cover it with my trembling one, staring at Momma as if she would come back through my sheer will alone.

Suddenly, everything goes still. The clouds stop twisting and turning, and the insects quieten. It's as if the very earth is holding its breath. A woman's voice echoes through the trees, reaching toward us with dark tendrils.

"Magic always comes with a price. A life for a life." The world starts again, and the clouds dissipate, taking the thunder and lightning with them.

Papa rears up, Momma's cooling body dropping to the ground. "No!" he screams back at the forest before turning to look at me, his fists tightly clenched. I stumble to my feet at the look of hatred and devastation on his face, then freeze in horror when an oily blackness slithers across his eyes, briefly turning his hazel eyes black. "This is your fault," he spits at me. His arm rears back, and he slaps me across the face.

Cassian catches me as I fall, my lower lip trembling at the assault. Fear tears through me as Papa turns his back on me to scoop Momma into his arms. Bitter tears course down my face as I slowly follow behind them, the anguish and confusion making me trip. Cassian continues to hold my hand tightly, and I can feel his gaze on me. I squeeze his hand but look straight ahead, unable to meet his eyes.

Alaric and the other guards make their way toward us, and I quickly glance down at my feet when his gaze clashes with mine. He tries to take Momma from Papa, but he screams at Alaric, refusing to let her go. Wiping away my tears, my throat tightens, threatening to strangle me. How am I to live without her? Who will tuck me into bed at night, checking under the bed for the monster I know lives there? Who will sing to me when I'm sad, or braid my hair just the way I like it?

The palace looms before us, its white granite facade glowing softly in the sun. I had always loved my home, filled with laughter and the songs Momma would sing. It was where I felt safe, where bumps and bruises were kissed with love, and I could always depend on it to protect us. For a moment, I imagine I see blood dripping down the walls before the vision disappears as quickly as it came. Shivering, I clutch Cassian's hand harder. I have the feeling the loving home I've always known is no more.

I had no way of knowing just how prophetic that thought would become.

Chapter 3

Morana

Three Months Later

Patting my hair to ensure it's in place, I blow out a breath and then lean forward to take the coachman's hand. Stepping down from the carriage delicately, I glance around, schooling my face to hide the disappointment at the emptiness of the palace's courtyard. I had hoped—in vain, it seems—that King Silas would have arranged some sort of welcome for us upon our arrival.

Sweeping my gaze across the courtyard, I notice little has changed since the last time I was here. Washerwomen scurry to and fro, their hands reddened and chapped from the harsh soaps. The blacksmith, his thick arms corded with muscle, heaves a heavy hammer to fashion a sword. Various servants dash from one side to the other, going about their chores.

It's all so very pedestrian. Where are the screaming crowds? The fanfare? Where are the nobles? I should be treated with the heralding of trumpets and the roar of crowds. This is not what I expected.

The king steps down from the carriage and joins me at my side. Taking his proffered elbow, I allow him to lead me up the stone steps and into the palace. I will quietly admit that the castle is indeed stunning. Far too bright for my tastes, of course. Ravenswing Castle, with its dark towers and glowering gargoyles, far better suits me. Adarvan Palace will do nicely for now, though.

The king leads me from room to room, passing richly decorated hallways and walls, past priceless art and artifacts. It takes everything in me to contain the excitement buzzing through my veins. After seven long years, the time is nearly nigh. Becoming queen of Valderán is just the first step. With my power, looks, and cunning, it won't be long before I conquer the other lands. In time, I shall rule them all, and they will bow down and worship me as their goddess.

Silas comes to a stop in the throne room like the good little puppet he's slowly becoming. Since our last meeting, I ensured his dreams were filled with images of me. Of me wet and glistening in the bath, or covered in blood during one of my sacrifices. He dreamed of untold sexual desires fulfilled, of passion and wild embrace. With each dream, my magic gradually seeped into his subconscious, preparing it for the day he's ready for me to take control. It won't be long now—once the last vestiges of feeling he has for Snow White and Elspeth disappear, he will be my creature, nothing more than an empty puppet ready to do my bidding.

The doors fling open as Alaric enters the room, Snow White in tow. Quickly dashing the smirk off my face, I replace it with a kind smile. Over the years, I had spent more time observing the king and queen than the little princess. Despite her eyes filled with sadness and mouth turned down with grief, her beauty shines inside her, which may become a threat to me as she ages. Gritting my teeth behind the false smile, I let my gaze roam over her. Her delicate skin is white as snow, her hair as black as ebony, and her lips the scarlet red of a rose.

But it is her eyes that fascinate me, having never seen their like. They are the same hazel color as her father's, but that's where the similarities end. A band of gold surrounds the irises, which are also covered in small gold flecks. At that moment, a sunbeam lances through the window, lighting her in its golden blaze. The light catches her eyes, and I take an involuntary step back when they seem to almost glow. Something pricks at my mind, but it is buried deep and refuses to surface.

Snow White lowers her head and drops into a graceful curtsey. "Papa, I am glad you are back. I've missed you." She steps forward, raising her arms, but he shoos her away. Devastation fills her eyes as she steps back, her bottom lip trembling. I bite my tongue in glee at the display; surely it won't be much longer until the king is ready.

"Snow, I would like to introduce to you my intended, Morana. We shall be wed tomorrow. She will be your new mother," Silas intones, barely looking at the girl.

"But, Papa, I do not want a new mother!" she wails, stomping her feet.

"Do not speak back—" he begins, but I place a placating hand on his arm.

"Let me, my love. Sometimes little girls need another woman to talk to." He sighs and pinches the bridge of his nose, waving me ahead. Stepping forward, I kneel in front of her with a rustle of skirts. "I'm sure we'll get along just fine, won't we, my dear?" I ask, locking my gaze with hers. Lowering my voice to a whisper, I add, "For, if you do not, I will arrange for you to be sold to the Beast of Granton."

Snow gasps and steps back, her eyes wide as they search mine. "He-he's not real," she stutters, swallowing hard.

Pulling myself to my feet, I pat her head. "Oh, but my sweet, he is. He roams the forests and mountains looking for lost children. I've heard he eats three or four a day!" She shakes her head, lip trembling once again. Now for the icing on the cake. "And I've heard that little princesses are his favorite." I snap my teeth at her, and she shrieks.

I put my finger over my mouth and back up, swallowing down the chuckle threatening to burst from me. Snow White stands frozen in terror, her eyes bobbing between me and her father. Alaric's brows lower menacingly, but he doesn't move, just gestures for the princess to stand at his side.

"Go back to your room, Snow. Tomorrow I expect you to behave accordingly. You will smile and be glad I have provided you with a new mother." After issuing his command, Silas presses a kiss to my lips, and I smile inside at the hurt on her face.

Alaric rushes her out of the room, her tiny sobs feeding the darkness within me.

I have spent the morning being poked and prodded, pampered and primped. The heavy navy and silver gown with long bell sleeves they've provided me has a square neckline that shows off my décolletage, its cinched waist highlighting my slimness. A silver circlet adorns the cascade of curls tumbling down my back, and a touch of soot darkens my lashes. I pinch my cheeks sharply to bring a little color to them, then brush away the maids before beginning the long walk to the chapel.

Two huntsmen stand watch at the main doors of the palace. They throw them open, bowing deeply. Tossing my head back, I march forward with anticipation. Trumpets herald my arrival, and I pause at the top of the stairs, soaking in the sight before me. The courtyard overflows with people, from nobles to knights, to villagers and servants. Even more line the curtain walls while others lean out of the windows in the towers. Flags wave gaily, and when the crowd sees me, a great cheer rises.

This is what I expected yesterday. I suppose a day late is better than nothing. Plastering on a victorious smile, I wave, the cheers growing louder. The two huntsmen escort me down the steps and onto the ornately embroidered carpet below, specially designed to protect my dress from the dirty slush left over from last night's snowfall. Hands reach out to touch me, to wish me good fortune. I inwardly shudder at the thought of their filthy hands on me, but I hide it well. I cannot let them see the true me. Not yet. But soon enough, they will fall to their knees before me, worshipping me.

The skies briefly darken when hundreds of ravens flock to the barren trees surrounding the palace, answering my silent call. Some settle on the towers, while others cover the chapel's roof. My babies deserve to be a part of my special day.

The chapel itself is small, made entirely of the same white granite as the palace. Narrow stained-glass windows line each wall while a multitude of cathedral candles bathe the room in a warm glow. Garlands of flowers dangle from the beams, and a harpist plucks a melody from her instrument.

If I had my way, there would be a suitable sacrifice chained to the altar, their screams preceding my walk down the aisle.

Silas stands waiting at the altar, looking robust and handsome. His light brown hair is peppered with gray, and his hazel eyes watch me with adoration. I duck my head in pretend bashfulness as the guests lucky enough to be invited stand, inclining their heads in respect as I pass them.

Nearing the altar, I peek at the princess sitting in the first pew. She glares back at me defiantly, angry tears swimming in her eyes. Mine narrow in return before I dismiss her, coming to a stop beside the king.

The priest, dressed in long golden robes and wearing a ridiculously large miter on his head, drones on and on about the sanctity of marriage. I repress the urge to roll my eyes, silently praying he'd get on with it.

I have more important things to do.

"It's time, my love," my new husband murmurs to me. The great hall bursts with wedding guests, platters of food piled high on the tables. A roaring fire in the gigantic stone fireplace keeps the winter chill away, and servants dart to and fro, bringing more wine and ale to the already inebriated masses. Ribald toasts are shouted while maids squeal—some in delight, some in horror—as the rowdier men drag them off to empty chambers. One maid is bent over a table as a group of men take turns fucking her, her massive heaving breasts bared for the whole room to see. A few are drunkenly dancing to the troubadour's music, tripping over the hunting dogs begging for scraps.

It's a disgrace.

I can barely contain my contempt for these people. They sicken me with their crudeness, but at the same time, their debauchery feeds the darkness inside me. A part of me wants to rip them all to shreds, paint the walls with their blood and decorate the room with their bowels. Another wants to join them, to drink and fuck and revel in madness.

Maybe I'll do both. Later.

Turning back to the king, I offer him a sultry smile, letting a little blush flush my cheeks. His eyes sparkle in delight while he takes my hand. Standing, I brush my hand down my dress, playing the hesitant maiden. The fool falls for it and rushes me from the hall, raucous laughter trailing after us.

When we reach the king's chamber, he pushes me against the wall, ripping at my stays. Silas greedily exposes my breasts before pawing at them like an untried youth. Rolling my eyes, I gently extricate myself from his grasp.

"Darling, we have all night," I purr, slowly removing my gown. When I'm down to my opaque chemise, I run a hand down his velvet doublet. "Let me help you undress." He nods like an eager puppy before his eyes glaze over.

I settle on the small stool in front of the dressing table and face the mirror. Biting my lip to prevent myself from laughing, I reach up and start undoing the pins from my hair. "Yes, love. Ohh, look at that beautiful cock. I can't wait for you to be inside me."

Through the reflection, I watch as he jerkily removes his clothes, then climbs onto the bed. "Yes," he hisses, as he begins fucking the bed. "You feel so good, my queen."

The last of the pins clatters on the table. I continue to watch Silas acting the fool, enjoying every second of the entertainment. While I brush out my hair, I toss in a few moans and yesses for authenticity and am unsurprised when he finishes quickly. He didn't even attempt foreplay. Looks like I didn't miss much.

Pulling myself to my feet, I reach my hands into the air and stretch out my back before slipping the chemise over my head. I toss it aside and stride confidently to the bed. He rolls onto his back, his flaccid penis glistening with cum.

"Was that good for you, Your Majesty?" I ask breathlessly as I straddle his waist.

"Yes," he acknowledges, eyes fixed firmly on my pert breasts. Men are all the same—base creatures, easily led and even easier distracted. They spend the first nine months wanting to extricate themselves from the womb and the rest of their lives trying to get back in.

Thin, black, tentacle-shaped wisps of magic trail out of me, swirling around my feet before moving up my body. Silas jumps below me when he spots them, but I quickly slap my hand over his mouth to silence his shouts. He grunts against it, body bucking under me, trying to throw me off. As the tendrils snake up his chest toward his throat, I remove my hand. Silas drags in a deep breath of air, and my magic seizes its chance. It pours into his mouth, bulging in his throat as it enters his system. He spasms under me, eyes so wide they threaten to tear the delicate skin around them.

Silas goes silent, his eyes now fully black. He lies still as I climb off him, and the corner of my mouth curls into a smirk. I lean over to kiss him softly on the lips. "Be a good boy now, Silas, and wait here for me. I'm not done having fun yet."

"Yes, my queen," Silas intones robotically, blackened eyes staring blindly at the painted ceiling.

Straightening my shoulders, I stride to the door, throwing it open. I make my way back to the great hall, my magic still swirling around me. During my time with Silas, the festivities continued, resulting in an orgy on the floor. It heaves with naked limbs, the occupants panting and moaning, thrusting and sucking.

Dark laughter spills from my lips and everything comes stuttering to a halt as the occupants mark my presence. "Come!" I call, and some of the braver souls do so. A timid maid tries to slide past me, an empty tray dangling from her fingers. The blush on her cheeks intrigues me, and I grasp her arm, forcing her to stop.

Lifting her chin with a finger, I stare into her blue eyes. She stands frozen, body shaking in fear. "You are lovely," I murmur to her, tucking a strand of golden hair behind her ear. "Tell me, are you yet a maid?"

Her eyes widen, and she replies with a small nod.

"Perfect," I hiss, removing the tray from her hand and tossing it aside. Pushing down on her shoulders, I make her kneel before me and push her face into my cunt. "Now, please your queen. If you do a good job, you shall be rewarded handsomely."

Several men step forward, their tongues practically hanging out as they watch. Some stroke their cocks, their desire to join us shining brightly in their eyes. The maid is hesitant in her actions, unsure what to do. I push her head tighter against me, grinding myself against her mouth.

That's the problem with virgins. No skill.

Grabbing onto the back of her gown, I haul her to her feet. Her mouth glistens with my juices, and I lick them from her before spinning her around. Running my hands up her middle, I grab her breasts, squeezing them painfully. Her head tilts to the side, a small moan escaping her lips. "Look at them," I tell her. "Look at all these men who desire you."

Pulling her dress up, I rip her underskirt off, baring her to the men. Without warning, I thrust a finger into her, making her cry out in alarm. I add another, viciously pounding them into her. Her shrieks echo throughout the room as she struggles to extricate herself from my grasp.

"Who's first?" I call out, and a giant of a man steps forward. His cock hangs out, thick and heavy, already leaking as he licks his thick lips. He's perfect. I shove her toward him, and he eagerly grabs her, ripping her gown in two before tossing her onto the nearest table. A line forms behind him, her screams beckoning to them like a siren's call.

Throwing my head back, I laugh, letting my magic loose. No one is safe from it; it glides and slithers through the room, affecting everyone. Their eyes turn black, then back to normal. The orgy continues, the ones previously abstaining now join in.

The smell of sex is ripe in the air. The sound of moans, gasps, and slapping flesh are loud, and I slither around the room, soaking in the sin. A particularly handsome man comes toward me, and I eye him with pleasure. Yes, he'll do. He lies on the ground at my direction, and I climb onto him, his cock filling me completely. Two maids join us, latching themselves onto my breasts, while another man comes from behind, pushing himself into my ass.

One of the king's huntsmen watches from across the room, and I beckon him closer. Batting my eyelashes at him, I open my mouth in invitation. He gulps, his eyes transfixed on our little orgy. He only hesitates a moment before thrusting his length in my mouth.

As the men pound into me and the women suckle my breasts, the pleasure continues to grow until it explodes, taking me with it. Opening my eyes, they catch the huntsman's, his face slack with pleasure as he feeds his cock to me. Blood fills my mouth as I bite down viciously, and he screams in agony.

Tearing my head back, I rip it from the root, and he crashes to the ground, blood spurting like a fountain. I spit it out, and the room goes silent as the onlookers stop to see what the commotion is. The two maids back away from me, eyes wide in disbelief as the huntsman's blood flows toward them. Whipping my magic out, I slit their throats before they can scream, cackling in satisfaction as they fall to their feet.

The man beneath me has stilled his movements, lying frozen in terror. The one at my back doesn't stop, too far gone in either drink or lust to notice what is happening around him. Flicking my hand back, he flies off me, hitting the wall with a painful thud. He slides down it, the light going out of his eyes, blood spilling from the crack in his skull.

"Your turn," I whisper to the man beneath me. Flicking my hand out, I grin when my nails sharpen into claws. Before he can do anything, I tear his steaming entrails from his gut. Blood-curdling screams rip from his throat as I keep pulling, piling them up next to him. Leaning forward, I place a gentle kiss on his forehead. "Goodbye, lover," I murmur before digging into his chest, ripping out his heart.

The screams stop, his head lolling to the side. Pulling myself to my feet, I run the heart over my lips, the blood painting my face. Everyone watches me warily, too scared to move or even blink. I meet their eyes, one by one, then tear into the heart with my teeth, the delicious flesh sliding down my throat. I moan in ecstasy, feeling my power increase with the bloody meal. After the heart is consumed, I smear blood over my face and down my breasts, then throw my arms into the air. Chanting a quick memory spell, I erase my presence from their memories before leaving the hall.

Moments later, screams echo throughout the castle as the partygoers wake up, processing their nakedness and the gruesomely bloody scene I left behind. Entering the king's room, I find him still lying on the bed, staring like the brainless moron he will soon permanently become.

"Good boy," I whisper, curling into his side.

Chapter 4

Snow White

Nine Years Old

"It's not fair!" I shout, bending over to pick up a stone. I throw it at a tree, gouging out a piece of bark. Tightness stabs my chest, making breathing painful.

"What's wrong?" Cassian asks, his eyes skimming the surroundings. He may only be thirteen, but he's always on watch, making sure I'm safe. We're out in the field adjacent to the one Momma died in, the one I refuse to step foot in again.

Clenching my fists tightly, I answer, "Nothing has been the same since my mother died. Papa ignores me. The evil stepbitch—"

"Language."

I narrow my eyes at him. "Bitch, bitch, bitch!" I scream back, the pain welling up inside of me bursting forth. "She's ruined everything! A-and I think she's the reason Momma died," I sob, my voice breaking as I let out the secret I've been holding on to for the last year.

Cassian finally stops searching for danger and meets my eyes. "Shush!" he whispers harshly, quickly coming to my side. Glancing up, I follow his gaze, noticing two ravens sitting in the branches of the tree I just damaged.

Raw terror scrapes at my heart, the feeling not unlike the raven scars I carry on my cheek—a constant reminder of my mother's death.

He flips his shaggy dark-blond hair out of his eyes before grabbing my hand and pulling me away from the tree. "You need to be more careful," he hisses at me. Once we're a safe distance away, he takes me by the shoulders. "She's powerful, Snow. I've seen some things I can't explain." His jaw ticks as his emerald-green eyes bore into mine. "Some of the huntsmen, who I have known since birth, are acting strange. Doing things they wouldn't have done before."

"Like what?" Scooping up my skirts, I sit on the thick grass, Cassian only hesitating a moment before joining me.

"I can't say," he says, eyes downcast while his cheeks flame pink.

"Cassian—"

"No, Snow. I can't tell you now. Maybe in a few years, okay?"

I growl with frustration. "Fine. Maybe I won't tell you what I saw, then." Folding my arms over my chest, I smirk at him, knowing how much he hates being left out.

"Tell me."

"No."

"Snow—"

"Nuh-uh."

Cassian sighs and throws himself back, tucking his arms behind his head, staring at the cornflower-blue sky. He turns his head, eyes beseeching me to let it go.

Pursing my lips, I join him on the ground. He moves an arm under my head to use as a pillow, and I snuggle into his side. Very quietly, I tell him what I had seen.

My stomach growls painfully. Some days the maid forgets to feed me. It's another thing I've noticed that's wrong. Before Morana came, my maid would wake me in the morning, bathe me, then help me dress and do my hair before providing breakfast. I was given my own suite of rooms after Momma died, consisting of my bedroom, closets, garderobe, and a solar. The solar is my favorite, with soft chairs near the window to look out over the gardens, and a case with my most prized possessions—a handful of books, a locket of Momma's hair, and little treasures such as the bird's nest Cassian brought me after a storm knocked it from a tree.

It is late, most of the castle asleep. I can no longer ignore the grumbling of my belly, so I grab a candlestick and pad silently out of my room and down the expansive hall. Jansa, my maid, never came at all today, leaving me to struggle on my own and as hungry as a church mouse.

I'm not sure why church mice are hungry, but it is something Momma used to say, so it must be true.

At the end of the hall lays two staircases; one leads to the main floor below, the other to one of the towers. My eyes narrow when I see a faint light coming from upstairs, along with a chanting voice. Too curious to consider what a bad idea this is, I set the candlestick down and quietly creep up the winding stairs, thankful I hadn't put shoes on. My bare feet are silent on the cool stone, leading me up to the room that should be empty.

When I reach the top, the light becomes brighter, illuminating the oak door that has been left halfway open. Peeking around it, I notice Morana standing in front of a tall mirror, one unlike any I have seen before. Its surface is silvery and ... it's moving. I slap a hand over my mouth before a gasp can escape. Peering intensely at it, I watch as smoke moves over the mirror before dissolving. A terrifying face appears, looking back at Morana.

It's not a real face; I realize after a moment of letting my heart settle back in my chest. More like a mask but with a moving mouth. Where the eyes should be, are large black holes, a red liquid leaking from under the eyes like tears. Blood, my mind whispers to me, and I swallow harshly, shivers of dread racing down my spine.

When she's finished chanting, Morana shifts out of the way, and I see a boy, around Cassian's age, kneeling at her feet. He faces the mirror, head bowed, his body trembling with fright. Morana grabs his hair, pulling him to his feet. He struggles against her but is no match for her strength.

"Mirror!" she calls out. "As I have agreed, a sacrifice for you." And with that, she wrestles the boy closer to the mirror. He drags his feet, whimpering. A small pebble dislodges under my foot, and the boy turns my way, his wide eyes begging for help. I crouch down, keeping my hand over my mouth, desperately keeping the scream locked in my throat at bay.

I can do nothing to help him, as much as I want to. I don't even understand what is happening, but a moment later, I do. Morana shoves the boy into the mirror, his screams abruptly cutting off when he disappears into it. I don't know where he goes, or what will become of him, but I can only assume the worst. I know what 'sacrifice' means.

Quietly inching away from the door, I quickly make my way back down the stairs. Scooping up the candlestick, I race back to my room, locking the doors behind me.

I'm not hungry anymore.

"Gods," Cassian whispers, his eyes wide. "Are you sure it wasn't a dream?" I elbow him in the stomach. He lets out a whoosh, the corner of his mouth ticking up. "Sorry, Snow. It's just, it sounds so fantastical." He goes very quiet for a moment, staring at the clouds. "What color was his hair? The boy?"

"Red." He freezes below me, his arm turning to stone. I lift my head, frowning. "What is it?" With his free arm, he brushes his hair back, his jaw ticking. I don't like it when he makes that face, it means he's upset. My heart hurts when he's angry or hurt.

"One of the pages disappeared last year. He was the nephew of one of the huntsmen, sent here by his family to begin his training." His voice cracks, and this time, I don't make fun of him for it. "His name was Quincy, and he had red hair."

I rest my head back on his arm and curl into him, offering what solace I can. Cassian remains silent as we watch the clouds race across the sky, both of us lost in our thoughts.

Thirteen years old

My bare feet scrape against the uneven slate tiles, pain lashing up my legs as I race through the palace. My chest aches with the labored breaths ripping from me, and a sob tears itself from my throat as I pass startled servants.

"Elspeth!" comes the deep roar from behind me, and my feet pick up their pace. I can't do this again. I can't let him catch me. Rounding a corner, I knock over a table, its contents spilling across the floor behind me. I skid, waving my arms for balance before moving on.

"Stop her!" the voice shouts, a ring of authority in his voice.

"Snow!" a voice hisses, urging me to slow. Cassian's arm reaches out of a door, begging me to come with him. I meet his wide eyes and shake my head.

"He'll kill you," I spit, and continue on. Seconds later, hands grab my arms, lifting me off the floor. Two huntsmen grin down at me, their eyes black and expressions vicious. "No!" I scream, tears streaming down my cheeks. "Please let me go."

They say nothing, holding me in place, waiting for *him* to catch up. "Take her to the black room," he orders, striding into the room. I desperately search his face for any kind of compassion, but there is none. It was ripped out of him years ago, turning him into the monster that stalks me through the halls of the home that once brought me so much joy.

Cassian sneaks out of the room he was hiding in and creeps along the wall, trying to get past unnoticed. Snapping my attention back to the man before me, I beg, "Please, Father. Don't do this." Bile rises in my throat, knowing he likes it when I beg. Not that it ever makes any difference; nothing I say or do will change the course he's set on.

But it does at least let Cassian slip away, and I'll take any small victories I can.

The huntsmen drag me down the halls until we reach a dimly lit corridor. My heart hammers painfully in my chest, my throat tight when I see the door looming ahead. *Be strong, Snow,* I command myself, but as much as I wish to be, my trembling legs give me away.

Opening the door, the huntsman on my left lights a single torch while the other tosses me into the room. I stumble and fall against the curtained wall, listening to their dark laughter as they leave, closing the door behind them. There's no use trying to escape; I can see their shadows beneath the door, guarding it until the man that was once my papa comes for me. Tucking my knees up, I rest my chin on them, hugging myself.

I don't understand how this has become my life. I know where it all went wrong—my mother's death and papa's marriage to Morana. My life should have been something out of a storybook, like the ones Momma used to read to me. I'm a princess, living in a beautiful palace. No life is without flaws, without heartache and strife. But I should have been dancing in the sun, twirling among the flowers. I should have been attending balls, having tea parties with friends, laughing with my mother, and riding horses.

Not trembling in the shadows, terrified of gaining his attention. Not doing everything in my power to avoid the stepbitch who regularly threatens to sell me to the Beast of Granton. Not tiptoeing around the palace on eggshells, fearful of making a wrong move. One that ends with me in the black room. He always makes me wait, which is the worst of all. He seems to know that leaving me in here, sometimes for hours, ramps up my terror and anxiety. Father feeds off it like a vampire craves blood.

A movement to my left causes me to jump to my feet, flinging myself back across the room. Father had thick black curtains hung on each of the walls. They're supposed to help muffle the sounds of my screams. Cassian's head peeks out from behind them, and my breath rushes out of me, leaving me light-headed. "What are you doing in here?" I whisper harshly, the fear ramping up again. If father finds him here . . .

"I couldn't stand to leave you alone," he says quietly. "I-I know what he's doing to you."

Shame colors my cheeks a deep rose, and my trembling fingers rest over my stomach. I drop my head, eyes filling again with tears. I didn't want him to know.

"Come here," he demands, holding his arm out. I shake my head, too embarrassed. Why do the floors not open up to swallow you when you need them to? "Snow. Now."

Swallowing down the lump in my throat, I slowly edge closer, keeping my gaze firmly fixed on my bleeding feet. When I'm close enough, he grabs the front of my dress and hauls me into his arms. I shudder against his broad chest, my hands lifting to clench the fabric of his doublet.

Cassian is no longer the scrawny, gangly boy he used to be. He's a man now, having joined the rest of the huntsmen a year ago. He's strong and powerful and still looks after me as he's always done. A secret part of me wishes he would take me away, somewhere I could be safe. Another land, perhaps, one where we could be free.

My stomach flutters as I rest against his chest, breathing in his scent. He smells of pine trees and fresh air, of hay and sunshine. I can almost remember what it was like to run through the fields, feeling the sun on my face.

Father has kept me prisoner in the palace for the last two years. He gave no reason, had no defense. My skin, already far too pale, has become even paler, and dark bags rest permanently under my eyes. Without exercise, sunlight, or even enough food to eat, I sometimes worry I'll waste away in a corner somewhere. Where I'll go unnoticed until the stench of my decaying body calls someone to investigate.

Cassian would never let that happen, my mind supplies. But Cassian is only one man among many. Far too many of the huntsmen are compromised by Morana's magic. And even if Cassian could get me out of the castle, he would be labeled a traitor. If caught, he would be hung, drawn, and quartered, his head mounted on a spike as a warning to others.

"I'm going to get you out of here, Snow. I promise you. I don't know how yet, but I will."

I shake my head against his chest, clinging harder to him. I can't let him do that. If enduring my father is what I must do to keep him safe, I will. Cassian has protected me as much as he could my whole life. It's my turn to do the same.

Hearing a noise outside the door, I quickly push him back behind the curtain, whirling around just as the door crashes open. Needing to draw on Cassian's strength, I quickly lower myself to the floor, tossing my hands under the curtains. Moments later, his hands meet mine, holding them, offering what support he can.

I clench my eyes closed, sending my mind away when Father rips my dress open. *Cassian and I race through the trees, our laughter joining the calls of rainbow-colored ghetti birds high in the branches. The sun beats down, warming me, and joy fills my heart.*

I ignore the stabbing pain, the sweat that drips onto my forehead, the filthy words he spits at me. Clinging tightly to Cassian's hands, I continue to disengage from the heinous act being forced upon me, keeping my focus on the imaginary landscape in my head.

When it's over, Father cries into my chest, patting my hair and calling me Elspeth. I stare blankly upward, watching the shadows of the flames flicker along the ceiling, my fingers twitching. Tears streak silently down my face as I cling to my only lifeline, the man hiding behind me.

Each time this happens, I feel a part of my soul shrivel up. I'm terrified that one day, there will be nothing left of me but an empty shell. Or even worse, that I'll wake up and discover that I've become a monster just like my father.

Chapter 5

Morana

My jet-black skirts tangle around my legs while I storm through the castle. Huntsmen and servants alike scurry like rats out of my way when they see the stormy countenance on my face. Grinding my teeth, I round a corner, shoving one of the maids out of my way. She falls to the ground, trembling, her eyes lowered in supplication.

"Y-your Majesty," she stutters out, hoping to appease me—but nothing will. Not today. I kick her in the stomach on the way past anyway.

I can't stop the mirror's message from replaying over and over in my mind. I had fully expected the mirror to reply as it always did to my question, so imagine my shock when a different reply was forthcoming.

"Mirror, mirror, on the wall, who is the fairest of them all?"

"You, my queen, although quite fair, can no longer hold the title, I fear. Another comes to take your place, fair of face and full of grace."

Fury, white-hot and scorching, tears through me, my eyes narrowing in disbelief. I will not allow this to be. "Who?" I hiss, readying myself to call my ravens to discover her location.

"Snow White."

I rear back, eyes widening in shock. It's easy to forget about her existence, she is so rarely seen. Searching my memory, I realize it's been over a year since I saw her creeping through the shadows early one morning. I've been busy with my own plans, setting up the pieces and placing my pawns. By being distracted, I've neglected to keep an eye on the happenings in the palace.

It's a mistake I won't repeat.

"Snow White!" The little bitch doesn't reply, and my pulse speeds up. How dare she not answer me? My long strides eat up the stone corridors, my shouts continuing to be ignored. There are only so many places she can hide.

When I've finally reached the end of my tether, I set my magic loose. The torches lining the walls flicker once, then extinguish themselves. Spinning around, I crane my neck, searching. *There.* One lone torch shines, and I storm toward it, only for it to wink out, the flame reappearing farther down the hall.

The torches guide me through the castle until I come to a darkened hallway in the belly of the palace. Two huntsmen guard the door, and it only takes a moment to utter a sleeping spell. When they're slumped on the ground, snoring heavily, I throw open the door and step inside.

I come to an abrupt halt when I see Snow White lying on the floor, her dress ripped open, and Silas on top of her, stroking her hair, calling her Elspeth. If the fury I had over the mirror naming Snow White the fairest was intense, what I feel now is all-consuming. My fists clench at my sides while my magic swirls around me in an agitated tornado. My chest heaves with heavy breaths, and my vision goes red.

"Whore!" I scream at her as I step closer. Sending a tendril of magic shooting into Silas, I wait for his eyes to turn black before leaning down and grabbing her by her long lustrous hair. Her body stiffens when she comes out of whatever trance she seemed to be in, her mouth opening and closing when she sees the ferocity of my anger.

Pressing my face close to hers, I spit, "Is this how you are trying to win your father's attention back? By opening your legs for him?"

Snow shakes her head, her wide eyes unable to hide the terror in them. "No, stepmother. I swear it, I did not ask for this. I did not want it."

I sneer back at her and turn her head, making her look at her father. Reduced to his puppet state, he sits on the floor, his flaccid cock dangling between his legs. His darkened eyes stare blankly, and a sliver of drool hangs from his lip. This is how he should be after all these years. I was wondering how he was able to resist my magic—even if only a little—for all this time, and now I know.

It was her fault. She's the spitting image of her mother, except for those freakish eyes of hers. Although I had removed all of the paintings and reminders of her after my marriage to Silas, I still remember her beauty.

"There's your father, Snow White. Take a good look. He's nothing but a drooling idiot. But you? You have betrayed me. I have allowed you to live, have allowed you to sleep under this roof and have food to fill your stomach. This is how you repay me?" I shake her hard, her head snapping back and forth with the force of my anger.

Her hand moves to rest over her stomach, and I go still. My gaze runs down her body, and I truly look at her. "No," I breathe, my magic starting to whip even faster around me. It's almost undetectable, but her belly is slightly swollen, and the fury comes racing back. Setting her on her feet, I grab her wrist and pull her from the room, ignoring her stumbling footsteps behind me as I drag her to the dungeons.

I cannot allow anyone to witness what I'm about to do. Although a good portion of the castle is under my full control, some are only able retain my spell for short periods. Others, not at all. And a few that I haven't bothered with, as I do need functioning protection should another country decide to invade. I've managed to frighten most of the population into obedience, but there are small pockets of resistance.

Should they discover Snow White's plight, I'll have a war on my hands. I may be the most powerful sorceress in the kingdom, but I'm not the only one. And the Restüra Continent, of which Valderán is but one country, has many more. It could become a problem should they make it their business.

Snow drags her feet the closer we get to the dungeons. "Please, Morana, I'm sorry. I swear I did not do this!" Her whiny cry sets my teeth on edge. Rounding on her, I growl, "You should have kept your legs closed. I'll make sure your father never looks at you with lust in his eyes again."

"Thank you," she whispers, her head lowered.

Oh, poor child. I think you misunderstand me. When I'm through with you, no man will ever want you. And I'll be the fairest in the land once more.

We arrive at the gates to the dungeon. Thick iron bars block the entrance, and I pull a set of keys from a hidden pocket sewn into my skirt. After it's unlocked, I drag Snow White down the dimly lit stone staircase. The room isn't as big as it could have been, but since the country has been at peace for over a century, it hasn't been required.

The low ceilings are arched, the stones perfectly placed to balance the weight of the palace above it. Small arrow slit windows line one wall, letting in the barest amount of light. Two cells are placed on the window side. Although the windows have no panes in them—allowing prisoners to freeze in the winter and be eaten alive by mosquitos in the summer—they are far too narrow for even a small child to fit through, so do not pose an escape threat.

Each cell contains a wooden bucket and a heap of moldy hay. To the right of the cells is a wall complete with chains and manacles, and to the right of that, several instruments are hung. A vicious barbed whip, large rusted pincers, a blood-splattered saw, and spiked gloves wait patiently to be used.

Swinging Show White around to the front of me, I push her up against the cool stone wall. She sobs quietly, the sound grating and most irritating. Leaning down, I rip the ruined dress from her and toss it in the corner. Snow immediately tries to cover her breasts and genitals, and cries out when I tear her arms away, locking the manacles around her wrists, then ankles.

"Why are you doing this?" she cries, her gaze flinching away from the sight of the tools.

"I am the fairest in the land!" I shout back at her, flinging my hair over my shoulder. "I will not allow anyone to best me. Especially not the daughter of that whimpering bitch, Elspeth."

"My mother was not a bitch," she growls back at me, finding a bit of backbone. I am almost impressed with her daring; it's been a while since anyone has challenged me.

"Oh, but she was," I sing, turning my back on her. "I saved her life, you know. The great Queen Elspeth, beloved by all . . . yet cried herself to sleep and refused to eat, simply because she could not conceive a child."

Snow frowns, a shiver working through her body. "I don't know what you're talking about."

Stepping forward, I lift her chin with a finger, a dark smile playing on my lips. "My dear sweet child. Has no one told you the truth? Your mother was barren, as useless as a glass of wine under water. When she locked herself in her room, starving herself to death, I came to her. I saved her, and with my magic, allowed you to be conceived." I poke her in the forehead. "So, you see, you owe your life to me. Without me, you would never have been born."

"Without you, my mother would still be alive!"

Stepping back from her, I chuckle darkly. "True, but that is neither here nor there. The past cannot be undone. But I will ensure no one takes from me that which is mine."

Chapter 6

Cassian

My heart feels as if it's being ripped in two. I squeeze my eyes shut, wishing I could block out the sounds of the king's grunts and groans as he defiles his daughter. I want to kill him, to inflict the kind of pain on him that he is on Snow. I want to strangle him with my bare hands and mount his head on a spike.

I want to pull her into my arms and take her somewhere far away, where we'll both be safe.

I remember the day she was born. My father, Alaric, brought me into the royal nursery when she was just a few hours old. The queen was resting in the next chamber from the birth, and a nurse sat next to the cradle, humming a lullaby.

My father had always been my hero; at over six feet, he was muscular and strong, and his heart was good. He was just and fair and always listened to my side before exacting any punishments. He did not stand for lying or cheating and made sure the other huntsmen followed suit.

I had been born in a shower of crimson, my mother's life force draining away from her as I tore myself into this world. My father could have blamed me, cast me aside, or hated the sight of me. Instead, he loved me fiercely, even though she was his one great love.

So when he led me into the nursery at only four years old and informed me that the infant princess was mine to protect, my heart almost burst with pride. I remember peering into the cradle, the baby looking back at me, her little fists waving in the air. I reached a hand in and she wrapped her minuscule fingers around mine. Then and there, I vowed to protect her.

At the time, the worst thing I could think to protect her from was a fall, and over the years, it became our little catchphrase: *I will always catch you if you fall.* Now I'm hiding behind this curtain, unable to do anything. I feel like an impotent fool. Not a man at all, but a coward, unworthy of being a huntsman.

My father would be ashamed.

On the other hand, there is nothing I can do. I have no weapon, and there are two guards at the door. If I were to kill the king, both myself and Snow would be labeled as traitors. I would willingly swing from the gallows if it meant she was safe, but I won't risk her life.

So I stay hidden and quiet, squeezing her hands so she knows I'm here, even though I want to vomit at the sounds. Her cries shatter my heart, forming a lump in my throat I can barely breathe around.

When the door is thrown open, I quickly let go of Snow's hands and silently get to my feet. Peering out of a crack in the curtain, I watch as Morana's magic swirls dangerously around her, the fury on her face clear. When she leaves, dragging Snow behind her, I cautiously creep out, warily eyeing the king. He doesn't move, not even a flinch when I raise my hand threateningly above him.

It would be so easy. The guards lie slumped at the door. I could take a knife and slit his throat. It would be over in seconds, and the princess would be safe. *But she was the last with him,* I remind myself. *You can't risk her life.*

Dashing out of the room, I race down the corridor, stopping at the corner to peek out. Snow and Morana look to be heading toward the dungeons, so I throw myself down the opposite hallway. I receive a few wide-eyed glances from staff as I run, my heart tripping over itself in its effort to keep up with me.

Reaching the servants' entrance at the rear of the palace, I jump down the stairs three at a time. Decorative shrubbery surrounds the base of the palace, and I push my way through it, setting a mental reminder to apologize to George, the head gardener. Crouching behind bushes out of sight, my ear near the dungeon window, I listen for Morana and Snow White.

Forty minutes later finds me with my head resting on my knees, my whole body shaking with both horror and fury. Snow White's terrorized screams still echo in my ears, and I find myself acting the coward once more, too scared to go to the window and look through. I can bear pain. The injuries I have endured as a huntsman I would suffer a thousand times over if it meant the end of her suffering. This, I cannot bear.

My mind screams at me to check on her, to make sure she's still alive. If she's not, I'll kill the queen myself, even if it ends in my death. Gritting my teeth, I force myself to move and crawl over to the window, blowing out a breath before peering inside.

Snow lies on her stomach on a heap of straw. I bite down on my fist to stop myself from roaring at the sight of her. Bloody welts mar her porcelain skin. Several strips of skin hang from her, the gashes deep and oozing. Her hair has been mostly shorn off; bald patches are mixed with short choppy strands, with one lone curl left. But what nearly destroys me is the blood trickling down her legs, pooling beneath her.

She's completely still, her face turned away from me. I'm not sure she's even alive.

I nearly jump out of my skin when a hand clamps down on my shoulder. Throwing myself back, my breathing catches in my throat as my eyes meet my father's. "What are you doing, son?"

Shame slithers through me at my helplessness. I gesture toward the window. "Snow—"

He pushes past me and peers inside, his gasp loud in the silence surrounding us. "Who did this to her?" he demands, turning away from the grisly sight.

"The king and queen."

"May the gods help us," he mutters, flicking his graying hair out of his eyes. He sits for a moment, then continues, "Things are getting bad here, Cassian. The orchards aren't being harvested, the king no longer hears petitions. The queen is removing the will of the people, and more than half of the huntsmen are under her spell."

I bow my head, knowing he speaks the truth. There has been unrest amongst the peasants and villagers, many going hungry. The king has become useless, and the queen has no regard for her people.

"You are my only child, and I would see you far from here," he continues, and I rear back in shock.

"You would send me away?"

He reaches out, grasping my fist. "I don't want to. You are all I have. But it's not safe here, and I predict it will only become worse." He glances back at the window, then searches my eyes. "Do you love her?"

"She's my best friend."

"I know. But do you love her?"

She's too young for the feelings I'm developing for her. Our shared childhood and close friendship have morphed into more intense feelings. Feelings I would never act upon, not until she's reached her majority. Not that I could ever act on them anyway; she is a princess, and I am merely a huntsman. I know my place.

But I can love her from afar and remain forever at her back, offering her my protection, as I will never be able to offer my heart.

"Yes."

He nods, staring off into the distance. Letting out a deep sigh, he says, "There are things I never told you about your mother. One day, I will tell you everything. But right now, I need you to do as I say."

I nod. "Of course, Father."

"You're a good lad, Cassian. And although you think yourself a man, ready to take on the world, you aren't." I splutter and he holds up a hand. "I was once seventeen too. I was brash and headstrong and thought no ill could befall me. I remember what it is like, son. But there is much you have to learn, things you need to accomplish if you're going to be able to help her and this kingdom. We need an army, one not tainted by Morana's magic. And we need a way to defeat her.

"Your mother was once an acquaintance of the Beast of Granton. When Morana's powers began to change our land, I wrote to him, and he agreed to allow you to stay with him for a time. He'll teach you what you need to know."

"I thought he was a myth." I'm stunned at the news. Every child knows about the Beast, stories of him are told to make them behave. "But what about Snow? I can't just leave her here."

"Cassian, what would you do? Steal her away in her condition? What if she dies while she's with you? I'll not see my son blamed for the death of the heir, nor watch you hang for it. I'll help her the best I can while you're gone."

I freeze, my heart and mind at war with each other. My father has never steered me wrong. Although my heart screams for me to storm through the palace and yank her from the dungeon, my mind heeds his words. What can I do? I have no magic, no army, no way to win this fight. Ignoring the pain in my chest, I nod in acquiescence.

"Good lad. Go to the stables and prepare Fire Heart. He's been bred for war, is swift and sure-footed, and will make a good companion for you on your journey."

"I can't take him, he's your favorite." Fire Heart is the grandson of my mother's horse, and Father's pride.

He clasps me on the shoulder before starting back out of the bushes. "You will do as you're told, Cassian. I trust Fire Heart will see you safely back to us."

Once he's gone, I turn back to the window, only to find Snow White standing on shaky legs, her face turned up to mine, tears coursing down her dirty face. "You are leaving?" she croaks in a hoarse voice.

Squeezing my arm through the window, I reach out, and she places her hand in mine. "I will be back, Snow. I promise you. I will find a way to defeat Morana and your father, and I will be the one to place the crown on your head."

"Please don't leave me," she sobs. "I don't think I can survive without you."

If my heart breaks any more today, I fear there will be nothing left of it. "I must. Be patient. Do what you can to keep yourself off of Morana's radar. Keep yourself safe, and I'll return soon."

I squeeze her fingers and she returns the gesture, hating when her hand slips from mine. It feels like an omen and not a good one.

Fire Heart, a midnight Friesian, stands at a towering seventeen hands high. His stall was specially crafted for his larger frame, and his onyx eyes watch me as I approach him. Holding out the carrots I liberated from the kitchen gardens, he delicately takes them from my hand, then whuffles around my chest, looking for more.

"Hey, boy," I murmur softly, scratching his forehead. It takes several minutes to get him bridled and saddled, and I lead him to the stable entrance, waiting for my father to return.

"Where are you taking Fire Heart?" a squeaky voice asks from behind me, making me jump. Turning my head, I spy one of the young stable hands. Freddie, I think his name is. With a mop of bright auburn hair and a profusion of freckles across his nose, he looks younger than his fourteen years.

I give him a sheepish smile and a wink. "A lovely new girl is working at a tavern in the next village."

The boy grins back and elbows me in the side. "Ah, then don't let me keep you. Give 'er a good seeing to!"

I pretend to laugh along with him, but his disrespect has me clenching my teeth when I turn away. Father would never allow such, but Morana's influence is more powerful than he.

Leading Fire Heart out of the stables, I go around the back, not wanting to draw any more unwanted attention. Moments later, Father joins me, carrying a heavy-looking pack over one shoulder. He sets it at my feet, then pulls me into a hug, pounding me on the back. "Godspeed, Cassian. I will miss you but trust you'll return soon with the aid we need."

"What if I don't succeed?" I voice the fear that has been nagging at me since he left me next to the dungeon.

He places his hand on my shoulder, his face serious. "You are my son, Cassian. And your mother's. She—she was special. And long ago I met an oracle, who prophesied that my son would one day reign as Valderán's hero. I have every confidence in you."

Swallowing down the lump forming in my throat, I give him one last hug, then swing up onto Fire Heart. Father attaches the sack he brought to the saddle, then slaps the horse on the rump.

"Take care of my son," he says to Fire Heart, and the horse nods, letting out a soft neigh as if he understands Father's words. Maybe he does.

A caw sounds from the tree nearest us, and Father stiffens. "Go now, Cassian," he hisses, removing a knife from his belt. He throws it, killing the raven instantly. "Now!" he shouts when I hesitate, and I race off, Fire Heart's heavy hooves pounding against the earth before any more ravens can follow us.

Chapter 7

Snow White

Four Months Later

My arms and legs are pinned to the wall, horror and panic racing through me. Morana is screaming filthy words at me, some of which I don't understand. Whore. Slut. She tells me I became pregnant solely to derail her plans.

My mind urges me to run, to do something, anything. I yank against the chains when a thick tendril of magic whips out of Morana. She flings an arm toward me, chanting words I cannot comprehend. The magic speeds toward me, and I throw my head back, a wild primitive scream ripping from my throat as the magic works its way inside me.

The chains rattle along with my screams, my eyes feeling as if they'll pop out of my head while the searing pain rips through my abdomen. "You think you'll birth an heir, ensuring your crown?" she yells, her face distorted in anger. The magic rips into me even further, and I feel a gush of liquid spilling down my legs. My screams grow even louder, the pain more than I can bear.

"Please!" I beg, my body stiffening, trying desperately to get relief from the agony.

"You will be begging for death before I'm through with you."

The magic leaves my body and I slump, my legs giving way. The chains save me from falling, my bare feet scraping against the harsh stone floor. I hang my head, desperately trying to force air into my lungs. Morana grabs my hair and rips my head back. I've never seen such cruelty on someone's face. Her eyes are flashing in anger, her brows low and lips curled into a snarl.

"Fairest of them all?" she mutters, brandishing a knife in her free hand. I flinch when she raises the knife high, convinced she's going to kill me. Instead, she hacks off a fistful of hair. She goes crazy, ranting and raving while she shears me like a sheep. Tears drip down my face in a never-ending stream while I do my best to hold still, fearful the knife will slip and end me.

After, she whips me mercilessly, demanding for me to scream. So I do, over and over until my voice deserts me.

My eyes fly open, my heart pounding with the leftover terror of the day Morana locked me down here. My throat is hoarse from screaming, as it is every morning. My mind refuses to let me forget and each night revisits the horrors on me.

The day after my imprisonment was my fourteenth birthday, which passed without fanfare or acknowledgment. My naïve self had thought I would be allowed back into my rooms, but I know now how foolish that was.

Pushing myself up, I unsteadily get to my feet, my back aching after lying on the moldy hay. I would give almost anything for the comfortable feather-filled mattress in my suite. After relieving myself in the bucket, I collect my small rock and carve another line into the wall.

Four months. It's been four months since I've been locked in this cold cell. Four months since Cassian left me, and four months of loneliness and pain.

At first, Morana visited me daily, torturing me with both whips and words. As the days turned into weeks, her visits became more and more sporadic, until they mostly petered off. Last month, she only came once.

Alaric is the only light I have now. He is unable to come by often, for fear of one of Morana's lackeys or ravens spotting him coming to the window. When he does, he brings little treats, like an apple or a book to read. I cherish the woolen blanket he was able to squeeze through.

The books are the only things that save my sanity. Without them, I would go quite mad. Inside them, I find adventure, love, and freedom, escaping the harsh reality of my prison sentence.

The huntsmen that drop off my daily meals and empty the bucket have been warned not to speak to me, so I go days, sometimes weeks, without a soul to speak to. I've taken to leaving a few crumbs at the window, hoping a bird or two might come and listen to me while pecking at my meager offerings.

My one hope is Cassian. He always keeps his promises, so I trust he'll be back for me. I just have to hold on.

Cassian

Waves of exhaustion roll over me. Fire Heart's steps are slow, his head hanging as we finally enter the Forbidden Forest. The journey here has been fraught with danger every step of the way and took twice as long as it should have. It's been four months since I left Snow behind. I thought I would have been back by now. Fear for her overrides all else—hunger, thirst, and fatigue are all nothing compared to the constant worrying. Did she heal from her injuries? Has she gotten an infection? Is someone caring for her? Is she alive?

Knowing I'll drive myself crazy if I keep at it, I do my best to bury the questions. I must do as Father asked if I have any hope of getting back to her.

Hearing a stream ahead, I urge Fire Heart on. The trees of the Forbidden Forest stretch their naked branches into the sky, the obsidian trunks hard and smooth like stone. I have never seen the like, and a shiver runs through me. Glancing up at the heavily clouded sky, the tops of the branches almost look like hands, desperately stretched out, begging for mercy that never comes. Pulling my cloak closer around me, I tear my gaze from the sight and focus on getting us to the water.

Fire Heart's ears prick up when we finally spot the stream, and he picks up his pace, eager for a drink. My flask ran out miles ago, and both of us greedily drink our fill before I set up camp. We desperately need to rest before trying to locate the Beast's castle in the morning. The map Father gave me, although good, is not as precise as it could be. I can't tell if we're right on top of the castle, or still miles from it.

After removing Fire Heart's saddle and brushing him down, I turn him out to let him graze as he will. He's well-trained and won't wander far. After hunting a rabbit, I return to camp and start building a fire. Fire Heart neighs a warning and I freeze, listening.

The forest has gone silent as if it's holding its breath. Nothing stirs, not even Fire Heart, every creature waiting for the perceived threat to pass by. The hairs on the back of my neck stand up and goose bumps dot my arms. My chest grows cold, and premonition whispers to me that something very, very dangerous is standing behind me.

Swallowing down the lump of terror forming in my throat, I reach for my knife but stop when a deep growly voice speaks. "Who are you, and what do you do on my lands?" Fire Heart rears back at the sound of the voice, the whites of his eyes showing.

"I am Cassian, son of Alaric, from the kingdom of Valderán." My voice rings out strong and sure, surprisingly enough. One must be thankful for small mercies.

"You're late," the voice grumbles, and I work up the courage to turn around. And inadvertently stumble back a step at the monstrously tall form. He steps closer, out of the shadows of the trees, and Fire Heart bolts in panic. "I seem to have spooked your horse."

I nod, my eyes wide. The half-man, half-creature before me must be at least seven feet tall. He sports a mane like a lion, and two ram-like horns curve from his head. He's almost twice as broad as I am, thickly corded with muscle, and razor-sharp claws tip the fingers on his massive hands. His human face is handsome, or would be if it wasn't for the coldness in his eyes and the heavy scowl he wears.

"Have you looked your fill?" he demands, his tails whipping around him agitatedly. I gulp, tearing my eyes away from him.

"I apologize, my lord," I murmur, realizing this must be the Beast of Granton. His fine clothes are a stark contrast with the—man? creature?—before me.

Beast gestures toward my things. "Come, my castle is not far. There is no point sleeping rough when you have a room waiting for you." He eyes the rabbit hanging from a tree and raises a brow, but says nothing more.

Quickly packing my bag, I whistle for Fire Heart, who sticks his nose out from behind a tree but refuses to come closer. Beast steps back into the shadows, and Fire Heart takes a hesitant step forward. "Come on, he's not going to hurt you," I call to him, and he disappears into the trees again. "By the gods," I mutter, dropping the bag on the ground. It takes me half an hour to catch him, but I finally lead him back, his hooves digging into the dirt, head swaying back and forth in a "no."

Stubborn mule.

Beast sticks to the shadows, as still as a statue, an amused smirk dancing across his lips. Fire Heart is not happy to be so close to the Beast, but he decides to be obedient and come with me. He makes sure to keep me between him and Beast, though. So much for a war horse and loyalty.

Chapter 8

Cassian

Eight Months Later

"Good!" Beast cheers in approval as I twirl my double-bladed war axes faster than the eye can see. Spinning around, I throw one and watch as it embeds itself deep into the hay bale Beast set up for practice.

"Again!"

Racing forward, I scoop up the axe and fling myself onto the side of Bastian Rock. It takes all my might to puncture the granite with the axes, using them to climb up the steep face of the cliff towering above us. Once I reach the top, I raise the axes in the air and roar. Beast answers and a wide grin splits my face. From the edge of the cliff, I throw both axes at once. They spin top over bottom before landing on the target.

Jogging down the gentler slope on the opposite side, I meet up with Beast, approval shining in his eyes. Handing my axes back, he tosses an arm across my shoulders, nearly knocking the breath out of me.

I never dreamed I would call the Beast of Granton my friend. When I first arrived, we were both wary of each other, but that quickly changed during my training. Father was right to send me here. It may only be a year since I left Valderán, but it feels longer. I didn't realize just how much more growing up I had to do, nor how ignorant I was of the world. Not that I'm a worldly person now; but the Beast ensured that I not only became highly trained with a variety of weapons but also broadened my mind through education. Mathematics, geography, philosophy, history, and even legends were taught.

A year ago, I thought I was a man ready to take on the world. Now I want to laugh at the thought. There is so much more to learn, things to see and new lands to discover. My previous naïveté shames me. How could I have ever thought I could take on the world? A wry smile plays on my lips as I shake my head at myself.

When my lessons first began, Beast had explained that I must start from the bottom and work my way up. Before, I would have thought myself beneath such things as farming, but now I understand its importance. I have much more respect for nature and the natural laws of our world and have become skilled in farming techniques, animal husbandry, weaponry, hunting, and survival.

The Beast didn't believe in being idle. If there was work to be done or things to learn, then he fully expected me to do so. He kept me busy from sunrise to sunset, only stopping when I fell into bed, too exhausted to move a muscle. My hands are now rough with callouses, and my strength nearly rivals the Beast's.

But even through all of this, Snow White was never far from my mind. The image of her covered in blood has never left me. Nor her tear-streaked face as she begged me not to leave her. My heart has marked each day I have been away from her, screaming at me to return.

Beast leads me back into his castle, then runs his hand through his mane. "There is something I have not yet told you—" he starts, heading toward the wide double staircase. "Come, I can explain better up here."

He guides me into the west wing, the one place he told me I was not welcome. I ride his heels, curiosity overwhelming me. The small hairs on my arms prick up as we make our way down the corridor. Although the rest of the castle is spotless, this wing looks as if it was abandoned long ago. More than once I have to duck to avoid the thick cobwebs swinging from the ceiling on an invisible breeze. Strips of aged wallpaper hang from the walls, and the rugs under our feet carry years' worth of filth.

Beast comes to a stop in front of a room and gestures for me to enter. "Have a seat," he commands, pointing to a wide wingback chair. He takes the one beside it, sitting back with his hands steepled under his chin. Eyeing me warily, he begins his story.

"I have not told you how I came to be like this." I watch his brows lower as he turns his attention to the window opposite him. He takes a deep breath and continues, "My grandparents were the rulers of Granton. The crown would have eventually fallen to me after my father crossed over into the beyond."

He leans forward and closes my jaw for me, his mouth curling into a wry smile. "Yes, I would now have been king, if it weren't for a man called Jessop. Jessop was a mere traveling merchant, or so we thought. A mighty storm swept the land one evening in winter. The temperatures were frigid, and snow piled as high as a man. I remember playing joust with my sister using giant icicles, and the ice on the pond being so thick it was as if walking on land.

"This particular night, the winds were viciously strong, and our family was gathered in the great hall, a roaring fire keeping us warm while we told stories. At one point, my sister slipped away, excusing herself to bed. I didn't know it at the time, but she had in reality been sneaking out to meet a lover. Her actions saved her life, so I cannot be upset over her deception.

"A booming knock came on the door, and the guards led in an old man. His white beard dragged on the ground, and his back was bent and crooked. He begged my grandparents for shelter for the night, and they graciously agreed. But the man who called himself Jessop was not as he appeared. In truth, he was a sorcerer. Not the most powerful, nor the wisest, but a sorcerer all the same.

"Now, my family had a secret, one which they kept even most of their knights and guards from discovering. The old man quickly discarded his disguise, revealing himself as a sorcerer, and cast a spell over the room which forced my parents and grandparents to shift."

I sit back in my chair, eyes wide as I listen to Beast's story. My gaze roams over his mane, horns, and tail, and I wonder at them. He sees the questions in my eyes and inclines his head. "We are shifters," he explains, and I gulp.

"I did not know such things existed," I murmur.

"Aye, well, of all the nations in the Restüra Continent, Valderán is the most isolated when it comes to magic and creatures. Other countries are far more diverse."

"What animal are you?"

"A manticore."

My brows pull down as I search my mind. "I'm afraid I'm not familiar with that."

Beast chuckles. "My family is the only of our kind, so that is not surprising. We have the body of a lion, wings of an eagle, and the horns of a ram. Fully shifted, we are a fearsome sight, and magic has no effect on us. What the sorcerer did not know, however, is that only family members over eighteen can fully shift. So when his spell was cast, my parents and grandparents were changed, but I, at fifteen, only partially changed.

"The guards and knights that did not know our secret, attacked us, while the ones that were privy to it attacked the others, trying to save us. It was awful and bloody, and when it was finished, my family lay slaughtered. The sorcerer escaped and has not been seen since. My first act as king was to have the men who killed my family hanged."

I can see it all in my mind's eye, and my heart goes out to the young Beast. "Yet you are not king now?" I ask curiously.

Beast laughs, the sound unpleasant and harsh. He gestures at himself. "Look at me. Anyone who saw me ran in terror, convinced I must be some kind of monster. Most of the staff fled, and within a year, the three villages surrounding the castle were empty. I relinquished the crown to a distant cousin who built his own castle on the opposite side of the country."

"And what of your sister?"

"She came back the next day, her lover in tow. When she saw my new form and the remains of the great hall, she fainted. Her lover told me she was with child, and I urged him to take her far from Granton. With the sorcerer still at large, it was imperative that they go and never return." Beast pauses and meets my gaze, and the intensity in them causes me to catch my breath. "I never heard from Aria or Alaric again, not until he wrote to me of you, begging me to take you in."

I freeze, the blood draining from my face. "You're my—"

"Uncle, yes. And you, a prince."

"By the gods," I breathe, my eyes tracing over his features, looking for something familiar. The firm jaw and cleft chin are the same, and I suddenly find it hard to breathe. Father rarely speaks of my mother, his heart still torn in two over her early demise. "Will you speak of her with me? My mother? I know so little."

Beast inclines his head. "But first, I must tell you that tonight is the first full moon after your eighteenth birthday." A mixture of fear and foreboding slither down my spine. "You'll experience your first shift when the moon reaches its apex. I will teach you how to control yourself and then we will hunt."

Snow White

My nails snap and break as I claw at the stone wall, desperately seeking escape from the pain. The tendrils of magic try to force themselves into my head, and a piercing scream tears itself from me.

Morana's chanting pauses as she hisses, "Why can I not get inside your mind?"

"Please, stop!" I beg, but she pushes the magic harder. It feels as if someone is trying to drill through my skull. Sweat drips profusely down my face and chest, and my back bows in agony.

Cassian, where are you?

Chapter 9

Snow White

One Year Later

Snow blankets the earth in its quiet sparkling cover. A shiver runs through me as I sit huddled in the corner, my knees tucked under my chin, my bare feet and legs purple from the cold. My former dress is now nothing but thin rags, not enough to provide any semblance of warmth. Morana found the blanket Alaric had given me and beat me relentlessly when I would not give up his name.

To further punish me, she also had the hay removed. In the summer, when it housed countless fleas, this was almost a blessing, but now I'd give almost anything to have it back for the little warmth it provided.

I absentmindedly watch my breath fog before me, the whorls and swirls distracting me for a moment before disappearing. It's becoming harder and harder to keep myself present and aware. Escaping into the depths of my mind, where freezing temperatures, lice, and hunger pangs do not exist, is becoming harder to resist.

Most mornings, I no longer bother to mark the day. There are already hundreds of scratches, and the sight of them leaves me both furious and depressed. I haven't seen Alaric in what feels like months, and I realized recently that I can no longer remember Cassian's face.

Hope is rapidly dwindling, and I am hanging on by a precarious thread. Soon there will be nothing left of me.

SIX MONTHS LATER

Laughing up at the deep blue sky, I twirl around, my blush pink dress swirling around me. Red, yellow, and purple wildflowers sway in the tall grass, and the ghetti birds sing in the trees. The sun casts a golden glow over me, warming me while a gentle breeze ensures it doesn't get too hot. A hand clasps mine, spinning me around, and I crash into a broad chest. Green eyes sparkle down at me, and my face splits into a wide grin. I knew he would return for me. His lips meet mine in a passionate kiss, and my heart swells with love. I have waited so long for this.

Snow.

Snuggling deeper into Cassian's chest, I revel in the feeling of his arms around me, holding me close. A joyful tear streaks down my face, peace enveloping me for the first time since Momma . . .

Snow!

Cassian scoops me up and races across the field with me. "You are so strong," I whisper as he gently sets me on his horse. The pounding of the horse's hooves is jarring, but Cassian holds me close, and I fall into a doze as we travel. I'm not sure where he's taking me, but it doesn't matter as long as he's with me.

We ride for what feels like forever. The moon follows the sun across the sky, over and over again, while Cassian regales me with tales of his adventures.

Snow White.

Eventually, we ride into a small glen surrounded by thick forests. A large white cottage with a thatched roof sits in the center, wild roses climbing up its walls in a profusion of color and scent. Deer, unafraid of our arrival, nibble at the grass, while a rabbit family pokes their heads up from a clover patch, their noses twitching in curiosity. It's an enchanting place, and I am delighted when Cassian carries me inside, kicking the door shut behind us. He lays me down on a soft bed, tucking warm blankets around me and drops a kiss on my forehead.

Wake up, princess.

Snuggling into the soft blankets, I fall into a deep sleep, where I dream of dark magic, blood, and the woman that is the source of all my pain.

Morana

"What do you mean, she's gone?" I yell at the huntsmen cowering before me. Unbridled fury courses through my veins, a sizzling inferno waiting to erupt.

One of the two huntsmen swallows, glancing at the other. "We-we went down to deliver her meal, and the gate was open," he explains, his voice wavering. He lowers his head, too weak to meet my eyes even when I step toward him menacingly. Wrapping a hand around his neck, I force him to look at me.

"She didn't get out by herself," I hiss in his face. "Who could have done this?"

He shakes his head, eyes wide in terror. "I know not, my queen."

Throwing him to the ground, I spit on his face. "Go through the castle. Find who is missing. She could barely walk, let alone orchestrate an escape. Someone is with her."

He gets to his feet and grabs the other, the two backing away with a bow before bolting.

Letting out a frustrated scream, I storm through the castle and up to my tower. "Mirror! Show me Snow White." The runes glow, and fog moves across the surface. Minutes pass and my fury increases with the wait. My hands curl into fists, my teeth grinding against each other as the seconds go by.

"I cannot locate her, my queen," the mirror finally answers.

"Is she dead?"

"I cannot say."

Throwing back one of the tapestries, I lean against the window and stare out over the kingdom, eyeing with satisfaction the destruction my magic has wreaked. Turning back, a thought comes to me. "Mirror, mirror, on the wall, who is the fairest of them all?"

"Morana, queen of Valderán, art the most fair."

I hum under my breath. Then she is either dead or no longer in Valderán. *Or some kind of magic hides her,* my mind reminds me. Until the huntsmen return to me with their answer, there is nothing I can do. If the mirror can't find her, I have little chance on my own.

Turning back to the window, I let the view calm me before heading to the great hall. Settling onto my throne, I patiently wait for the huntsmen to return. An hour turns to two, and even several glasses of the finest red wine cannot stem my annoyance. Tapping my foot in irritation, I mutter under my breath about the incompetence of the fools I'm surrounded with.

An eternity seems to pass before they finally come stumbling into the hall, practically tripping over each other in their haste to reach me. Rolling my eyes, I silently beg the dark gods to give me patience. They fall to their knees before me, breaths coming out in sharp pants and hands trembling at their sides.

"Well?" I grind out when they remain silent. The one on the left swallows audibly.

"Both Alaric and Cassian are missing, Your Majesty."

Sitting up straighter, I cast my mind back. Alaric was here yesterday, I'm sure of it. But Cassian . . .

"When was the last time Cassian was on duty?" I bark out.

The two huntsmen exchange glances. One shrugs, while the other replies, "I haven't seen him in quite some time, my queen."

I narrow my eyes at him. "Define 'quite some time,' huntsman."

"I cannot recall the last time I saw him. When I realized this, I asked around. No one can remember seeing him for at least a year. One stable lad mentioned he remembered Cassian taking one of the horses out to visit a girl, but neither he nor the horse seems to have returned."

The men scamper off when I absentmindedly wave them away. If Cassian has been gone for so long, it's strange Alaric never voiced his concerns over his missing son.

Unless he wasn't missing, and Alaric knows exactly where he is.

Storming out of the hall, I find myself once again in my tower, demanding the mirror tell me where Cassian is.

"He does not reside within the boundary of Valderán," the mirror replies.

Simpletons. I am surrounded by simpletons. Pinching my nose, I demand, "Well, then where *does* he reside?" I'm going to wear a hole in my favorite shoes with all the impatient tapping I'm doing today.

After several minutes, the mirror responds, "He was in Granton, my queen, but now sails for the Forbidden Isles."

My body stiffens. No one goes to the Forbidden Isles. A group of gods-forsaken islands, they are desolate and inhospitable. There's only one reason anyone would be idiotic enough to go there.

My screech rings through the palace. "Bring me Alaric the huntsman!"

Throwing back the tapestries, I lean out the window, bracing my hands against the stone sill. Dawn breaks, weak tendrils of light reaching up from the horizon to tear back the darkness. Already steady shouts come from outside the castle's gates as villagers with pitchforks and torches vie for my attention.

"Give us food. Stop taxing us to death. Where are our children?" I mock under my breath. I am tired of their demands. Their petty little grievances mean nothing to me. A month ago, they were there in their hundreds, but as my magic slowly seeps into the land, its insidious claws working through the soil, their numbers have dwindled. Now a mere fifty or so remain, the others having either perished or succumbed to my control.

Stepping away, I ring for my maid to ready me for the day. After she leaves, I turn toward the bed, my mouth curling into a smirk. Silas lays propped against the headboard, pillows cushioning his back. His black eyes stare at nothing while a line of drool steadily spills from the corner of his mouth.

It took far longer than I could have imagined, but now that Elspeth has been dead all these years, and I removed Snow White from his sight, he has finally become the puppet I so needed him to be.

There's nothing left of the man. He's a shell for me to use and fill, then discard until I have use for him. The people have been clamoring to see their king, and I've heard the whispers they think to keep from me. They speculate that he is dead, perhaps by my hand, or some foul poison. Or that he has perhaps been imprisoned, kept from his people.

Today, I find myself thirsting for amusement. The people want to see their king? I will give them their king. And a show they won't soon forget.

Chapter 10

Cassian

Waves crash against the sides of the ship, the spray a welcome relief from the intense heat of the sun. Breathing deeply of the brine-scented air, I stand at the bow of the ship, looking out over the seemingly endless ocean before me. The mermaid figurehead, with her generous breasts and mane of red hair, keeps vigil over the rolling white-capped waves, protecting us from storms on our voyage.

After Beast finished filling me in on all the secrets my father had kept from me, he spent the next few months training me on all things shifter. My first shift was painful and terrifying, but breathtaking and thrilling. I learned how to fight in this new form of mine, how to hunt, and even how to fly.

I've shot up several inches, and am broader and even more muscular than before. All hints of boyishness have been eradicated, and a part of me grieves for the lost innocence of youth.

When Beast declares I have learned all I can from him, he once again takes me into the west wing. He withdraws a large golden bowl from a shelf and sits it on the mahogany table next to me. It has an unusual design; while the base and sides appear to be like any other bowl, the edge *is flattened and has runes carved into it. Pulling a flask out of a drawer, Beast carefully fills the bowl, then waves a hand over the top.*

"*Ask it to show you your heart's desire,*" *Beast commands.*

Leaning forward—and feeling particularly ridiculous—I do as he asks. When the liquid in the bowl lights up, I jerk back in surprise, then lean forward when a picture emerges. An emaciated girl with short, butchered hair curls into a corner, her mouth open in a scream as she weakly fights off disembodied hands that reach toward her. It takes me a moment to realize it's Snow White, and my eyes immediately fill with tears as my heart wrenches painfully in my chest.

I could easily pass her in the street and not recognize her. Staring at her image, I document the abuse she's suffered. Someone will pay for what they have done to her.

Gritting my teeth, I leap to my feet, glaring at the Beast. "*All this time you have had a way for me to see her, and you denied me?*"

Beast comes to his feet, knocks his chair over, and leans his fists against the table as he glares back. "*And what would you have done if I had shown you when you first arrived? Hmm? Gone running back to her? You would have been killed, and she would be left with no hope, or dead alongside you.*"

"*I could have—*" *I start angrily, then stumble back a step when Beast growls.*

"*You could have what? You barely knew how to fight. Your education was laughable. What would you have done the first time you shifted without any guidance?*"

I lower my head, shame filling me. The Beast provided me with so much, had stuck with me through painful shifts, and had patiently taught me everything I know. I wouldn't get far without the help he's provided me, and I know it.

Beast moves around the table and places a hand on my shoulder. "Your feelings for the girl are clear. I've taught you everything I can, but there's one more thing you must do before going to her."

My fists clench on hearing this. She needs me. She must think I've abandoned her, forgotten about her and my promise. She needs to know I'm coming back for her. "What else?" I ask wearily.

"A message arrived yesterday. The Oracle has requested your presence. I have arranged a ship to transport you to the Forbidden Isles."

My eyes fly wide. "It will take months to get there! I've already been gone far too long."

Beast's nostrils flare. "Do you wish to know what my spies have informed me? Valderán is dying. The sorceress calling herself a queen is slowly poisoning the land and the people. Once she has fully conquered the kingdom, she will move on to the next until the whole continent falls before her. Think you can defeat her on your own? Or do you just plan on rescuing the princess and hiding her away? What will you do when Morana has destroyed everything?"

I study my feet, my cheeks turning red under his questions. I need to stop thinking like a love-sick child. "Apologies, my lord."

Beast barks a laugh. "Pretty words, nephew. I can't say why the Oracle wishes to see you, but an invitation from them doesn't come lightly. You will sail first thing in the morning."

A squawking gull lands a few feet from me, bringing me back to the present. It tilts its head, its beady eyes sizing me up. For a moment I wonder if Morana controls more than just the ravens, and a shiver rolls through me. The thought is a terrifying one—never being able to ascertain whether you are being spied on.

The gull, apparently deciding I'm inedible and uninteresting, takes off, soaring up into the cloudless sky. My inner beast wishes to be free to do the same, and I silently reprimand him to settle down. It will take months to arrive at the Forbidden Isles, and although I may be powerful in my alternate form, I can't fly that far. Seamen are already incredibly superstitious; I don't fancy my chances of making it off this ship alive should they discover I'm more than just a man.

That night, I toss and turn in the small bunk of my minuscule cabin. Nightmare has come visiting and drags me down into the dark depths with him. Images of death and blood, of mouths open in terrible screams, dance around me. A bitterly cold pain slashes through me, and I cry out, desperately trying to stuff my intestines back into my gut. A sinewy shadow falls over me, and I back away, pleading for my life. Sharp claws dig into my chest, ripping my heart from me.

I throw myself into a sitting position, cold sweat dripping down my face, my heart hammering madly in my chest as Nightmare releases me from its grasp. Bile rushes up my throat, and I leap to my feet, emptying the contents of my stomach into a bucket, the sound of my father's screams replaying over and over in my mind.

Chapter 11

Morana

Descending into the dungeons, I kick a decomposing rat out of my way. My lip curls with disgust at the soft squelch it makes, and I lift my skirt higher. Grabbing a torch from the wall, I allow its flickering light to guide me into the dark, damp tunnels.

While the palace previously only hosted the two cells Snow White had been imprisoned in, I have since reopened the original dungeons. You will find no windows here, just pitch-black hunger and despair. Rats gnaw on both the living and the dead, while fleas and lice torment the living with the never-ending itching.

Luminescent mold, in a variety of neon colors, grows profusely down the walls, their weak glow the only light available. Frail moans and feeble pleas for mercy accompany me to the cell at the farthest end.

Alaric covers his eyes, protecting them from the light of the torch when I reach his cell. Before he can speak, I thrust out my magic, boring into his skull. He throws his head back, his eyes bulging as he fights against it. I cackle. Does he truly believe he can best me? No one is more powerful than I.

Alaric, as the lead huntsman, has never once caused any trouble over the years. Therefore, I left him alone, which was one mistake I won't repeat. "Why is your son heading to the Forbidden Isles?" I hiss.

"I will tell you nothing," he spits back defiantly. His neck snaps back at a painful angle when I force more magic at him. Screeching with irritation, I cut the flow when I realize he's one of the few immune to it. No matter. I have other means.

Flicking my wrist, he flies back against the wall, glowing bands of magic pinning his wrists and ankles to the wall with unbreakable manacles. He glares at me, gnashing his teeth, fists clenched rebelliously.

"Where have you taken Snow White?"

Alaric clamps his mouth closed, refusing to answer. He wishes to do this the hard way? Fine. My nails grow into claws, and I tear the shirt from him, then swipe down his chest, leaving jagged lines of bloodied flesh behind. He grunts in pain, but his mouth stays firmly closed.

A red mist lowers over my vision, and I scream my questions at him—each unanswered one earning more strikes. Blood splatters across the moss-strewn walls and drips from the low stone ceiling. Panting heavily from exertion, I finally stop when he passes out, greedily taking in the gruesome sight before me. Alaric's head hangs low, his body limp, crimson strips of flesh dangling from his torso. My stomach clenches with taboo hunger.

Scooping up the water bucket in the corner, I toss it over him. Alaric comes to, weakly spluttering. "I have no more use for you, Alaric the huntsman. But know this: I will hunt down your son and the princess. And when I do, I will tear them limb from limb and hang their heads on spikes on the palace gates."

His eyes go wide when I rush at him, swiping my claws into his belly. His entrails spill out, and he screams as he fights against the restraints. I rip the steaming mass from his body, tossing them on the floor, then tear into his chest and cleave his heart from his body.

His body slumps, the light quickly leaving his eyes. The heart quivers in my hand and then stills. I breathe in the rich metallic scent, then bite into it, taking Alaric's strength and life force into myself. Once it's consumed and the hunger appeased, I paint my face and neck in Alaric's blood before sweeping out of the dungeon, leaving his mangled body behind without further thought.

Flowers and candles deck the great hall, the long tables decorated in fine linens and the best dinnerware. Trumpets blast, and the doors are thrown open in front of me as I step out of the palace.

Small groups of villagers stand by the gate, shouting and chanting. I raise my arms high, magic blasting from me. It dips and swirls, moving from one person to another. Guards, huntsmen, villagers, servants—it matters not. Blessed silence descends, and I breathe in deeply before calling out, "King Silas has heard your pleas! Come, come, one and all. A feast awaits you."

The dead-eyed masses come pouring in, taking seats at the various tables. I gently pull back on the magic, just a little, enough for the people to not be total puppets. I need them to be on the brink of awareness.

Silas sits on a golden throne on the dais, his crown placed at a jaunty angle, a bottle of wine before him. He looks around almost bewilderedly, his consciousness struggling against the hold I have on his mind.

I join him, gesturing for the people to stand. "A toast to our most beloved king!" A weak cheer joins the raising of glasses, and my eyes narrow at their disrespect. "To our king!" I shout angrily, and those closest to me jump. They cheer louder this time, and I fall back onto my throne, satisfied with the effort.

Servants scamper out of the kitchens, bringing bowls laden with a thick stew. Hardy bread and cheeses accompany it, and the starving villagers waste no time digging in. Silas sits silently beside me, his dour face ruining my mood. "Here, my love, eat your stew. We must keep your strength up."

I must have released too much of my magic, as he ignores my command, his eyes locked on the flames burning merrily in the man-sized fireplace. Squeezing his leg under the table, I lean closer. "Now, Silas. Eat your meal."

He finally does as I request, woodenly spooning the stew into his mouth while returning his gaze to the flames. I studiously ignore the liquid dripping down his doublet, and instead focus on the people lapping up their meals like the good little dogs they are. I must pay my respects to the kitchen staff; the stew is wonderfully flavored, rich and intoxicating.

When everyone has gorged themselves on food and drink, I raise to my feet, dragging Silas up with me. Excitement buzzes through my veins, and I have to stop myself from jumping up and down like a child. The murmurs die down, and the room goes silent. A wicked grin splits my face when I lean over and yank down the curtain behind us.

Three spears rise from behind the thrones, the skin of a man bound to the furthest two, holding it out on display. The middle spear holds Alaric's severed head, his face forever frozen on a scream.

Tugging back my magic, my gaze bounces from one person to another, eagerly watching as they wake from my spell. Their eyes go from Alaric's face to his saggy skin, to the empty bowls in front of them.

The sickening realization enters their eyes, and cries of dismay and retching fill the room. I throw my head back, dark laughter pouring from me.

The next day, there are no protesters at the gates.

Chapter 12

Snow White

A m I real? Or just a fragment in someone's dream? Perhaps I am a ghost. Maybe... as slippery as an eel, the thoughts slide away.

I brush my hands down my arms and shudder at the papery skin stretched tightly over bone. It feels unfamiliar, as if my body is not my own. My hands fall away and disappear into the black nothingness surrounding me.

It wraps around me in an embrace, promising sanctuary. It whispers to me of danger and despair, encouraging me to take shelter in its arms. *It is safe here, no one can harm you.*

It's a lie wrapped up in the guise of safety.

Something prods at my lips, a faraway voice begging for someone named Snow White to eat. *Go away.* They force something into my mouth, insisting I swallow it. My tongue runs along the soft flesh, testing the foreign object. At their persistent urging, I bite into it, and a juicy, sweet taste bursts on my tongue. It tastes familiar, I'm sure I know . . .

They are back again, this time with a sharp object. I flail at them weakly, barely able to move my arms. They hold me down as I twist and turn, terrified screams ripping from my throat. *No. Don't. Please don't hurt me.* They shave my head, muttering about fleas.

Once they're gone, memories begin to trickle in. The harsh metallic taste of blood coating my mouth. The never-ending pain ripping through my body. The meaty sound of the leather whip striking my back. The spectral shade of Death reaching for me. Beckoning me to follow it. *Not yet.* There is someone I must find. Cas—

The thought floats away and I go with it, the darkness wrapping itself around me like a comforting blanket.

Safe.

Time passes. Night, day, night again. They won't go away. Lucidity comes and goes, but every time I slip into the darkness, they call to me, begging me to return. They pull me from the safety and force me into the awareness. Into being. Eat. Piss. Bathe. Tears run down my icy cheeks as I plead and beg. *Stop, please. Leave me be.* Still, the hands come, rubbing lotions into my skin, forcing food into my mouth, making me swallow.

Let me go back into the darkness.

"No, Snow White. You must fight this! Morana is destroying your kingdom."

Morana. I flinch back at the name. I know this, I know . . . crimson streaks running down my legs. Agonizing pain. My babe. Darkness comes roaring up, reaching for me. *Take me.*

Hands shake me. I turn to them but see nothing but the walls of my prison. Look at all the pretty white lines. "Wake up!"

Shivers rack my body. I need . . .

"What do you need?" The voice is soft and caring. Not like *hers*.

Him.

"Who?"

Green eyes flash in my memory. A fleeting smile. A promise. Feminine voices murmur and someone tucks another blanket around me. Warmth begins to seep into me.

"What did he promise you?"

My vision blurs. Why does my chest hurt so? I begin to rock as the pain escalates.

"Tell us who you need," they plead.

I hum, then giggle at the raspy sound. *Someday my prince will come.* But he's not a prince. No, he's . . .

"What is he?"

Gone. He is gone.

Despair tightens my throat, choking the life from me. This time the hands cannot stop me from plunging back into the darkness. I swim happily in its depths, where there are no lies, no broken promises, and no memories.

Chapter 13

Cassian

Five Months Later

"Land, ho!" a deckhand shouts from the crow's nest, and I quickly set down my cup of tea and jog out of my cabin. Seamen stream past me, eager to see land after so many months at sea. Someone hands me a telescope and points into the distance.

Ignoring the shouts of elation around me, I peer through the scope, greedily searching for land. *There.* I can just make out steep mountains rising from the water, and my heart thuds in my chest.

So close. Excitement bursts through my veins, making my head swim. Passing the telescope to one of the crew, a smile stretching wide across my face, I join in the cheers for the captain. One man pulls out a fiddle, and some of the men link arms, dancing in joy. Another uses an axe to open a keg of ale, and the cheers grow louder as mugs are thrust under the golden stream.

Taking mine over to the railing, I lean over, my eyes trained on the islands in the distance. My thoughts turn to Snow White, as they so often do. Lately, I have been having dreams of her, most of them disturbing. I do not know whether they are a figment of my sleeping mind's imagination, or if there is some truth behind them. Visions of her encased in darkness, screaming, fighting unknown assailants. Others of her staring blankly at the ceiling, the rise and fall of her chest the only sign of life.

Gods, I miss her. She was my constant companion for most of my life. The one person I could truly be myself with, the one who knew my secrets and didn't judge. It's been a little over two-and-a-half years since I left her. She'll be seventeen soon, almost a woman grown. She won't be the child I left behind, just as I am no longer the starry-eyed youth I once was.

I cannot help but wonder how she has changed, how she is still the same. Will she hate me for leaving her? For abandoning her when she needed me most? My jaw ticks at the thought. I can't blame her if she does.

Over the past few years, I have agonized over the decision. I've replayed what my father told me, the things Beast said to me. Their insistence that I grow up and find a way to get help was valid. Older and wiser now, I understand that. But could I have not brought her with me? Snow could have healed from her wounds in Granton. She would have been safe from her father and the queen. She could have grown up in peace, and I could have been at her side if she needed me.

If there is any validity to the dreams I'm having, then Snow White is no longer the girl I once knew. The dreams are filled with pain, terror, and confusion. Some of the more recent ones seem to indicate that she is lost within herself.

Logically, I know I could not have taken her with me, for the simple fact I would never have gotten her out of the palace alive, not once she was in the dungeon. With many of the huntsmen under Morana's spell, the guards posted outside, and the blasted raven spies everywhere, we wouldn't have stood a chance. Even if we had made it out, it wouldn't have been long before the ravens found us.

It destroys me to know I couldn't help her then, that I could do nothing but sit idly by while she was raped and abused. My eyes narrow at the vast expanse of sea, and I hurl my mug into the waves. It hits the water with a splash, and I vow then and there that once we're together, no one will ever lay a finger on her again.

Not if they want to keep breathing.

The captain pulls up to the jetty on the morning of Snow White's birthday. The sun has just freed itself from the horizon, the calm sea reflecting the pinks and golds of the sunrise. Seagulls scream overhead, diving into the water in search of their breakfast.

The crewmen moor the Jolly Roger, tossing the anchor into the sea before throwing a ramp down so we might disembark. I eagerly jog down the ramp on shaky sea legs and make my way off the jetty, nearly falling to my knees in gratitude on the rocky beach. After months at sea, it's a relief to be on solid ground again. A hand claps me on the back and I nearly go sprawling. A flash of silver catches my eye, and I spin around, meeting Captain Hook's amused gaze.

"Good to be on land again, aye?" the ostentatious pirate says, grinning at me.

"Aye," I reply, trying to ignore the ridiculously large feather bouncing in the oversized tricorn hat Hook seems to favor.

A shout from the ship catches the captain's attention, and I take the opportunity to look around. Beast had warned me that the Forbidden Isles were desolate. The expansive beach stretches around the cove where we docked, which is shaped much like a horseshoe. Jagged granite mountains stretch into the sky, the tops blurred into the low-lying clouds. At the base of the mountains is a small village—if "village" is indeed the correct word for the tiny settlement.

A white lighthouse presides over it all, standing tall and proud at the edge of a cliff on the left of the horseshoe. At its base is a large inn, a blacksmith's smithy to its right. A few small stone houses with thatched roofs are dotted here and there, a couple of scraggly trees between them. On the right-hand side of the horseshoe are market stalls. I cannot see from here, but the scent of freshly baked bread competes with the salty scent of the sea, and my stomach rumbles loudly, reminding me that I have not yet broken my fast.

There is nothing else. Why anyone would choose to live in such a place astonishes me. I could not live without the soft grass beneath my feet, the sound of the winds singing amongst the trees. A stab of homesickness pierces my heart and steadies my resolve. I will find this oracle and then return to Valderán, rescue Snow White, and somehow, defeat Morana and save the kingdom.

Easy, right?

Sweat pours from my brow, stinging my eyes. I wipe it away irritably, then swing my arm back, slamming the axe into the cliffside. *Don't look down.* My feet scramble against the loose pebbles, threatening to send me careening to the bottom. As I'm currently about two hundred feet up, that wouldn't be ideal.

It's been six weeks since I left the captain and crew behind in the village. Captain Hook assured me they would await my return, and I must take him at his word. I'm not sure he realized just how long my journey would take, even if the innkeeper warned me of it.

We had been sitting near the fire, drinking ale and playing dice when the owner of the establishment approached me. He had overheard I had been summoned by the Oracle and pulled me aside.

"The way to the Oracle is treacherous, lad. There be nothing but sharp cliffs and jagged rocks, ready to tear into an unsuspecting man. Magic behaves oddly here, some spells going awry."

I thought of my inner beast, and the corner of my mouth lifted in a smile. I was planning on shifting as soon as I was out of sight of the village and flying the rest of the way. "Thank you for the warning, good sir. I have no magic to speak of, so will be quite all right."

The portly innkeeper's gaze sharpened. I hesitated when it seemed he was peering into my soul. "It is not only magic that behaves strangely here," he muttered just loudly enough for me to hear. I stiffened, searching his eyes. Was it possible he knew my secret, or did he speculate? I had returned to the table, uneasiness settling in my gut like a bad omen.

A second omen came the following day. I was purchasing bread, cheese, and various types of dried meats from the small marketplace when an elderly lady approached me. Her gnarled fingers held on to my sleeve with a strength that belied her years. Her eyes were a faded blue, her silvery-white hair plaited into a long braid trailing down her back.

"Beware the trickster, my boy," she uttered before letting me go and walking away, her walking stick tapping loudly on the cobblestone street.

"Wait!" I sprinted after her, her movements surprisingly quick. When I caught up to her, panting, I begged her to explain herself.

She took pity on me and stopped, peering up at me. "The trickster, boy. Pay attention."

"Who is the trickster?" This earned me a knock over the head with her stick. My eyes narrowed as I rubbed my head. What was that for?

"Anyone who wishes to see the Oracle must first pass the trickster. Beware. Should you look him in the eye, you will be cast from the Forbidden Isles, never to return. Whatever you do, Cassian of Valderán, whatever you might see or witness, do not meet his gaze."

Two warnings should have persuaded me, but as I packed my bag and set off with a cocky swagger, I had every intention of returning no later than the following night. Once I was out of sight of the village, I quickly stripped, folding the clothing into the bag which I placed around my neck. After glancing around to ensure no one was around, I shifted, letting my manticore out with a roar.

For three days, I flew high, reveling in the freedom of flight and the feel of the wind rustling through my fur. Until I smacked into an invisible wall and fell from the sky. Terror had clawed at my throat, and I was convinced that was the end of me.

Two days were wasted recovering from the fall. Thank the gods for the shifters' ability to heal. That was the last time I was able to shift, and since then, I have been making my way on foot, navigating the rugged and uneven landscape.

Scrambling the rest of the way up the cliff, I finally heave myself over the top, collapsing on my back. Staring up at the cloudless sky, I allow my racing heart and breath to calm. The sun has passed its zenith and is starting to make its descent. With a sigh, I push myself up, my muscles groaning.

Strange things come out at night. Things whose howls make the hairs on the back of my neck stand up and my blood run cold. Dragging myself to my feet, I scan the area, my breath leaving me in shock when I spot a large cave in the distance. I rub my eyes to make sure it isn't a mirage—I've been fooled once already—but it doesn't waver. A part of me urges to keep moving as long as there is sunlight left, but the idea of being safe inside a cave, where I might light a fire and sleep peacefully, is too much to overcome.

Adjusting the bag around my neck, I forge onward, my steps dragging with exhaustion. Sweat drips down my back, dampening my tunic. On and on I trudge, the walk taking longer than I would have expected it to. When I finally swipe the perspiration from my eyes and glance up, the cave is still the same distance it was when I started. When my fatigued brain realizes I have passed the same set of apricot-colored stones for the fifth time, I collapse to my knees, head hanging in defeat.

"Cassian, son of Alaric. Welcome," a quiet voice hisses. I snap my head up, my gaze wandering around, seeing nothing.

Something titters in amusement, and I am no longer a mile from the cave but outside its entrance. Something moves within, something not human. *Beware the trickster,* the old woman's voice whispers, and I have just enough presence of mind left to lower my head, keeping my gaze firmly on the ground beside me.

Minutes tick by and nothing happens. No more voices, no movement. I swallow, trying to wet my parched throat, but the fear coursing through me stops me from moving. I've come too far to lose now. I don't know if this is the trickster I was warned of, but I can't take any chances. I just wish I could have slept first—in my exhausted state, I may make a mistake.

I clench my fists as my mind thrusts a picture of Snow White in front of me. I will do this. I will get past this so I can get back to her. Determination pushes the fatigue away, and I reach into my bag, gulping down some water from my flask. "I'm ready," I call out, just as the sun dips below the horizon.

"Cassian!" Snow White calls out to me, making me jerk. I raise my head until I'm reminded of the old woman's words. I squeeze my eyes shut and lower my head back to my knees. "Please, Cassian, help me!"

Something tugs on my sleeve, and I freeze, holding my breath. Snow's screams reverberate across the hills, playing on my nerves. These are not normal screams, but otherworldly ones, which I am sure will haunt my dreams for years to come.

Sweat drips from my forehead, gently soaking my hose. The screams come to an abrupt end, the tail of them echoing over the peaks. Silence envelops me, so thick I can only hear the thumping of my heart ringing in my ears. Just as I uncoil my muscles, the sound of metallic scraping sparks my nerves.

"Cassian," my father groans, "please, son. Help me." I crack my eyes open, keeping them focused on the ground. His feet appear in my peripheral vision, and I stare in horror as blood splatters on the ground. "Please," he begs, his voice thick and guttural, as if filled with liquid.

Fingers twist into my hair, trying to force my head back. I curl into myself, using all my strength to pull myself away. My father's feet disappear, but the blood remains, thick and sticky on the dusty ground.

The sounds of angry howls, yips, and snarls assault my senses as giant paws circle my huddled form. Hot, foul breath ruffles the hair behind my ears, and saliva drips onto my tunic. A rough tongue licks the back of my neck, sending shudders up and down my spine. I clench core muscles to prevent me pissing myself as icy terror grips my heart. My inner beast roars, begging me to let it out. Not that I could, anyway—whatever magic blocks my shift is holding him prisoner. Eventually, the animals disappear, silence once more descending. I exhale the breath I have been holding all at once and greedily suck air into my starved lungs. The quiet doesn't fool me, I doubt the trickster is finished just yet.

Minutes tick by, ramping up my anxiety. My lowered gaze swings back and forth over the small amount of earth I can see, waiting, wondering. The trickster must get bored with my continued silence, for moments later, a ring of crackling fire encircles me. I hastily pull my feet under me, curling into a tight ball as the scorching heat shimmers around me. Panicked wails of anguish and terror sound from the depths of the flames, Snow White's and my father's voices pleading for mercy and salvation. The scent of acrid smoke mixed with burning flesh fills my lungs, making me choke and splutter.

It takes everything in me to stay still, eyes downcast. I was brought up to protect, to become a huntsman, my sole purpose to serve and defend the royal family. Alaric passed Snow White into my care when I was nothing more than a toddler myself, and I have always taken my duties seriously.

My rational mind knows she is not here before me, burning alive in the dancing flames. But her screams awaken something primal within me—the thing that whispers that she is mine. The raw need to leap up and tear her from the flames is so forceful, I have to lock myself down. My muscles tense tightly, but I grit my teeth and wait it out.

As quickly as they appeared, the flames die out, leaving me cloaked in the cover of night. A soft hand strokes down my face, cupping my cheek. "My beautiful boy," an angelic voice says softly. "It's okay. You can stop fighting now. I'm here."

Shock rocks me to my core. I desperately want to look up. To see the woman who died birthing me, to just once lay my eyes on her. Do I look like her? Are her dimples mine? My eyes burn with unshed tears, and the hand moves to my head, gently stroking my hair. I clench my eyes shut tightly, blowing out shallow breaths.

This creature, or god, or whatever it is, is not just some trickster. Its cruelty is endless. It has somehow bored into my mind and ripped out my jagged pieces, displaying them before me, mocking me for my weaknesses.

"Who are you?" I cry out, and my mother's hand disappears. A horrible scraping sound slides around me, and something hairy brushes my ear. Keeping my head lowered, I open my eyes. Eight thin hairy legs stand before me. The creature paces around me, hissing at me in a language I'm unfamiliar with. Its feet poke and prod at me, trying to force me to look at it.

"Cassian, will you not look at me?" it wheezes, stopping in front of me. "I see you met that meddling crone in the village. Did she tell you not to meet my eye?" I remain silent, giving it nothing.

Malicious laughter, low and dark, rolls over me. "She is a jealous old hag. She envies my powers and tells all newcomers to the islands to avoid me. I am Anansi, messenger to the sky god, Nyame. She has seen your struggles and wishes to award you for your bravery. All you have to do is meet my gaze, and I will bestow all her gifts unto you."

Do not listen to it, Snow White's voice murmurs in my mind. *Come back to me.*

Just then the sun peeks over the horizon, and Anansi squeals, disappearing back into its cave. "Well done, Cassian of Valderán. You will find the Oracle due north, two day's walk from here."

I jerkily get to my feet, swaying as the fatigue returns in force. "Thank you," I reply to the trickster and stumble away from the cave, turning myself north.

Chapter 14

Snow White

A flicker of light dances beyond my closed eyelids, causing me to recoil into the soft pillows behind my head. My hand opens and closes over the velvety blanket covering me, and for just a moment, I think I'm in my room in the palace.

Cracking my eyes open, I blink against the brightness, struggling to bring the room into focus. My vision slowly sharpens, and the ceiling above me comes into focus. Dark wooden beams run down its length, breaking the white expanse. Three arched Gothic windows line the wall opposite me, and I can just make out the forest beyond.

I'm most definitely not in my room. My heart thrashes in my chest, closing off my throat. I gasp, desperately trying to claw air into my lungs as my gaze swings wildly around the room. I tear the blankets back, determined to escape, only to find my horrified gaze locked on the thin sticks that used to be my legs.

A low moan rips from my mouth as I inspect my arms and hands, finding them in a similar condition to my legs. They tremble violently with the exertion of raising them, but I carry on, gently touching my face and hair. Sobs rack my shoulders when my questing fingers find protruding cheekbones and butchered hair.

I don't understand what is happening. My mind feels sluggish and lazy, as if I've been asleep for a very long time. My body is not my own, and I don't know where I am. A myriad of thoughts slither around my brain, but holding on to one is impossible. They are as slippery as eels, here one minute, gone the next.

I manage to push myself into a sitting position, shifting the pillows behind my back to be more comfortable. My eyes ping-pong around the cozy room, taking in the gleaming wooden floor, braided rug, and small dresser with a vase of wildflowers sitting cheerfully on top.

Blue, blue skies with white fluffy clouds. Run, run, run. Shrieks of laughter under a golden sun. Rainbow birds and a flower crown; green, green eyes spinning me 'round and 'round.

My breath catches in my throat when memories begin to tear themselves out of the dark recesses of my mind. Raw, pent-up emotions claw their way through to the surface, threatening to drown me. I quickly push them back down, mentally backing away. But underneath, there lies a swirling mass of red and black, a boiling, bubbling fury so great it threatens to annihilate me. Its intensity terrifies me, so I shove it aside along with the memories, determined to examine them later.

The wooden door cracks open, and a child with extraordinary white-blonde hair backs into the room pulling a cart of sorts with her. My brows shoot up when she wheels around and I discover she isn't a child, but a dwarf. Her cornflower-blue eyes widen dramatically when she sees me sitting up, and her face splits into a wide grin.

"Sisters," she calls. "Come quickly, the princess is awake!" She abandons the cart in the corner of the room and dashes toward me.

I yank the blankets up, my eyes peeking from over the top. My hands shake nervously when I hear a stampede of footsteps pound outside the doorway, and moments later, six other women pour in. All are rather short in stature, and all have the same blue eyes. Their hair colors range from the deepest black to the palest blonde, with auburns and browns thrown in for variety. Each is stunningly beautiful, and I cringe, feeling dirty and ugly in their presence.

The one with the white-blonde hair speaks first. "Princess Snow White, I am Hilda. These are my sisters, Kelda, Linne, Nissa, Runa, Selma, and Thyra." Each woman raises a hand when her name is called and offers a range of smiles—some big, some small, and some right in between.

My gaze bounces between each of them, and some of the fear I first felt dissipates with the friendly smiles and glances. I've known enough evil to recognize it quickly, and these women show no signs of such infestation. I inch the blanket down until it's tucked against my chest and give them a tremulous smile in return. "Hello," I croak out, my voice rusty from disuse. "Where am I?"

The women all start talking at once, hands moving excitedly. Hilda, who seems to be in charge, clears her throat and looks pointedly at her sisters. They sheepishly close their mouths and lower themselves to the floor, tucking their legs under them. Hilda snags a nearby chair and places it by the bed before lowering herself onto it.

"What do you remember?"

Dropping the blanket to let it pool in my lap, I take a deep breath and push back the darkness surrounding my mind. Searching through vague memories, I pluck one out and examine it. "I was in the dungeons at the palace."

She nods encouragingly. "Do you remember how you got here?" My brows lower, thinking, then I shake my head slowly. "Alaric the huntsman brought you to us. He found you unresponsive and was worried you wouldn't survive much longer. He smuggled you out of the palace and brought you here."

Forcing a swallow down my throat, I ask quietly, "And where is here?"

The sister with rich auburn hair pipes up. Linne, I think her name is. "You are in Monarch Glen."

"I'm afraid I am not familiar with that. Are we still in Valderán?"

The sisters all nod as one. The one with hair as black as mine says, "We're a hundred miles or so from the kingdom of Alba, in the far northeastern corner of Valderán."

It takes me a moment to place where we are, having to reach deep to remember the geography lessons my tutor once gave me. Sadly, my education has been somewhat lacking the past few years.

Vague half memories of being on horseback play in my mind, and I wonder if that is when Alaric brought me here. My heart warms when I think of the many kindnesses Alaric afforded me over the years. He may not have been able to visit me often in the dungeons, but I always appreciated the small gifts he brought and the scraps of news he shared about Cas—

My body freezes, my mind scrambling away from the name. Rage bubbles in my veins, and I once more choke it down. The sisters gasp around me, some backing away. "Your eyes," Thyra murmurs.

Hilda rises from the chair and steps forward, worry evident in her features. She gently lifts my chin and peers into my eyes. Her brows lower for a moment, then her face clears, a small smile replacing the frown. "Ah. I suspected as much."

"What? What is wrong with my eyes?"

The sister with hair the color of rich chocolate whispers, "They're *glowing*."

Turning back to Hilda, I ask, "What do you suspect?"

She brushes a hand down her sage-green dress, then fiddles with her apron strings before meeting my gaze. "You are looking quite exhausted, Your Highness. Let us leave speculations and serious discussions for another time." I open my mouth to protest, but she waves a finger at me. "We have plenty of time for that later. You need to heal and recover first. Once you're back on your feet, we'll talk. There are things you need to know, and a war is coming our way. We, and all your subjects, are going to need you, Princess. Will you recover and stand with us when the time comes?"

I'm not sure what she is talking about. War? Glowing eyes? I don't like being ignorant, but the determination shining in her eyes prevents me from arguing. A slight movement from the far corner of the room catches my notice, and I imagine I see my mother's shade, her hand outstretched toward me, eyes pleading. I blink and she's gone, and I return my attention to Hilda, straightening my shoulders.

"Yes."

Morana

Ignoring the maid who has come in to light the morning fire, I snuggle deeper into the covers, unwilling to open my eyes and greet the new day. Instead, I examine the dreams that visited me last night—visions from my ravens, snapshots of various places around the country.

Two-thirds of Valderán has fallen to me. Each day, the poison I have poured into the earth slithers farther and farther in every direction, infecting the minds of nobles and peasants alike. Rivers turn to blood, a frothy crimson that rolls over rocks and pebbles in a vicious current that will sweep even the mightiest of men out to sea. Trees, once laden with the famed honeyed apples Valderán is known for, now stand barren, the trunks black and withered.

The once emerald waves of grass are now brown, the bees and butterflies having since moved on to greener pastures. Flies, on the other hand, have arrived in swarms, feasting on the carcasses of animals too weak from starvation to survive.

I have my reasons for destroying this country. Ones I have buried for so long I sometimes struggle to remember the origins. But the desire for vengeance still burns strong in my breast, unwavering and undeniable. I will conquer this land. Every man, woman, and child left standing will fall to their knees before me, their heads bowed in supplication. They will repent for what they did to me. Their eyes will be opened to their treachery, and their screams will be heard across the continent as they burn in the flames of atonement.

My teeth grit when my mind turns to Cassian and Snow White. The mirror tells me that Cassian is still in the Forbidden Isles, but Snow White is nowhere to be found. This gives me hope that she is dead, most likely perishing when Alaric stole her from the palace. My lip curls when I think of the huntsman. Even now, his empty skull decorates the gates, having been picked clean by the birds.

Throwing back the blankets, I ignore the drooling idiot next to me and slip out of bed. I wrap a robe around me, then make my way up to the tower. It has been too long since I have abated my curiosity.

"Mirror, mirror, on the wall, who is the fairest of them all?"

"My queen, I cannot lie, there is one more beautiful than thy."

No. It cannot be. "Tell me!"

"Snow White lives and has rejoined the light. She lives with seven others and rebuilds her might. I cannot say where she is for sure, some magic protects her, keeps her location obscure."

My hands slowly form into fists as I stare at the mirror in shock. Never mind that it was speaking in its ridiculous rhymes again—I swear it does it solely to annoy me—but the news that Snow White is indeed alive has floored me.

Turning, I dash to the window and mentally call my ravens. They come in their thousands, hovering around the palace.

"Find Snow White!"

Chapter 15

Cassian

I ran out of water last night. My tongue sweeps over my cracked lips, and my legs wobble beneath me as I try to keep to my feet. The pack resting on my back seems to grow heavier with each step, even though it's lighter than it was when I began this journey.

The sun scorches the earth with its rays, presiding mercilessly over the azure sky. The granite mountains have made way for sandstone ones, the rich red and orange rings stretching far above me. There is no vegetation here, not a single blade of grass, nor a tree whose shade I might shelter under. My sweat dries faster than my body can produce it, and I feel as if I'm losing my sanity. Mirages abound in every direction, each one a false prophet, pointing toward salvation that doesn't exist.

Dropping to my knees, I lower my head. I need to rest for a moment. Just a moment. Two small dusty feet appear in front of me, a girlish giggle reaching my ears. I use the last of my strength to raise my head, only to see a six-year-old Snow standing in front of me.

Her braided black hair hangs over her shoulder. A flower crown rests jauntily on her head, and an impish grin shows off her missing front teeth. What trickery is this? Does Anansi come again to test me?

The girl holds an arm out, and when I don't take her hand, she stomps her bare foot and waggles her fingers at me. "Come, Cassian, son of Alaric."

I stare at her almost in wonder. How did they make her so perfect? I remember that dress and the crown that I wove for her. Even her voice is as I remember, raspy and lispy with the missing teeth.

"Come," she says again, and I force my aching body to my feet.

"Who are you?"

"I am the Child. Now, follow me, my sisters are waiting."

I am not sure if following her is the wisest decision, but perhaps these sisters will have water. And food. Maybe a safe place to rest for an hour or two. I stumble after her, and after several yards, the girl vanishes before my eyes. I spin around, but she is nowhere to be found.

"Cassian of Valderán, please, follow me."

My jaw scrapes against the dusty ground when I turn toward the voice. Now, Snow White is an adult, maybe twenty. She stands strong and sure, her beauty blinding. I struggle to force down the lump in my throat.

"And you are?"

She turns, beckoning me to follow. "I am the Maid."

As with the Child, as soon as we've walked several yards, she vanishes. Before me stands a similar cave to the one Anansi hid in. A frail voice calls out to me, "Cassian, lost prince of Granton, enter."

Stepping through the arch, my eyes take a moment to adjust to the darkness within. A single torch sputters and flares against the cave wall. The Child and the Maid stand beside an old woman who I recognize from the village.

She winks at me with Snow White's eyes, huffing a laugh at my surprise. "Well met, lad. I am the Crone, and with my sisters, are the Oracle that you seek." I sway on my feet, and the Crone gestures toward a large rock. I take the offered seat, my gaze swinging between the three.

The Child and Maid step back, revealing a cauldron behind them. It's squat and wide, steam curling from its surface. Pushing myself to my feet, I step forward, brows lowering when I get a better look at it. It's made from some kind of dark metal that seems to devour any light that touches it. The rim is flattened, covered in runes, almost identical to the scrying bowl Beast has.

"You have seen something similar before," the Child states.

I incline my head. "Yes, in the Beast of Granton's castle."

She waves a hand over the cauldron. Neon-blue lightning streaks across the surface, culminating in tiny sparks. The opaque liquid inside clears, and I watch as the Child begins to speak.

"Many years ago, long before even Silas and Elspeth were born, or their parents before them, a sorceress was created." The cauldron shows me a stunning woman, magic flowing around her. "She was corrupted by the power within, became dark and vicious. Those that got in her way were annihilated." The scene changes, showing great massacres and suffering. "The cries of the dying were heard by the All-Father, Odin, who sent his son Baldr to investigate. Baldr was never seen again."

The Child lowers her head, a tear running down her cheek. "Odin's wife, Frigg, was devastated when her son disappeared and blamed the sorceress. She sent the Valkyries to collect her soul." The cauldron shows me seven women riding magnificent horses through the sky. I have never imagined such, and I observe in fascination as the women and horses descend toward a dark castle built up against the side of a mountain. "Unfortunately, the sorceress had been informed of their impending arrival and stole the horses away. The Valkyries were weakened without them, and they too vanished. Like Baldr, they too have never been seen again."

The Child retreats into the shadows, and the Maid steps forward. "In the far northeastern corner of Valderán, nestled amongst the Regency Mountains, you will find Snow White sheltering in Monarch Glen. Magic hides the cottage from prying eyes, but beware—Morana has commandeered thousands of ravens to seek her out. Should she step out of the boundary line, she will be found."

The Maid whispers words over the cauldron, and a scroll rises from within it. "Take this map, Cassian. It will show you the way." I reach out and grab the scroll, tucking it into my bag.

A low buzz of excitement begins to spread throughout me. Finally, after all these years, we will be reunited. The Maid steps back to join the Child, and the Crone, for the second time, whacks me over the head with her stick.

"Pay attention, lad." I scowl, rubbing the small lump quickly forming on my scalp. Her face is serious, but her eyes sparkle with mirth. "Morana will not be easily defeated, her powers are too great. You must find the horses and return them to the Valkyries."

My brows lower. "If they haven't been seen in generations, how am I to find them?"

The Crone rolls her eyes. "Did the Maid not just present you with a map?" She raises the stick again threateningly, and I swing out of her way. "Pay attention!"

"Yes, ma'am," I reply sheepishly, ducking my head.

The Crone sighs. "Children," she mutters under her breath, shaking her head. She murmurs over the cauldron in a language I do not understand, and this time, a sheathed dagger emerges. "Do not lose this," she states, gesturing for me to add it to my bag. "You must use it to shatter the glass from the inside. If you do not, all else will fail and Morana will control all of Restüra."

I rack my brain. "What glass do you speak of?"

"From the inside, Cassian. You must break it from the inside."

With that, the torch sputters out and the cave descends into darkness. "Wait!" I call out. "What glass?" There is no reply, and I sigh deeply. Stepping forward blindly, waving my hands in front of me to act as my eyes, I feel—nothing. The cauldron that was in front of me moments ago is gone. Moving to the wall, where I remember the torch being, also nets me nothing. The stone wall is bitterly cold, with no remnants of warmth remaining from the fire.

Turning away, I trip over the rock I had been sitting on, landing heavily on my knees. I find my bag, but it's heavier than it should be. I manage to get it open, feeling around inside. My flask is full, and I find a loaf of bread and dried meat wrapped in a cloth, along with a woolen blanket.

I fall on the food like an animal, tearing into the bread. I'm more careful with the water, knowing I must conserve it until I can find more. When I've sated my hunger and thirst, I curl up on the cold ground, pulling the blanket over me.

I'm out before my head hits the earth.

The feeling of tiny legs crawling over me startles me awake. Little spider eyes stare into mine, and I grimace, flicking it off me. It scuttles off into the shadows while a shudder works down my spine.

After relieving myself and eating the last of the bread, I dig through my pack. A small piece of paper flutters out, and I catch it before it hits the ground. It seems the Crone has left me a note. A grin spreads across my face. *Yes.* My shifting ability has been returned.

Quickly undressing and tossing the clothes in my bag, I shift, reveling in the power running through my body. Stepping out of the cave, I stretch my wings and roar, the echo carrying for miles around.

Moments later, I'm in the sky, heading back to the little village and the Jolly Roger. *I'm coming, Snow White.*

Chapter 16

Snow White

Ten Months Later

Standing naked in front of the patinated mirror, I slowly run my gaze over my body. Rays of sunlight stream through the open windows, accentuating the shine of my newly grown hair, now reaching just past my chin.

The claw marks on my cheek have faded, but are still visible. My cheeks have rounded out slightly from the hollowed craters they were when I arrived here. My bowtie lips are as red as ever, while my eyes betray the suffering I've endured, no longer sparkling with life as they once were.

The rest, care, and nutritious food I've had with the sisters have transformed my emaciated body into a healthy one. Turning to the left, I peer at my back over my shoulder, wincing at the sight of the hundreds of scars crisscrossing it. At least they have healed now, but I hate having to bear the constant reminder of what Morana did to me.

It doesn't make sense. All these years later, it still confuses me. Morana may walk around calling my father her love, but I know she has no real feelings for him. She cares for no one. She knew he violated my body and stole my innocence—the most heinous act a parent can inflict on a child. She had to know I didn't want him to touch me.

How could she place the blame at my feet? Why was I punished and tortured? Was it because I was with child when she had none? Was it jealousy over my beauty? By the gods, I wish I were ugly. Perhaps then my father would have left me alone, let me be the child I was supposed to be. And maybe Morana would have turned a blind eye to my existence.

After my mother died, Cassian was the only one I could truly count on. He knew me better than myself, was the keeper of my secrets, and the owner of my heart. Long before I even understood what that meant.

But he betrayed me. He left me behind almost four years ago to suffer unimaginable pain. The torture, the starvation, the bitter cold, the loneliness . . . the descent into madness. It was the sisters' care that brought me out of the nothingness and restored me to life.

I don't know where he is. He's most likely forgotten about me, perhaps off having grand adventures. Or maybe he's fallen in love and has a family. My eyes flash gold as the anger bubbles up. I slam them closed and breathe deeply, settling the rage down. He doesn't deserve my anger, nor my tears. Cassian made his choice, and it wasn't me. The feelings I might have once had for him have been burned to ashes, blown away on the breath of my screams. He left my heart with a gaping wound, and I have gleefully filled it with hatred.

Wherever he is, he better stay there.

Once I'm calm, I turn away from the mirror and sit on the edge of my bed, pulling on fawn-colored hose, then slipping on sturdy leather boots. Yanking a cream oversized tunic over my head, I then wrap a belt around my waist, pulling it tight. Lastly, I tie my hair behind my ears with one nod toward femininity—a red bow.

As I tuck knives into my boots and add another to my belt, I consider how much I have changed. Gone are the frilly dresses and intricate hairstyles. I no longer dance in meadows or read books by the fire.

Now, I train.

When I had settled into the cottage and started gaining my strength, the sisters regaled me with stories of their past. Once upon a time, they were mighty warriors known as the Valkyries. They towered over most men, and one of their missions was to collect the souls of the bravest warriors, escorting them to Valhalla.

We had all been sitting around the fire in the common room, tears streaming down the women's faces as Hilda recounted the story. Even the deer had come to listen, sticking their curious noses through the open windows.

They told me of Baldr and their mission to collect Ravensly's soul for her alleged role in his disappearance. How she had ensnared their horses, whisking them away. The sisters sobbed as they explained they were almost as one with their horses and removing them also eliminated most of their powers.

In revenge for coming after her, Ravensly, who was Morana's ancestor, turned the Valkyries into dwarfs. They were swept up on a foul wind and deposited—none too gently—in Monarch Glen. Using the last of their magic, they summoned the cottage into being and threw up a shield that would block the majority of prying eyes from being able to find them.

Very few knew of their location, and only a very powerful oracle would be able to breach the shield.

Only the return of their horses, should they even still exist, would restore the Valkyries to their former selves. They prayed often to their god, Odin, for his help, but either he wasn't listening, or he too could not find the horses.

So, for now, the sisters train me. Every day begins with a run, followed by breakfast. Then I spend the rest of the morning with Selma, working on various weapons skills. Although the Valkyries favor spears, I prefer a bow, but knives are also my forte. After lunch, I'll either practice horsemanship with Nissa, hunting with Runa, or tracking with Linne.

But it is what comes after the evening meal that I love the most. We gather in the common room, talking, laughing, telling stories. It took me several months to join in with them, too traumatized and nervous to contribute. But one day I giggled at a particularly hilarious story, and since then have opened up more.

For the first time since Momma died, I have a family. One that I will protect at all costs.

"Good!" Selma shouts as my knife finds its target in the dead oak tree. We don't practice on living trees, as you never know which one is home to a dryad. The shy nymphs are tied to their trees, and we don't want to damage them. "Now see if you can hit the same mark again." She stands off to the right, her dark-blonde hair tied up in intricate braids, eyeing my posture and aim. I jog over to the tree, grab the knife and return to my starting point. Flicking my wrist, I send it flying. It lands about an inch from the first mark, and I purse my lips in irritation.

"It's close enough, Snow."

"Close isn't good enough," I growl back at her. Retrieving the knife, I go again, and this time, it embeds itself in the first mark. Selma gives me a cheer, and I reward her with a satisfied grin.

"I think we should try the spear—" she cuts off, raising her eyes to the sky. I hear it then, the raucous calls of ravens. Fear pierces my chest, and my mouth goes dry watching hordes of them fly over us. I'm well inside the boundary, which means they can't see me, but the dread remains. I'm not ready to face Morana yet.

The Valkyries informed me several months ago about Morana's magic poisoning the land and how she was either killing or controlling the citizens. My heart cries out for them. They are my people and my responsibility as their princess. Hiding away here feels cowardly, and I can feel their deaths in my soul.

Cassian was meant to come back with an army, or with some way of defeating Morana. With him gone, I will have to find some way of doing it myself. I'm finally strong enough, but I need warriors at my side. The Valkyries would join me in an instant if only there was some way for me to locate their horses. It would be an honor to have them fight at my side.

As we stroll toward the cottage, the perimeter bells blare, forcing us to pick up our pace. They are one of Nissa's inventions, a warning system if anyone approaches. The rest of the sisters pour out of the house, their spears at the ready. Hilda tosses my bow and quiver, and I loop them over my back. We each split up, racing to our designated section of the boundary.

Think of a bowl sitting on the ground. That is what our boundary is. It reaches above the tallest trees and spreads roughly a mile around the cottage in each direction. Runes mark the trees to prevent us from accidentally leaving the boundary.

I climb one of the taller trees, settle on a thick branch, and scan the perimeter. The density of the forest makes it difficult to see, so I quickly calm my harsh breaths so I might listen. Moments later, the birds fall silent and my heart rate picks up. Quietly removing the knife from my belt, I wait.

The sound of hooves reaches my ears. My gaze follows the direction of the noise, landing on a magnificent black horse. Its silky mane flows in the gentle breeze, a hulking figure with a hood pulled low over his face on its back.

I bide my time, and when they pass under my branch, I sail off it, knocking the man from his horse. The stallion nickers and prances to the side, its nostrils flaring angrily. Straddling the man, I hold the knife to his throat, raising my eyes to meet his. Jade-green eyes stare back at me. I grow unnaturally still, the blood draining from my face. He reaches up and gently brushes a lock of my hair from my face, breaking the spell. Scrambling off him, my ass lands on the ground as I stare at him in disbelief, my heart lodged in my throat.

"Hello, Snow."

Chapter 17

Cassian

The last ten months have taken their toll on me. The journey back across the ocean was fraught with peril.

Black roiling clouds fill the sky, thick sheets of rain drenching the crew as they hastily tie down the sails. Vicious winds whip up the waves, some reaching heights of ten feet. My stomach burns with acid as the ship rolls beneath me, and I desperately clutch the railing for dear life. Hook, on the other hand, stands braced at the bow, arms flung wide, daring Triton to do his worst, even as his men fight to keep the Jolly Roger from capsizing.

We eventually limped into port, months later, the ship battered and bruised, and if I had been grateful for land when we first arrived in the Forbidden Isles, I was doubly so upon our return to Restüra.

After spending a night at an inn, I found a page waiting for me the following morning, Fire Heart in hand. The bags attached to the saddle were laden with provisions from the Beast, enough to see that I wouldn't starve on my journey.

Prior to setting off, I asked the map to lead me to Snow White. I had watched in slack-jawed wonder as a golden line appeared. It snaked and slithered over the map, a serpentine line stretching from my current location to Monarch Glen, nearly at the border of Alba. Adrenaline had coursed through me at the thought of being so close. I had set off immediately, Snow White my sole focus.

Every time I was forced to stop frustrated me. But I could only push the poor horse so far. He may have been bred for endurance and war, but often needed a full day or two of rest before carrying on. I'm not exactly the lightweight I was at twelve.

As soon as I stepped foot in Valderán, I felt a difference in the air. It was heavy and oppressive, and all of my instincts screamed at me to *get out*. The bitterly cold breeze rattled and pinged off me, as if it was sentient, searching me and learning my secrets. I had immediately covered myself, keeping the hood of my cloak pulled low over my face.

Just in time, too, as the ravens followed the wind, their aggravating squawking grating on my nerves. I kept myself as uninteresting as possible, slowing Fire Heart's pace to a crawl. After several days of this, the birds disappeared, having decided I was no one of importance.

Throughout my journey to Monarch Glen, my eyes were opened to the destruction Morana has caused. It's been several years since I've been in Valderán, and seeing my home destroyed makes me want to rage at the gods. How could they allow this to happen? Do they not care for us mortals? Have we, with our greed and petty squabbles, angered them so much they have turned their backs on us?

The destruction of the land has not yet reached the entirety of the country. I have only seen glimpses of it—a forest burning here, a river running red there. For the most part, this far north remains untouched. But inns and pubs are filled with displaced citizens fleeing the destruction. They tell tales of friends' eyes turning black before committing heinous deeds. Of children's bodies left to rot by the side of the road, women captured and defiled.

Orphaned children roam in feral packs, pouncing on unsuspecting travelers and bludgeoning them to death for the few coins in their pockets or the food in their sacks. One such group, along with their leader, has become so feared that most refuse to even utter the gang's name, terrified it might tempt the gods to send them their way. The Lost Boys. I have been fortunate to not have met them or any other troublesome youth on my journey. Of course, my size and the two war axes strapped to my back might have had something to do with it.

And now, after all this time, I am finally here. Lying on the warm ground, the emerald-green, sun-dappled canopy above me, and the girl—woman—I have dreamed about for so long straddles my chest, her small knife to my throat.

The Oracle hadn't done her justice in their imitation of her. Her ebony hair no longer flows down her back, but rests just under her chin. A rosy hue kisses her cheeks, and her ruby lips beg to be kissed. Her beauty could rival that of any goddess. Snow's hazel and gold eyes are the same familiar ones I remember, although the expression in them is not.

They tell a story I'm almost afraid to hear.

The moment my fingers touch her, a roar echoes inside. *Mine.* Snow White tumbles off me, landing on her backside. She stares at me with a mixture of fury and hatred, then jumps to her feet. Her hand tightens around the blade, and she bares her teeth at me.

"Don't ever touch me," she hisses, then turns on her heel and races away, quickly melting into the forest.

Although I have no right to feel it, hurt pours through me as I push myself to my feet. I knew she might hate me, but to see it—*Go after her. Mine.*

My head swings wildly around, looking for the voice. It's deep and rumbly, the words mispronounced slightly, as if not spoken by a human tongue. *Bring her back!*

"Who is that?" I rage out loud, spinning around, seeing nothing but trees and ferns.

You didn't think I was you, did you?

My eyes widen at the mocking laugh. I rub my knuckles over my chest, and the laughter comes again. *I am Aren, your manticore. Now, go get our mate.*

"I don't understa—"

By the gods. Are you always this dense? You, Cassian. Me, Aren. We are two and we are one. Now go after our mate or I'll force a shift and go get her myself.

The voice goes silent, and I waste several seconds wondering if I'm going mad, if the Crone had hit me one too many times with her stick. *Now!*

"Okay, okay," I grumble under my breath. Swinging up onto the saddle, I circle Fire Heart around and gallop after Snow White. The forest closes in around me, prickly bushes snagging my hose, branches threatening to unseat me.

An arrow shoots past my face and Fire Heart rears, pawing at the air. I clamp my legs around his sides, holding on for dear life. He settles with a snort, and I whip my head around, searching for the threat, the blood pounding in my veins in a steady rush.

"I deliberately missed," a disembodied voice shouts. "You are not welcome here. Leave, and I will spare you your life."

"I have come for Snow White," I call back, searching amongst the branches for the owner of the voice.

An arrow lands in the ground, inches from Fire Heart's hooves. "Second warning. There will not be a third."

Grinding my teeth, I rein Fire Heart around. He prances irritably, snorting in displeasure. *Plead our case. Don't let them stop you.*

"The Oracle of the Forbidden Isles has sent me to aid in the fight against Morana."

Silence descends, and the horse shifts under me. Leaning forward, I pat his neck, murmuring assurances to him. The sound of a twig snapping jerks my head around, but I see nothing. "What is your name?" the voice eventually asks.

"I am Cassian."

"Alaric's son?"

"Yes. Do you know him?"

Three dwarfs drop from the trees, landing lightly on their feet. One carries a bow, the other two, spears. I eye them warily, a nagging feeling tugging at my memory. Something about them seems familiar, but I can't place why.

"I am Hilda," the one with the bow says. "We have known your father for many years. He brought Snow White to us some time ago and entrusted us to her safekeeping. He told us you would return for her one day with aid." She looks around, brows lowering into a scowl. "We expected an army with you."

"I don't have one—yet," I reply, suddenly remembering why they look familiar. "You are the Valkyries." I smile triumphantly. Not only did the map lead me to Snow White, but also the daughters of Thor. We're one step closer now.

The three women exchange glances, the two with spears raising them. Hilda waves a hand at them, and they lower them again, to my relief. Hilda tilts her head, studying me. "How is the Oracle these days?"

"Helpful but vague. Has a way with sticks."

The women titter, blue eyes sparkling. "Hmm. Seems she has not changed overmuch, then. Come, you must be exhausted."

I follow them through the forest, bringing up the rear. By the time we reach a clearing with a charming cottage sitting in the center of it, four more women have joined our ranks.

It's clear women own the cottage; flowers in a riot of colors border the cottage and the path leading to the door. Ruby roses climb the walls, magnanimously leaving space for the windows. The lawn is neatly cut, and everything is pristine. If bachelors lived here, I can attest it would not look quite so charming. A shudder runs over my shoulders when I think of the huntsmen's quarters at the palace.

Snow White leans against the front door, her arms folded across her chest and wearing a heavy scowl. I bring Fire Heart to a stop and just stare at her, drinking her in. After so long apart, it almost feels surreal that she's standing here in front of me. I'm tempted to pinch myself to ensure it's not a dream.

"I'll not sleep under the same roof as him," she spits out.

Hilda sighs and pinches the bridge of her nose. "Snow—"

Snow narrows her eyes, turns, and once more races into the forest. "I've got this," I say, swinging my leg over Fire Heart and dropping to the ground. "We need to have a long overdue talk."

The woman with auburn hair chuckles and grabs my horse's reins. "I'll put him in the stable for you. Take your time." She winks at me, and I salute her before running after Snow.

My long strides eat up the distance, and it's not long before I have her in my sights. She glances over her shoulder, her eyes widening when she sees me chasing her. "Leave me alone, Cassian!" she shouts, picking up her pace.

Aw, Snow. I'll always catch you, remember?

My heart rate picks up, my lips curving, the thrill of the chase making my blood sing. I gain on her, my long strides no match for hers. Reaching out, I grab her shoulder and spin her, backing her against a moss-covered tree.

Her eyes spit fire at me, and I smirk back at her. She tries to shove past me, but I capture her hands and forcefully hold them above her head. Her chest heaves and my gaze catches on it for a moment, my mouth going dry. Tearing my eyes away, I meet hers. If looks could kill, I'd be six feet under.

I press my forehead against hers, struggling to calm my breathing. My heart beats fanatically, both from the run and her closeness. I pull in a deep breath, her light jasmine and gardenia scent flooding my senses.

"Did you just sniff me like an animal?" Snow asks caustically, trying to wriggle out of my hold.

"And if I did?" I move closer to her, boxing her in. Her eyes widen, pupils expanding. My body reacts immediately. I grit my teeth and move back slightly, willing myself to calm down.

Snow splutters, obviously not expecting my answer. "Well-well that's just weird."

I press her hands tighter against the tree, and she gasps. I breathe deeply again, and Aren growls in my head. *Kiss her already.*

No, I argue back. *I won't take something she isn't willingly giving. Her father took her choices away, I won't do the same.*

Aren harrumphs and settles down. Gods, this is so strange. I used to tease one of my fellow huntsman's sisters for talking to herself. At least no one answered her back when she did so. Especially not an overgrown lion-ram-eagle beast with an attitude.

Are you calling me fat?

Hold your tongue, I return.

Snow White stares at me as if I've lost my mind. Unable to remember what she said last, I change topics. Looking deeply into her eyes, I murmur, "I have fought for four years to get back to you. You may not believe me, but it's the truth." Her cheeks explode with a rosy flush. "You have every right to be furious with me. But heed this, Snow. I will only allow you to be angry for so long." I press into her, crushing her chest to mine. I angle my face so my lips are a hairsbreadth from hers. "But after that time is up, I'm coming for you. We both know you're mine. We were written in the stars. You are my destiny, and I am yours. So take the little time you have left. Hate me. Rage at me. Hit me if you feel the need to. But when your time is up, it's up."

Snow's nostrils flare, and her hands fist in my grasp. Her tongue darts out to wet her lips, and I inwardly groan. I force myself to let her go and back away. She slides to the right, edging away warily.

"Oh, and Snow?" She comes to a stop, head turned away. "Remember, I'll always catch you."

Chapter 18

Snow White

Two Months Later

Keeping my back to the wall, I silently creep down the upstairs hallway, lifting my legs over the floorboards I know squeak. My heart thrums in my chest while I tiptoe down the stairs. Although it's early, I can hear Nissa and Linne chatting quietly in the kitchen, the scent of freshly baked bread making my stomach rumble.

A male laugh echoes through the cottage, grinding on my nerves. Gritting my teeth, I move off the final step and catch my breath when my weight makes the floor creak. I should not have to fear walking around the cottage. I was here before him. He's everywhere I turn. Leaning arrogantly against a tree while I train. Obligingly tasting a sauce Runa makes. Chopping firewood to fill the log store for the winter. It seems like I cannot even relieve myself in peace.

The Valkyries have been more than welcoming. You could never call them anything but self-sufficient, but I guess having a big, strapping man around to do all those pesky chores you hate comes in handy. Between avoiding him and completing my own duties, the past few weeks have flown by.

I'm not stupid, I know what he's doing. Ingratiating himself with the sisters, hoping they'll allow him to move into the house. Getting them on his side so he can get closer to me. *We both know you're mine. We were written in the stars,* I mock silently, crossing my eyes. I ignore the heat that infuses my cheeks when I think of his words. They mean nothing. He's all talk.

But oh, do those words haunt my dreams. In the depths of the night, I want so badly to believe them. The day he arrived here, a countdown started, an invisible clock ticking down the seconds until he makes good on his claim. I'm simultaneously horrified and intrigued.

Hearing footsteps, I freeze, barely daring to breathe. The cottage and the little bubble we live under are my safe place. Somewhere peaceful, tranquil, healing. A home. Something I haven't had since Momma died. That great overbearing oaf has robbed me of that. Now, here I am, sneaking around like a mouse, hoping to not get caught by the cat. He sleeps in the stable with Fire Heart, but still manages to worm his way into the cottage for meals. I swear Cassian has put some sort of spell on the sisters, as they have all fallen for his charms.

He is *very good-looking*. I roll my eyes at myself. Yes, okay. I will admit that he has grown up nicely. Gone is the boy with bony shoulders and the breaking voice. Cassian now stands tall, at least six foot five. Thick muscles cord his broad shoulders and long, powerful legs. His hair has darkened a little, closer to a light, golden brown than the blond he once was. The only thing the same are his eyes. The beautiful green eyes that change depending on his mood. Usually a jade color, they can change to a brilliant emerald when his passions are running high.

I give myself a mental slap. Why am I thinking about him? He abandoned me. He doesn't deserve a single thought.

Just as I resolve to shove away all thoughts of the thorn in my side, I'm pushed against the wall. "Good morning, Snow," the devil himself murmurs, lightly brushing my cheek with his fingertip. A shiver runs down my spine, and heat coils in my stomach.

Annoyed at my traitorous body, I push Cassian away. "I thought you were going to leave me alone until my time is up," I snap at him, wishing my hair was long enough to flick.

Cassian raises a brow and chuckles darkly. "Oh, Snow. This *is* me leaving you alone."

I swallow down the panic that threatens to strangle me. My eyes dart around the corridor, seeking help. There are seven other people in this house but never anyone around when I need one. "Yes, well, how about you grant me the greatest gift you've ever given me?" He frowns, tilting his head to the side. "Your absence."

"Snow White!" Linne gasps, coming out of the kitchen, wiping floury hands on her apron. My triumphant grin at the devastated look in his eyes quickly melts, replaced by chagrin.

Hanging my head, I mutter an apology and run down the hall, throwing the door open and leaping outside. Guilt hounds my heels. This isn't me. When did I become the vindictive person that spews hatred? *You could always hear him out,* my logical side advises. *He left you behind to be tortured and abused,* my darker half sneers. Clutching at my head, feeling as if I'm being torn in two, I tear across the lawn, heading for my favorite spot. Plunging into the forest, I knock branches out of my way, stumbling as my vision blurs. The trees thin, and I fall onto the thick grass of the miniature clearing I found exploring one day.

It doesn't come as a complete surprise when Cassian cautiously lies down next to me. I peek at him, but he's staring up at the sky. "Remember when we were kids and we'd spend hours finding shapes in the clouds?" he murmurs.

My voice gets stuck behind the lump in my throat. Turning my gaze heavenward, I nod. Cassian turns his head toward me, but I stubbornly stare at the sky, refusing to meet his eyes. He scoots closer, then gently pushes his arm under my head and pulls me into his side. I stiffen but then the lingering anger deserts me, leaving nothing but heartache in its wake.

I roll onto my side, burying my head in the crook of his arm. Covering my eyes, I choke on a sob, my shoulders quivering. Cassian's arm comes around my shoulders and pulls me tighter to him. "Shh," he whispers. "I'm here now. All will be well."

Great racking sobs rip from deep within me. I cry for Momma, for my lost childhood. I weep for the destruction of my innocence, for the suffering I was forced to endure. I wail for four years of lost hope and the loss of my childhood friend who I missed watching grow into a man.

Cassian holds me throughout, letting me relieve myself of years of pent-up torment. There's nothing pretty or dainty about these cries. They are soul-deep and threaten to send me spiraling back into the darkness I once took so much comfort in.

Eventually, the crying turns to hiccups, then the hiccups to sighs. I push myself into a seated position. Cassian watches me solemnly, hesitation dancing across his face. We may have spent all these years apart, but he's still my Cassian. I still know him. He wants to comfort me, but he's scared I'll lash out at him.

The guilt returns with a vengeance. I have been terrible to him. I've mocked him, pushed him away, thrown spiteful words at him. *You don't know why he was gone for so long,* I remind myself. *Maybe if you actually listened to him, you'd find out why.*

Reaching out a trembling hand, I place it on his cheek. His eyes widen, a small smile on his lips. He covers my hand with his and closes his eyes, breathing out a deep breath. "Why did you leave me?" I whisper brokenly. "And why did you never come back? I waited for you. I peered out the window in the dungeons, day after day, praying to any god that would listen for you to return and save me from Morana. But you never came."

The muscle in his jaw ticks, and he opens his eyes, locking on mine. "It's a long story, Snow. I have so much to tell you. But it's imperative the Valkyries hear it too, and I'd rather only tell it once."

I nod, lying back down beside him. A brilliant white cloud glides past, lit by the sun. "That one looks like an elephant chasing a cat," I whisper. Cassian hugs me tighter as we stare at the sky.

Chapter 19

Cassian

The past few weeks have been hell and a lesson in restraint. After my ridiculous promise of allowing her time to be angry—which I regretted by day five—I made it my mission to stalk her. She's like an untrained horse, skittish and nervous. She needs to learn I'm not a threat to her. I won't hurt her. And I'll never willingly leave her side again.

So I did just that. At first, I watched from the shadows, letting her feel my presence without seeing me. Then I subtly changed my line of attack. Suddenly, I was everywhere.

She was training? I was watching. She was feeding the chickens? I was a few feet away, chopping wood. Bathing? I was outside the door, my heavy footsteps pacing up and down the hall. I would have taken up sleeping on the floor outside her door at night if the sisters would have allowed it.

For two months she has refused to look at me, turned away from me, or used her razor-sharp tongue to eviscerate me. I won't deny there haven't been times I've wanted to shake her into silence, force her to listen to me, then kiss her senseless until she forgives me. But I've restrained myself. My guilt over having to leave her behind has dogged me after all these years. It's never waned, no matter how many people tell me I had no other choice. I know I couldn't have taken her at the time. My brain assures me repeatedly that I have nothing to feel guilty about. My heart, on the other hand, disagrees.

So I understand her anger. Her hurt. Her mind and heart are at war with each other, just as much as mine are. While mine argue over guilt and regret, hers quarrel over betrayal and injustice. Snow doesn't know if she can trust me again, and I vow to do whatever I need to show her she can.

But after two months of bickering and avoidance, finally having her in my arms feels like a giant leap forward.

For the first time, all nine of us gather around the dining table. Previously, Fire Heart kept me company as I ate my meals in the stable, grateful to be fed at all. It was Kelda's and Thyra's turn to cook, and my stomach rumbles at the rich smells of freshly baked bread, hearty venison stew, and roasted vegetables. Hilda sets down jugs of mead and water amongst the little vases of flowers Snow picked to decorate the table. Several conversations are going on at once, and it has a decidedly festive feel to it. Perhaps because we have all come together, or maybe due to Snow White's quiet laughter and sparkling eyes.

It seems our little getaway this morning has done the trick. This is the first time I've heard Snow's laughter in years. My heart warms at the sound, and I want nothing more than to sit back and enjoy every moment. But a quiet urgency has taken up residence inside me. I don't regret the time I've spent here—seeing Snow smile is everything—but I'm very aware of time passing. It's easy to forget the outside world while ensconced in this idyllic little haven. I could easily spend many more months here, wooing Snow as she deserves. We could get lost in the golden glow of sunny days, of finding each other again.

But every day we're here is another day Morana's magic is creeping closer. People are dying, starving to death, while the country withers away. Others are being turned into the queen's puppets, while more resort to thievery and murder. Valderán desperately needs help. Morana needs to be defeated, and Snow must take her rightful place as queen.

Snow White's eighteenth birthday is in two days. When I informed her there was a clock on her anger, I chose her birthday for when her time is up. We can't wait any longer.

Turning my attention back to the meal, I fill a bowl of stew for Snow and hand it to her. She peeks up at me through her lashes, her cheeks turning a charming shade of pink when she thanks me. I wink at her, then turn to my meal.

After we've eaten our fill, we retire to the common room. A fire burns cheerfully in the fireplace, and two of the Valkyries light candles placed sporadically around the room. The low-beamed ceiling and glow from the fire lend the room a particularly cozy and intimate feel. The sisters take seats around the room, and I usher Snow into a comfortable-looking chair. There are no further seats. For a moment, I debate lifting Snow and putting her on my lap, but decide against it.

Our truce seems too new and fragile for such liberties. Instead, I settle on the floor at her feet and begin my story.

I start at the last time I saw Snow, outside the dungeon window. Tilting my head back, I look up at her. "I never wanted to leave you," I begin. "I argued with my father. I wanted nothing more than to steal you away, take you with me." A tear slips from her eye, and she gives me a tremulous smile.

"Alaric convinced me there was no safe way to extricate you from the dungeon. Your injuries were severe, and between the huntsmen, servants, and ravens, the chances of us getting out alive were slim to none. He was terrified we would be given the traitors' death."

I tell them of my journey to Granton, how I met the Beast in the forest. Snow White gasps. "You met the Beast? Was he terribly frightful?"

My fists clench when I remember how Morana used to threaten to sell Snow to him as if he were some kind of mindless, raging animal that couldn't control himself. "I was nervous at first, but over time, we became great friends." Everyone listens raptly as I share the Beast's story. A few sniffles are heard at the tale of the destruction of his family.

When I reveal that I am Beast's nephew, Snow pushes my shoulder. "Wait. You're a prince?"

I turn to meet her eyes, my lips curving into a smile. "Kind of? I don't know. Am I still a prince if the crown was given to another?"

"Yes!" everyone shouts out, amidst much laughter.

I wave my hand. "That's neither here nor there. Finding out I'm a shifter was a much bigger shock." The room erupts into chatter, and I wait for them to calm down. Once they do, I explain what kind of shifter. Aren demands I tell them what a handsome and fine beast he is, and I relay that to the women.

"Show us!" Runa calls out, and the other Valkyries cheer.

I throw my head back, laughing. "No one wants to see me strip down so I can shift."

The room goes deathly still for a moment, then Kelda murmurs, "I wouldn't mind." The room is filled with catcalls and ribald jokes. Snow stiffens behind me. She narrows her eyes at me, a rosy flush staining her cheeks. I wink at her and then raise my arm, encouraging the others to quiet down.

"Once Beast had taught me what he could, we received a message from the Oracle, demanding my presence in the Forbidden Isles." The sisters all listen, delighting in the tale. When I explain about Anansi and the trial I had to endure, Snow places a hand on my shoulder. The simple gesture warms my heart. Clearing my throat, I continue, relating what the Oracle had told me.

"I was then able to shift again, and quickly made my way back to the village, where Captain Hook was still waiting. It took us longer than expected to make it back to Granton, as the seas were unseasonably rough."

Hilda rolls her eyes and snorts. "Triton and his temper. It doesn't surprise me to hear his tantrums are continuing to plague sailors." Linne and Thyra nod.

"And then I made my way here," I conclude.

"We haven't left Monarch Glen in decades," Hilda informs me. "Your father told us of what Morana is doing to the kingdom, and we've heard some rumors here and there when we trade with the village at the edge of the glen. Can you tell us any more of what you've seen?"

"It seems the destruction is only recently making its way to the north. I witnessed a burning forest and saw a river frothy with blood. I heard tales of wild children killing passersby for coins or food and thousands making the journey to Granton and Alba to escape the wrath of the queen."

Snow White's hand tightens on my shoulder. "Why is she doing this?" she whispers. "Destroying the kingdom for what purpose? So she can rule over a wasteland?"

Unfortunately, no answers are forthcoming. Morana must have her reasons, even if I suspect she's not in her right mind. She's angry, bitter, jealous—yes. But I've always thought something was missing in her. Maybe she's a knife short of a set, or perhaps her mother didn't hug her enough as a child. It does make me wonder, though, if she has a grudge against the royal family, or against the kingdom itself.

A high-pitched ringing starts up, grating on my nerves. The women surge to their feet, running from the room. "What's going on?" I ask, jumping up, looking around in alarm.

"Move!" Snow snaps at me, pushing me aside. "Stay here." She races after the sisters, and I'm fast on her heels. She scoops up her quiver, throwing it over her back, and grabs her bow before dashing out the door. She quickly melts into the night, following the sisters. All eight of them vanish in the blink of an eye as if they were never here. Silence reigns supreme—only the light rustling of leaves in the cool breeze and the soft chirping of a cricket give any indication of life.

A shout goes up in the west. *Let me out,* Aren demands urgently. Something in his tone makes me obey, and I quickly remove my tunic and hose, tossing them over a bush next to the door. I run and leap, shifting in mid-air. When our paws hit the ground with a thud, we go still, scenting the air. Catching Snow's scent, we lope forward, following it. This is the first time I've shifted since Aren made his presence known to me. Besides helping the sisters around the property and stalking Snow for the past eight weeks, I've also been having conversations with him, getting to know this other entity that cohabits my body.

It's an unsettling feeling, having him take over. My consciousness, although fully aware, is suppressed while he takes the reins. He confided in me that he's always been with me, just muted. Even when I first started shifting, he wasn't able to make his presence known. Some shifter law, I suppose. It's not until they meet their fated mate that they're able to come forward as their own entity.

It must have been hell for him, trapped for over twenty years, unable to do anything but watch the world pass him by.

It was, he replies. *But do not pity me. It is the way of our kind.* I shut up and let him find Snow. Our mate.

Chapter 20

Snow White

When the alarm sounded, I reacted instinctively. Still coming to terms with having Cass around, I didn't think twice about leaving him behind. I can hear him behind me, but I can't think about him or his revelations now. Someone has entered into our little bubble, and we have no way of knowing if they be friend or foe.

Our cottage is miles away from the village at the edge of the glen and from any other homestead. The Valkyries explained once that they do occasionally get the random traveler passing through to Alba, but it's rare. Having the bells ring twice in the space of two months is unheard of.

I scramble up the same tree as last time, finding it the easiest to climb and the most accommodating for perching. The moon is only a thin crescent hanging in the velvety midnight-blue sky, the stars glimmering brightly like diamonds. Their light is scant but enough to see a few feet away at a time.

Squinting my eyes, I scan the small area I can see, excitement bubbling in my veins. I live for moments like these. As a young child, I was outgoing and curious, secure in my place in the world. After Momma died and my world came crashing down, Morana and Papa taught me what terror is. I withdrew and became a timid mouse, too scared to stand up for myself. I cowered and whimpered, then escaped into the darkness.

You were weak. No. I quickly squash that line of thinking. I wasn't weak, I was a child. I did what I had to do to survive. And that is exactly what I did.

The one upside of Cassian not taking me with him is the Valkyries. They brought me back from the brink of death and restored both my health and mental state. They taught me to not give up, how to fight, how to be strong. When it comes time to face Morana, I know I will have the strength to do so. And I have them to thank for it.

Now I love to fight. The rush, the adrenaline, the power—it makes me feel alive. There's nothing better than sparring with the sisters, or like now, waiting with bated breath, my heart thumping in anticipation, my mind focused and clear—after so long of being trapped inside myself—ready to drop from the sky to confront whoever has encroached on our haven.

The muffled sound of a twig snapping makes my head whip to the left. I quietly pull an arrow from my quiver and notch the bow. Tilting my head, I listen hard but hear nothing else. It may have been a rabbit or other small creature.

"Princess Snow White of Valderán, I bid you greetings. I am Merlin, most recently from the Principality of Kisfeld. I have heard of your plight, and have come to pledge my aid."

I shriek, nearly losing my balance. My bow falls to the earth with a clatter as I wrap my arms and legs tightly around the branch. Hanging my head over the side, I peer down. A man stands below me, wearing a long hooded robe. His magnificent white beard is long and thick, trailing down to his stomach. His hair, mostly covered by the hood, is just as white. He carries a staff in one hand, the other hangs loosely by his side. At first glance, he appears to be a harmless old man, but ancient power radiates from him. A tremor runs over my shoulders at the familiar feel, so similar to Morana's.

"We are about to have company," he states in a calm voice. I suddenly find myself standing on the forest floor, my bow in my hands. I look around wildly, brows lowered in confusion. "You must calm him," Merlin continues. "He will not listen to me."

"Who—" A roar shatters the stillness of the night. Terrified birds shriek, flocking into the sky. Icy terror claws at my chest and I find it difficult to swallow.

"There," Merlin murmurs, pointing his staff to the right. I turn, raising my bow. "You won't need that," he states matter-of-factly. His calmness soothes me, which is even more disconcerting, considering he is a stranger.

The thick ferns part, and I inadvertently step back, gasping. A low growl emits from the creature before me, followed by a gruff bark-like sound. My eyes widen comically as I look up, and up again. On all fours, he stands close to eight feet tall. His fur is a light-gold color, his thick mane a few shades darker. Spiraled horns grace his head, curving backward and to the side. Wings are tucked tightly against him, and his tail waves agitatedly.

He steps closer, lowering his head, mouth open in a snarl. His teeth are wickedly sharp and as long as my hand. "Greetings, Aren and Cassian. I am Merlin, come to offer my assistance. I mean no harm to you and yours."

The beast narrows its eyes at Merlin and then turns toward me. He tilts his head, jerking it to the side, clearly indicating for me to move away from Merlin. Well, that's just like Cassian, trying to protect me. Instead of obeying, I slowly advance toward him, reaching out an arm. My fingers delve into the soft fur on his chest, and a heavy rumble comes from his mouth. He's purring. I tilt my head back, grinning up at him, and he lowers his head so I can meet his eyes. Even in the darkness, I can see the jewel-like emerald color.

He's magnificent.

Aren shifts to the left, blocking me from Merlin's view. "I think we should hear him out," I murmur, scratching his chest. "We need to start building our army. If he's willing to help, then we should at least listen." He chuffs, returning his glare to Merlin. I sigh. Aren seems like he might be even more stubborn than Cassian.

I wasn't sure that was possible.

Releasing a deep sigh, I put my hands on my hips. "How about shifting back so we can have a conversation?" He shakes his head and begins to growl. "Please?"

"I think he needs these," Hilda says, materializing out of the darkness. She hands me Cassian's clothes, and the lightbulb goes off.

"Ohh." My cheeks burn, and I'm grateful it's dark. Aren makes a peculiar noise, and I realize he's laughing at me. I toss the clothes over his back, and he exchanges glances with Hilda, who instantly understands what he wants.

"Yes, I'll keep her safe," she assures him. I narrow my eyes and grit my teeth. *I can keep myself safe, thank you very much.*

The other women join us while Aren disappears into the forest. All this time, Merlin hasn't moved, just waits patiently. A few minutes later, Cassian joins us, standing by my side.

"Who are you?" Cassian demands, crossing his arms over his chest.

I elbow him in the ribs, making him double over. "Be nice."

"Are you still ticklish, Snow?" he whispers, his breath fanning my hair as he straightens. "Revenge is sweet, you know."

I gulp and turn back to Merlin. "Sir, can you tell us why you have come?"

The Valkyries gather around my back, keeping their weapons handy. Merlin inclines his head toward each of them, saying each of their names at every nod. He strikes his staff against the ground twice and toadstools appear, growing larger and larger until they are the height of a chair. There is one for each of us, and we take a seat. Two torches appear behind Merlin, floating in mid-air, allowing us to get a better look at the newcomer. My mind spins when I sit down. Lions and princes and magical torches. Oh, my.

"I am a traveler," Merlin begins. "I have been roaming both the Restüra and Reaveton continents on a personal quest. During the course of these travels, I have heard much of Queen Morana and her vendetta against Valderán.

"The Oracle is a personal friend of mine, and she informed me of your visit with her, Cassian. I, myself, hold a considerable amount of power, and I take offense to anyone who chooses to yield their magic to cause harm. I wish to make myself of service, if I may." Merlin's gaze rakes over the sisters. "I am sorry for what was done to you. I have roamed these lands for hundreds of years and recently heard of a legend that might interest you."

Hilda straightens her shoulders. "What might that be?"

"Do you know the Carrion River east of Clawback Mountain?"

"Yes."

"It is said that seven creatures live beneath its waters. Kelpies, they are called. They are the most beautiful of horses—pure white with golden manes. They wander the banks of the river, and anyone foolish enough to try to ride them, quickly meets their death beneath the rippling waves as the horses drown them. Legend has it they are driven by mindless fury, seeking revenge on the one that made them so."

Linne sobs, burying her head in Selma's shoulder. Thyra whispers, "They have been this close all these years?" The sisters erupt, dismay palpable in their cries.

Hilda wipes a tear from her eye and clears her throat. "Are they trapped there?"

Merlin's mouth curls in a sorrowful smile. "Indeed." Nissa cries louder, and Kelda rubs her shoulder. "But I have in my possession seven golden bridles. Should you go to the river and clip the bridles on them, both the horses and you will be free from the curse."

Everyone goes quiet. "Our powers will be returned?" Hilda asks at the same time Nissa says, "We can go home?" The sisters erupt again, chatting excitedly. Linne jumps up, throwing her hands in the air in a happy dance. Runa and Selma embrace. The cries are replaced with laughter and excitement.

My heart clenches in my chest, and I look down at my feet. I'm happy for them, I am. Truly. I swallow thickly, and my vision blurs.

But I've just lost another family.

Chapter 21

Snow White

Two Days Later

The morning of my eighteenth birthday dawns bright and clear, the newly awakened sun coloring my bedroom with the brilliant oranges, pinks, and golds of the new day. I stretch languorously, the warm feather quilts tempting me to stay abed. I give in for a moment, letting my mind wander where it will.

The Valkyries left with Merlin at dawn yesterday morning after his revelations the night before. He had refused our offer of staying in one of the sister's rooms, assuring us he was quite comfortable in the tent he conjured outside our boundary. The ladies were eager to commence their travels after so many years apart from their steeds. They promised to be back within a few days as Merlin would be assisting with the transportation.

I'm not exactly sure what that entails, but magic must be involved, as the trip would normally take weeks, if not longer. Especially since the few horses they keep in the stables had to be left behind.

Cassian and I have been left to our own devices. Hilda dragged him off before they left. I couldn't hear their conversation, but Cass looked thoroughly chastised by the end of it. She gave me a meaningful look as well, which caused my cheeks to heat and made me duck my head.

A coiling tension has been slowly brewing between the two of us. A glance, a touch. The possessive gleam in his eyes. It makes me want to run, to hide, shivers of something I don't understand sliding down my spine. At the same time, it intrigues me, makes me squirm, heats my belly with promises of . . . something out of my grasp. Run, stay. Hide, explore.

I'm a mass of contradiction wrapped up in a storm of feelings too big, too great.

I've barely had time to even sort out what I feel. Young Cassian was my best friend and confidant. I loved him with the mindless abandon of youth. My world revolved around him; he was the sun, and I, merely a planet trapped in his orbit.

Then he was gone. And no matter how unfair it may have been, the betrayal I felt was real. He had been the one constant in my life, there each day, until he wasn't. I spent years hoping, praying, desperate for his return. Needing him to be the one that saved me. That childish love and belief burned on the pyre of despair and was blown away on the winds of hopelessness.

Now he's come back. Taller, older, wiser. A shifter and a prince. He comes with promises and pretty words and hounds me with his presence. I've discarded the hatred—which, if I'm honest with myself, was never truly such—and forgiven him for leaving. I may have previously lost myself to the darkness, but I am of sound mind. I can see he had no other choice.

But there is still a sliver of mistrust at the back of my mind. He swears he will never leave me again. I so desperately want that to be true. I've overcome the horrors my father visited upon me and have risen from the ashes of the terror Morana inflicted. I crawled my way out of the darkness, trained to become strong.

That strength is no match for my heart, though. It begs me to let Cassian in, to allow him to prove himself. My body yearns for his touch, my lips desperate for his kiss. I may have let him closer recently, but a tiny part of me still fights against the primal, raw chemistry between us.

I cannot breathe when he is nearby. I cannot breathe when he is far.

The sun has returned. Will I bask in its warmth, or burn to ash amongst its flames?

After completing my morning ablutions and dressing in breeches, boots, and a tunic, I fling open my bedroom door and immediately fall to the floor with an oomph. Cassian jumps to his feet, axe in hand, his shoulder-length hair mussed and eyes wild. I blink up at him and clap a hand over my mouth, unable to stop myself from giggling.

"Were you sleeping outside my door?"

He runs a hand over his face and tosses me a sheepish look. "Maybe?" He tucks his axe back in its holster and reaches an arm out, pulling me to my feet. Cassian backs me into the wall and runs a finger down my cheek. "Good morrow, Snow. Happy birthday."

My breath catches in my throat. *Kiss me. Let me go. Save me. Destroy me.* His eyes search mine, then drop to my lips. My tongue darts out to moisten them, and his jaw ticks. I tentatively place a hand on his cheek, the short beard he's grown since arriving here tickling my fingers. Cassian lets out a deep sigh, leans forward, and places a kiss on my forehead.

My heart lurches, disappointment racing through me. I swallow it down and give him a tremulous smile. He winks and takes my hand, leading me down the stairs. "Come, I have much planned for the day."

"Like what?" I ask curiously.

"Breakfast first," he tosses over his shoulder. After settling me into a chair in the kitchen, he bustles around the room, deftly cooking up a batch of oatmeal. I watch in fascination, my chin resting on my hand as he portions some out into bowls to cool. Next comes a honeydew melon, fresh from the gardens, which he chops and divides evenly. He glances up, catching my eye. "What?"

I shake my head. "Nothing, just surprised, I suppose. I didn't know you could cook."

Cassian raises a shoulder. "Beast taught me. And a good thing too. It's come in handy more than once during my travels." He takes a seat opposite me, pushing the bowls of fruit and oatmeal in front of me. I stare at the food for a moment and sigh. He reaches across the table, placing a hand over mine. "What's wrong?"

It's my turn to shrug. "It's silly."

"Look at me, Snow," he commands quietly. I look up, green clashing with hazel. "Nothing about your feelings is silly. Don't dismiss yourself like that. I want to know what's going on inside that beautiful head of yours."

I duck my head, hating the blush that stains my cheeks. "Sometimes I forget," I start, keeping my eyes firmly fixed on my lap, "that you've had this whole other life without me. You're Cassian, but not the one in my memories. You've had adventures and experiences that I'll never know about, learned things I didn't know you knew." I gesture toward the food. "I know it's foolish, doesn't make sense. It's been four years—of course, you have lived your life. It's little things like this that remind me of it." I lean back, keeping my head bowed. "You've even returned a prince. I find it difficult to reconcile the old Cassian with the new."

His chair scrapes against the flagstone floor, and I can hear him moving around the room. He kneels before me, and gentle fingers lift my chin. "I am still me," Cassian murmurs softly, locking his gaze on mine. "I am still the boy that danced amongst the flowers with you. I am still the one that watched over your cradle with a wooden sword clenched tightly in my hand. I'm still the Cassian you spilled all your darkest secrets to. As for being a prince—" He makes a dismissive noise in his throat. "That means nothing to me. It's a lost title, something that might have been. It holds only one significance."

I swallow down the lump forming in my throat. "What?"

He places both hands on my cheeks. "I have loved you always. But I was nothing more than a lowly huntsman. I knew I could never be anything more than that—a protector, someone to guard your back."

I rear back, shaking my head. "That meant nothing to me! How could you think—" He cuts me off by placing a hand over my mouth.

"I know my status didn't register with you. But think. Would your father have allowed such a match? Or the people? Do you honestly believe anyone would accept such a thing?"

My eyes narrow. Is he saying . . .? My chair screeches as I push back, coming to my feet. I back away, shaking my head. A multitude of pictures run through my mind. Cassian holding my hands during my father's assault. Holding me while I cried into his chest. Dancing with me, chasing me. Arguing with his father outside the dungeon window.

My back crashes into the wall as more memories come. Early ones of me standing in my cradle, arms thrust out for him to pick me up. Cassian scooping me up when I fell. Cassian hiding me away when Morana would roam the halls, screaming my name. Sleeping outside my door to protect me. Haunting me around the cottage, always there, always ready to catch me.

Tears course down my cheeks. *I have loved you always.* Those were his words just moments ago. Intense waves of feeling slam into me, making my knees buckle and my breath hitch painfully. He rushes forward, catching me before I hit the floor.

I'll always catch you.

"You love me," I gasp out in wonder, my hands fisting in his navy doublet. I've been so blind. His hands slide into my hair, tilting my head back.

"Of course, I love you. It's always been you, Snow." His lips come down on mine, and my heart soars. I wrap my arms around Cassian's neck, twining my fingers in his soft hair. His kiss deepens, urging me to open for him. I acquiesce, and his tongue slides into my mouth, dancing with mine. Frissons of heat spark under my skin, shooting straight to my core.

Cassian pulls away and rests his forehead against mine. Our breaths mingle, and I take the moment to revel in the feeling of rightness.

When he steps away, I drop my arms, already missing the feel of his around me.

After choking down the cold oatmeal, Cassian leads me outside, our hands firmly entwined. Squinting against the sun, I ask, "So, what plans have you been hatching?"

Cassian chuckles and grins down at me. "We both missed out over the last few years. I thought we could show each other our new skills." He tosses his free hand out, and I glance around curiously. We're in the training yard, and he's laid out an assortment of weapons. My bow and a quiver full of arrows. Two wooden swords, his axes, and a couple of knives.

My lips stretch into a wide smile. "You're on." Dashing over to the stack of weapons, I scoop up the swords, tossing the bigger one to Cass. He catches the hilt with one hand and spins it around, his face splitting into a grin.

With a laugh, I rush forward, and our swords clash with a loud crack. I jump back before bringing it down sharply. Cassian blocks me. He spins away, then rushes at me, tapping me on the waist. I growl and narrow my eyes at him. Cassian laughs heartily and gestures to me to come for him. Over and over our swords collide. My arm trembles as

I block one more blow, and we lean into each other over the blades, panting heavily. "Yield," Cassian demands loftily.

"Never," I gasp. I back away from him, dragging the sword on the ground. He lowers his head and licks his lips, his eyes turning from sage to emerald. He stalks toward me, a deliciously evil grin spreading across his face. My heart skips a beat and the exhaustion flees.

"You will," he says in a deceptively calm voice.

"I am your princess. You will be the one that bows before me," I throw back haughtily, straightening my shoulders and leveling him with a cool look.

Cassian barks a laugh and tosses the sword to the side. My eyes grow wide and I gulp. "Run."

"What?"

"Run, princess mine."

Chapter 22

Snow White

Exhilaration rushes through my soul as I spin on my heel and dash into the forest. My feet pound against the moss-covered ground, my heart drumming rapidly while my laughter soars amongst the trees. Deer, rabbits, and chipmunks scatter, racing to hide from the beast stalking me.

A roar shatters the silence of the forest, sending delicious thrills of excitement through me. My gaze catches on an ancient oak tree a few yards ahead with thick branches low enough for me to reach. My feet pick up their pace while my lungs gasp for air, and as I near the tree, I leap up, my hands scraping along the rough bark. I pull myself up, my feet scrambling against the air for purchase. I manage to swing myself onto the branch before darting farther up, allowing the thick canopy of leaves to hide me from view.

Aren can't run as fast as I can through the woods, not with his height and girth. The trees are too close together to allow him easy passage. If he truly wanted to catch me, he wouldn't have shifted. I settle down to wait, allowing my heart and breaths to calm.

The sound of snapping twigs below alerts me to his presence. Peeking through the thick foliage, I spy him stealthily padding toward my tree. I bite my lip, making sure to keep still and my breathing calm. The tree shakes, and I tighten my legs around the branch. Aren's front legs rest on the trunk, his gaze triumphant as it locks with mine, his teeth glinting in the sun in a leonine smile. Or, that's how I'm interpreting it.

He growl-barks at me, a low rumbly sound with the edge of command. Dropping back down to all fours, he looks at me expectantly. "All right, all right. I'm coming," I grumble, climbing back down the tree.

When I'm almost at the bottom, the alarm bells start blaring, and my heart leaps into my throat. Aren spins around, growling. Dropping from the last branch, I begin to run, but Aren leaps ahead of me, shaking his head. He lowers himself to the ground, his head jerking toward his back. I delicately step on his thigh, then swing my leg over until I'm straddling him, making sure to avoid his wings. I wrap my hands into his thick mane and tighten my legs when he stands.

We quickly head back toward the training grounds, the shrill shrieking of the alarm piercing my skull. Once we're out of the trees, Aren makes a beeline for the weapons. As we near them, I lean over and, balancing precariously to the side, scoop up my bow and quiver. I pull myself up, notching an arrow after placing the quiver over my back. Aren's haunches flex, his muscles rippling under me as his wings spread. I quickly hold on to his mane again, a thrill of excitement running through me. He surges into the air, and even though I'm worried about whatever has set the alarms off, I can't stop my shout of joy as we fly upward, his magnificent wings flapping steadily as we climb higher.

In only seconds, we are above the tree line, and I look around in awe at the landscape before me. The Thogrun Mountains line the north, their craggy peaks forever covered in snow, no matter the season. There are rumors they are the home to an army of dwarfs who mine for precious jewels in the caverns hidden within. Monarch Glen stretches out to the east and west, a mixture of ancient forests, bubbling streams, verdant meadows, and brackish lakes. The air is crisper up here, the scent of pine heavy on the winds that snarl my hair and try to unseat me from my perch.

Aren roars a challenge, and my head snaps to the left when I hear horses neighing in return. My eyes fly wide in wonder as seven pure white horses with golden manes and tails race toward us, their hooves pounding against nothing but air currents.

They are as tall as Aren and just as majestic. One horse breaks off from the others, taking the lead while the rest fall back. My eyes mist with tears and I clutch tighter to Aren's mane. Hilda sits tall on the back of her steed, no longer childlike in stature. Her icy-blonde hair whips around her in the wind, untamed by the golden circlet adorning her brow. She holds a mighty spear in one hand and clutches the reins in the other.

"Meet us in the training grounds," she calls to me, and I nod.

Aren banks to the left when suddenly a movement to the right captures my attention. A raven rears backward, flapping its wings furiously, its beady gaze locked on mine. Recognition lights its eyes and it caws loudly.

A wave of ferocious anger rips through me, explosive and volcanic, heating me from the inside. Aren roars, swiping at the bird, but it easily dodges out of the way. Before I even realize what I'm doing, I lift my bow and aim, the arrow piercing its heart. Satisfaction replaces the anger as I watch it plummet to the earth.

One of the things that kept me going during my time in the dungeon was the thought of revenge. I wanted justice for my mother, for the life torn from my womb, for the beatings I took at the hands of the psychotic queen. I lost it for a while, becoming too complacent during my time with the Valkyries. I've needed my time here, to heal and gain strength, to recover from the depression that had its claws sunk so deeply in my psyche, and to train so I could become ready for the war that is coming. At the same time, being here has almost been like a dream, the outside world easily forgotten. But seeing Morana's spy hit the ground in a shower of ebony feathers has rekindled the flame and reawakened the urgency to save my kingdom.

I hope the raven had time to relay my image to Morana. I hope she's even now standing in front of her magic mirror, raging at the sight of me killing her raven. And I hope she realizes I'm coming for her.

Aren shakes his head, his muscles bunching under me. I hold on tight as his wings fold back and we descend toward the ground. When we land, I clamber gracelessly off his back, my legs like jelly. Aren lopes into the trees, and a few minutes later, Cassian comes out, buckling his belt around his waist. His eyes find mine, searching my face, and I offer a side smile back. He comes to a stop beside me, our fingers brushing together.

Large shadows glide over the grass, turning it from a shamrock green to pine. Placing a hand over my eyes, I squint against the sun and watch as the Valkyries land on the other side of the training ground. They dismount their horses and walk toward us, and I grab Cassian's hand, entwining our fingers. Hilda, Kelda, Linne, Nissa, Runa, Selma, and Thyra fan out in a semi-circle, and my gaze passes from one to the other.

I'm by no means short at five feet eight inches, but they now tower over me. Each is dressed in intricate battle leathers adorned with gold accents. They all wear a circlet around their foreheads, with a different colored jewel mounted in the middle. Bracelets adorn their upper arms, inscribed with words written in a language I'm unfamiliar with. Some carry swords, others, spears.

Hilda steps forward, her mouth curled into a wide smile. I stare up at her with my lip trembling, blinking back tears. I can sense the farewell coming, and I'm not ready for it. The Valkyries have become my family, like the sisters I could have only dreamed of having. She wraps her arms around me and I swallow hard. She backs away, holding on to my shoulders. "Happy birthday, Snow."

"Thank you." I search her eyes. "You're leaving, aren't you?"

"Come into the house, we have much to discuss," she answers, avoiding my question. All of us return to the cottage where we find Merlin in the kitchen. The good tablecloth has been placed on the table, along with a large vase overflowing with pale pink and mauve peonies. An intricately decorated, three-layer cake rests on the countertop, surrounded by platters of salamis and cheeses, crusty bread, and pots of butter and honey.

I stop and stare at the bounty, amazed at how quickly he has been able to put this together. Magic must be handy indeed. Cass draws out a chair for me, and I take my seat. He squeezes my shoulder gently before sitting next to me. The others take their seats, and after the food is passed around, talk turns to their trip to the Carrion River.

"Merlin transported us to the river," Runa explains, slathering butter on a thick slice of bread. "When we arrived, the horses were nowhere to be seen." She bites into the bread, effectively silencing herself.

Kelda picks up the story. "I don't know about the rest of my sisters, but as soon as we stepped onto the sandy banks of the river, I had the most powerful sense of foreboding." The others nod, concurring with her. "The clear skies quickly became dark, thick with heavy clouds. A conspiracy of ravens, many hundreds strong, swarmed around us, squawking. They tore at our hair and faces, determined to prevent us from reaching the edge of the water."

I wrap a slice of salami around a piece of Rauchkäse cheese, the smoky flavor complimenting the salami perfectly. I barely notice what I'm doing as I listen raptly to their story.

Thyra sips her wine, then sits back, running the edge of her finger around the lip of the glass. "I'm not exactly sure what Merlin did, but he used his magic to freeze the birds. Silence descended over the immediate area. It was as if time itself stopped."

The corner of Merlin's lip lifts. "Only above the water. Beneath it carried on as normal."

Nissa's eyes light up. "It was an . . . interesting experience." She tilts her head to the side. "Merlin gave each of us a bridle. They were unlike anything we'd ever seen. So delicate it looked like a strong wind would snap them, but strong enough to subdue the horses. We were afraid they wouldn't remember us, or that the spell they were under would prevent them from coming to us."

"So what did you do?" Cassian asks, refilling his glass with more wine.

"The simplest thing we could think of—call them," Hilda replies. "Each of us was more than willing to jump into the water to find them. After so many years apart, we were anxious to see them once more."

"But we didn't see the point of getting soaked if we didn't have to," Linne interrupts.

Hilda huffs a laugh. "Indeed. I went first. Mine was trained to answer to my whistle. After releasing it, we waited, and moments later, the river became frothy, the ripples turning into waves as Torsten leaped from the dark water. He reared in front of us, forelegs lashing out. It was as if he didn't know who I was, and I could feel my heart cracking."

Kelda, sitting next to her, places her arm around her shoulders. "They're like our family," she explains. "Knowing they've been prisoners to the river all this time, forced away from us and their homes, and that they've been this close was difficult for us to bear."

The others murmur their assent. Hilda threads her fingers through her cloth napkin and then continues, "Torsten wouldn't allow me near him. He kept backing away or lashing out with his hooves. Eventually, Linne and Nissa distracted him, and I was able to throw the bridle over his head. Once on, it clipped into place, and he settled down. The fury and wariness left his eyes, and he came to me at once, nuzzling into my shoulder. We did the same for the rest of the horses, calling them out of the Carrion one by one until they were tamed."

My brows lower. "But that was two days ago. Why did it take you so long to return?" I ask curiously.

Selma and Thyra stand to clear the plates from the table. Once it's clean, Merlin flicks his wrist, and the cake floats over to the table, settling down gently in the middle. Thyra hands out fresh plates and forks while Selma cuts everyone a slice.

Hilda catches my eye. "We went to Asgard to see our father, Thor. We have brought back gifts for you and Cassian." She reaches under the table and brings up a satchel, then comes to her feet, stopping by Cassian. She lifts out two axes, intricately carved with runes. His eyes widen as he takes them reverently, turning them over to view the etchings.

"These are incredible," he breathes, unable to take his eyes off them.

"They were made by Sindri, the dwarf that made Thor's hammer, Mjolnir. Never throw them without the intent to kill, as they never miss their mark," Selma says.

Reaching over Cass's head, Hilda hands me a small wooden box. Like the axes, it is carved, not with runes, but with delicate flowers. I trace my finger over the carvings, then carefully lift the lid. Inside sits a silver necklace, the chain thin and dainty. Hanging from it are five disks, each engraved with hieroglyphs.

Linne stands and walks over to me, taking the box from my hands. She puts the necklace around my neck, and it settles between my breasts. "Never take it off. The day will come when you must rely on it."

I glance up at her. "What do you mean?"

She places a hand on my head, her eyes beseeching. "I cannot tell you more, for that is all the seer Ulfhild told us."

I let out a sigh. Why is everyone so cryptic? Once we finish the cake, Hilda informs us it's time for them to depart. I square my shoulders, determined not to fall to pieces. Each of the Valkyries hugs me before collecting their weapons.

"Fear not, Snow, you will see us again. We go to spread the word that the Princess of Valderán is coming to claim her crown. We will speak to Thor and our uncles and brothers, to see who might come to your aid."

"Thank you." I do not trust myself to say anything further, for fear I may do something to humiliate myself, like attach myself to their legs and beg them to stay.

Cassian and I stand in the doorway, his hand on the small of my back as we watch them mount their horses and fly away. I do not turn my gaze away until the tree line blocks them from view. Letting out a weak breath, I allow Cass to lead me back inside, where we find Merlin standing in the middle of the miraculously clean and tidy kitchen.

"Tomorrow, we leave," he informs us. "It will take time to reach the palace, and we'll need to collect your army on the way."

"I don't have one yet."

"You will," he says with a wink.

Chapter 23

Morana

Black candles grace the windowsill and shelves in the bathing chamber, the flickering light bouncing off the stone walls and warm hardwood floors. Shadows drench the corners, concealing the bodies of the virgin boys who so generously donated their life force to ensure I remain young and beautiful. Warm, thick blood fills the large tub to the brim, coating my skin in its life-giving essence. I lift and twist my arms into the air, fingers dancing in the cool air, my gaze transfixed on the crimson drips sliding into the tub. Scooping some of the blood into my cupped hands, I slather it generously over my face, my tongue darting out to taste the coppery liquid running over my lips. The heady taste and scent awaken the hunger deep inside me, and I bring my hands to my mouth over and over, the rich blood sliding down my throat and quenching my thirst. When I have drank my fill, I breathe in deeply, then slowly slide under the surface, remaining under until I am forced to rise for more air.

Gentle power thrums through my veins, invigorating me. Sweeping through the castle, I smile and greet the servants. Change is afoot. I flick my wrist toward the doors leading to the courtyard. They fly open with a reverberating crash and the guards standing just outside jump at the sound, spinning around with their swords raised. My magic flicks out, tossing them to the ground like insignificant insects while I descend the steps, my burgundy dress swishing around my long legs.

As per usual, the servants scurry to hide when they clock my presence. One goes so far as to dive into a mountain of horse dung, much to the despair of the one that had just cleaned it up. He cries out in anger, the sound grating on my ears. The fool has not seen me yet, so busy is he berating the coward.

My eyes narrow dangerously. No one should ignore my presence. I curl my fingers and a wisp of magic solidifies before flying toward him. Blessed silence reins once more. The man spins around, stumbling on unsteady legs. I cackle at the terror in his widened eyes, watching in glee as his questing fingers tremble at his mouth, feeling the thick black thread that has sewn it shut.

His gaze meets mine, and my mouth stretches into a smirk. Another flick of magic takes out his kneecaps, his muffled screams caught in his throat as he crashes to the ground, writhing in agony.

Tossing my hair over my shoulder, I sweep out of the courtyard and head for the mausoleum. Dead grass crunches under my slippers, and barren shrubs huddle miserably in the once glorious flower beds, their wizened branches black and ugly.

A soft sobbing stops me in my tracks, my gaze bouncing from one bush to another, searching for the source. Ah. A tiny nature fairy the size of a butterfly weeps inconsolably under a rotting camellia. Their job is to keep nature balanced and can often be found in flower gardens. I lash out my foot, sending the fairy flying with a squeal. My shoulders quiver as a malicious grin stretches across my face.

The mausoleum is set in its own grounds to the side of the palace. The imposing structure was once as brilliantly white as the palace, but the poison in the ground has discolored it to a sickly gray. Four columns hold up the stone awning over the entrance which sports heavy wooden doors deeply engraved with various gods of death and the underworld. On the right-hand door, the Shinigami sit surrounded by cherry blossoms. Hel stands proud by her hellhound while Hades glares at any visitors from his throne. Anubis, Kali, and Pluto grace the left-hand door, decorated with skulls and scenes of the underworld.

My eyes roll to the heavens. They are nothing. The time of the gods has long since passed. My magic blows the doors open and I sweep inside, dismissing the insignificant figures. I am far more powerful anyway.

The inside of the mausoleum is cavernous, bigger than the building outside suggests. The ceiling reaches thirty feet high and is divided in half by a supportive stone beam. The right side is painted with the image of a glorious castle in the sky, surrounded by golden rays of the sun and puffy clouds. Tree branches in the foreground are covered with rose vines and house miniature Fae.

The left side is darker. Thick, gray clouds swirl in the background, showcasing a dead tree, its bare branches reaching into the sky like skeletal hands. Two sinister vultures peer down into the room, their eyes seeming to follow you if you dare look up at them.

But they are nothing I haven't seen before. I have been here often, sometimes to vent, other times to gloat. My fingers drift over one coffin, then another, the dust and decay of dead royalty coating my hands. I come to a stop in front of a pair of coffins. Inside lie King Aramaus and Queen Bridgette, the great-grandparents of King Silas.

A smirk settles over my face. He's not much of a king anymore. I knock on their coffins. "What say you now, Your Majesties? You were warned when you came against my family. Now your grandson's wife lies cold nearby. Your kingdom is in tatters, the land dying under my poison. Your people are fleeing, while others rot in the fields. And Silas is nothing more than a drooling moron, a puppet for me to play with."

I imagine their faces pale with despair. Oh, how their knees would wobble, their cries would rent the skies with their grief. They would have bowed before me, begging my forgiveness.

But it would never come. They took from me the only thing I could have loved. Their arrogance, their greed, cost me everything. Now, their kingdom will pay for their mistakes, and their descendants will feel the force of my wrath.

My eyes flick over the man lying on the cobblestones as he uses his arms to drag himself over the uneven ground. His muffled mouth makes whiny, pleading noises, which I ignore. He's already forgotten. Loud cawing snaps my head up and my spine straightens when ravens pour into the courtyard, screeching at me. Lifting my skirts, I race up the stairs and through the palace. Huntsmen throw themselves out of my way as I storm up one flight and then another before climbing the steep, twisty steps of the tower.

"Show me," I demand the mirror, and its foggy surface begins to glow. Slowly, the fog dissipates, and my heart freezes in my chest when an incredibly beautiful woman aims a bow at me, her eyes flashing with a golden fire. My body freezes, and I stare at Snow White incredulously.

Gone is the skeletal waif that languished in a huddled ball in the dungeon. Her ebony hair shines in the sunlight, her cheeks rosy with health. But it's the look in her eyes that arrests me. It is one of determination and retribution, one that promises vengeance. She cocks her head to the side, a defiant slant to her brows as she stares at me through the raven.

Her arm draws the bowstring back before releasing it. The arrow flies toward me, breaching the mirror's surface. I duck, the arrow whistling over my head before it lodges in the wall, vibrating from the impact. Bloodied feathers rain from the ceiling, carpeting the floor just before the raven's body drops to my feet.

I slowly stand, my brows deeply furrowed. What she just did is impossible. Nothing can come out of the glass. Whirling around, I dash down the stairs, my hair flying out behind me. I stumble to a stop outside a locked door and fumble in my pocket for the key. I open it with shaky hands, tamping down on the confusion and fear racing through my mind.

Stepping quickly inside, I lock the door behind me and take a moment to catch my breath. The circular room was once used for storage, but I had it cleared out years ago. On the left is a narrow but tall fireplace, a heavy wrought-iron hook attached to the side, waiting for a cauldron to be placed on it. A long wooden table made from thick planks sits to the right, its surface covered in beakers and bowls. A chest sits nearby, filled to the brim with all sorts of potions and poisons.

Animosity and enmity replace the fear as I gaze over my precious stash. I breathe deeply of the herby scents and an evil smile grows on my face as a plan forms in my mind.

I pluck a dozen apples out of the air, red and ripe, each one perfect in form and size. Flinging an arm up, they settle into a basket as flames burst to life in the fireplace. I toss various ingredients into the cauldron, chanting ancient words over the potion. Steam rises from the pot, its whorls shaping into a screaming skull. When it's ready, I dip all but one of the apples into the poison, marking the safe one with my fingernail.

Striding over to the ordinary mirror hanging on the wall, I stretch my fingers out and wave them over my face. I watch in satisfaction as my height lowers several inches. Heavy lines appear around my eyes and forehead, my teeth yellow, and my shoulders slump. My dark hair turns gray and my eyes turn cloudy.

You want to come for me, Snow White? I throw my head back, cackling. *You don't stand a chance.*

Chapter 24

Cassian

Glancing up from the book I'm reading, I get lost in the fire crackling in the fireplace. The dancing flames and sparks hypnotize and entice me, and the scents of burning wood and pine cones fill my senses. The orange glow barely lights the room, providing just enough light to see by.

Besides the low sizzling and snapping of the fire consuming the logs, the rest of the cottage is hushed. Merlin retired to his tent several hours ago, and Snow White followed shortly after, peeking shyly over her shoulder at me as she ascended the stairs. I had not yet been tired enough to find my own bed, and instead, got lost in a story about love and revenge, pirates and giants, princesses, deadly poisons, and rodents of unusual size.

A deep yawn threatens to crack my jaw, and I lean back in the chair, the book dropping to my chest. The warmth of the fire seeps into my bones, my eyes grow heavy, and a wave of exhaustion hits me with the force of a blow.

A loud piercing cry startles me out of my dreams, jerking me painfully awake. I jump to my feet as it comes again, my head turning toward the ceiling. The weariness vanishes immediately as the cries turn into terrified screams. My heart leaps into my chest and I tear out of the room, swing around the banister, and race up the stairs.

I don't bother to knock. Throwing Snow's door open, I skid to a stop when I see her scraping her nails against the wall. "Let me out!" she cries, the terror and desperation clear in her voice. She spins around, her eyes wide and unseeing. "No," she moans, backing into the wall. "Papa, no, please!" Her head thrashes from side to side and tears course down her face. She slides down the wall and hugs her knees to her chest. "Cassian, where are you?"

The plaintive sorrow in her voice breaks me, the searing pain in my chest enough to make my head spin. Rushing to her side, I gently scoop her up. She freezes in my arms, her body stiff and unyielding. "Gone, gone, gone," she whispers, still caught in the grip of her nightmare.

Laying Snow carefully on the bed, I place the heavy feather quilts over her before crawling in beside her. She shivers violently, sobs racking her shoulders. I pull her into my arms and cradle her gently, murmuring softly to her. She quietens and her body relaxes against mine.

"Please don't leave me," she whispers against my neck, and I flinch, the old shame and guilt rearing their ugly heads.

"Never. I'll never leave you again." I pull her tighter to me, and her arm comes around my neck as she nuzzles into my chest. She sighs and slips back into sleep, while I stay awake to protect her from the demons that haunt her dreams.

The dawn chorus pulls me from my dreams, and I groan, rolling onto my back. Patting around the bed, my brows furrow when my questing hand finds only cool sheets, and no Snow. Squinting my eyes open, I peer around the empty room. "Snow?"

The door to the bathing chamber creaks open, and Snow White sticks her head out. Her eyes darken with anxiety, and she chews on her bottom lip, a blush staining her cheeks a deep burgundy.

Pushing myself up, I swing my legs over the side of the bed and rub a hand over my face. "What's wrong?" Snow ducks her head, then straightens and meets my eye. She takes a hesitant step forward, then another, clothed only in a towel wrapped tightly around her. Her bare feet pad quietly over the hardwood floors until she comes to a stop in front of me.

Her hand nervously clutches the towel as she meets my confused gaze. She takes a deep breath, then blurts out, "I can't do this anymore, Cass. Every night I'm terrified of going to sleep. I relive his touch over and over." I reach out and take her hand, rubbing my thumb over her knuckles. "I need—"

"What do you need?" I ask quietly when she pauses.

She pulls her lips into her mouth while her eyes plead with mine. "I-I need you to take it away." She drops my hand, then lets go of the towel. It drops to the floor in a puddle at her feet, and it takes everything in me to keep my eyes firmly on hers. "Please, Cassian. Make me forget. Help me erase the memory and replace it with you."

Swallowing thickly, I carefully rise to my feet. Her hands tremble at her sides, but she remains still, watching me with a mix of determination and terror. Gently laying a hand on her cheek, I run my thumb over her lips. They part under my touch and my cock stirs in my hose. "Are you sure?" I murmur, my gaze coming back to hers. She nods jerkily. "If you want me to stop at any time, tell me, and I will."

"Okay," she breathes, her tongue darting out to wet her lips. Ever so slowly, I lower my head to hers, taking her lips in a soft, tender kiss. She opens for me with a sigh, and I take the invitation to slide into her mouth. She tastes of fresh mint and honey, and I press closer to her, sliding one hand into her hair, cradling her head. I lose myself in her taste and touch, my heart soaring knowing she trusts me to do this for her.

Claim our mate, Aren growls. I push him away. I'm not going to rush this. It matters not that I've waited for this moment for years. I won't scare her away or do anything to make her uncomfortable.

Snow takes a slight step back, putting her palm on my chest. I freeze but relax when the corner of her mouth lifts. "Remove your shirt."

"As you wish," I murmur, grasping the edge and pulling it over my head. Her eyes widen and she hesitantly runs a finger over a scar on my chest. I quiver under her touch, the need to touch her strong. I still haven't allowed myself to fully look at her, too worried I might spook her.

"What is this from?"

"Beast was teaching me to fight. I didn't dodge away from his claws quickly enough." She presses her lips to the jagged edge of the scar.

My teeth clench from keeping my hands at my sides. Snow trails her fingers over my chest and down to my waist, then moves around to my back, her hand leaving trails of heat behind. She comes around my other side, her fingers now edging into the top of my hose.

"Now these," she whispers, backing away to watch. I'm not sure I've ever moved so quickly in my life. They join my shirt on the floor, and I stand before her naked, our breaths shattering the silence. I finally allow my gaze to wander from the curve of her neck to her full, ripe breasts and the pendant that lay between them. Her coral nipples pebble, begging for my touch. I rake my eyes over her flat stomach to her hips, then to her core and down the length of her long legs.

She is exquisite, more than I could ever have imagined, the dreams I had over the years failing spectacularly against reality.

Snow does the same, her gaze gliding over me before landing on my hardened cock. She blushes prettily but doesn't look away. "Can I touch you?" I lower my head, and she reaches out with a trembling hand, stroking her finger down my length. I groan at the touch, and she jerks back, eyes flying wide. "I'm sorry," she whispers.

My lips curl up. I step toward her, running a hand through her hair. "You didn't hurt me, Princess. You can touch me however you like." She searches my face, then pushes up on her toes. Meeting her halfway, our lips meet. Her chest brushes against mine, her softness to my hardness. Bending my knees, I lift her, her legs wrapping around my waist. Her core presses against my abdomen, leaving evidence of her arousal on my skin.

Our kiss turns frantic, hot, heavy, mouths open and breaths ragged. Intense waves of love, desire, and need thunder through me. She is the blood that pounds in my veins, the stars that glimmer in the night sky.

She is my world, my everything. The years apart, the loneliness and longing were all worth it for this one moment here.

I carry Snow to the bed and tenderly set her down. She peers up at me, worrying her lip. "Are you sure?" I ask once more. I'll accept nothing but her complete and willing consent. She hesitates for just a second, then nods.

"I want this. I want you, Cass."

I take a moment to stare at her, determined to keep this moment in my memories until the time comes when my soul departs this world. The first rays of dawn trickle through the east-facing windows, bathing the room in a golden glow. They light Snow White with tender kisses of pinks and golds, illuminating her body as if the sun, too, worships her. Her short ebony hair spreads wantonly over the feather pillows, while her glorious body is spread out like a feast, just waiting for me to partake of.

Walking around the bed, I climb in beside her, then pull her into my arms. My eyes lock with hers, and I let her get comfortable with our bodies pressing together. I run a hand through her silky hair, then brush over her brows, then down her cheek. She watches me back, the gold flecks in her eyes more prominent.

I ghost my lips over hers, little nips and butterfly kisses. Turning her head to the side, I glide my mouth down the elegant column of her neck before opening my mouth and sucking the skin at the base, leaving my mark on her. Aren purrs with approval, the sight of our mark exciting him.

Moving down to her breasts, I force myself to stop and glance up at Snow. She smiles encouragingly, her eyes hooded with desire. I cup one breast in my hand, its pillowy softness making me groan. My mouth waters at the sight of her nipples, and I deftly suck one into my mouth. Snow's back arches off the bed, one hand fisting the sheets while the other tangles in my hair. The bite of pain as she pulls it, excites my cock, which has grown so hard I fear it might snap.

Breaking away from her breasts, I press wet kisses down her stomach, dipping my tongue into her navel. Sliding down the bed, I gently press her legs apart. Snow slams her knees together and stiffens, panic fluttering across her features.

"Will it hurt?" she asks, fear tinging her words.

"No, sweetheart. I promise." She pulls her lips into her mouth, worry etched on her brow. "Do you want me to stop?" Her shoulders rise as she pulls in a deep breath, then shakes her head.

Her body relaxes, and her legs part just a little. Backtracking, I leave them as they are and instead, run my hands down her legs before kissing the length of them. The tension in her body further loosens, and she starts making little sounds of pleasure at my touch. I part her legs again, and this time, she lets me.

I tease her with my mouth, using my tongue over the tops of her thighs. Her breaths come faster the closer I get to her core. Her heady scent makes my head reel, and when I cannot stand it anymore, I part her lips with my fingers and put my mouth over her clit. Snow lets out a half-squeal, half-moaning sound that makes me chuckle against her hot flesh. She squirms under me as I taste every inch of her, so I place a hand on her stomach to hold her still.

I pull her clit into my mouth, sucking firmly. "Cassian!" I smile inwardly and keep going. Her arousal leaks from her core, and I make sure to lap up every drop. I have waited years for this, hungering for her taste and touch. I'll not waste a single morsel of the meal laid out before me.

Snow's hands come back to my head, my scalp prickling with the force of her tugs. "It's too much," she cries as she tries to shimmy out of the hold I have on her, but I tighten it. She's not getting away, not now that I've tasted her. She's mine. I growl against her heat and swipe through her damp folds, then press a finger into her scorching heat.

Her hips rock as I add a second finger. Twisting my wrist around, I search for the little rough patch I know will make her scream. *There.* When I swipe over it, I swear Snow's soul leaves her body. She arches off the bed, shouting my name. Her core clamps down on my fingers as her orgasm crashes over her, her cum filling my mouth and sating my thirst.

But one orgasm isn't enough. I want her needy and begging, desperate for me to fill her. Grinding my cock into the bed to ease the pressure, I attack her again with my mouth, my eyes rolling back at her taste. I will never have enough of her. Snow moans, one hand slapping the bed as I lift her ass so I have better access to her.

Shift your horns so she has something to hold on to, Aren suggests.

"Do you need something to hold, Princess?" I ask, tearing my mouth off her long enough to ask. She gives me a jerky nod, her body writhing under me. Lowering my head, my eyes flutter closed as I allow my horns to grow. It's a handy trick Beast taught me. I can shift my horns, tail, and claws if I need to.

Her lips part as she takes in my new form, then immediately grabs them. Once again, I almost come. Aren's rumbly laugh bounces around my skull. He left out that her touch would feel like she was holding my cock. I go back to feasting on her, drawing another orgasm from her. When her body is languid and trembling, I move between her thighs.

"Can I have you now, Snow?"

Her eyes are closed, her breasts rising and falling rapidly as she comes down from her high. "Please," she whispers.

Placing my hands behind her knees, I lift her so that my cock lines up with her core. Her hands grip my horns tightly, her body tensing with apprehension. Although it nearly kills me to hold back, I slowly push into her, my eyes almost crossing at the intense pleasure of being inside her. Inch by inch I feed my cock into her. "Open your eyes, Snow. I want you to know who is inside you."

Her eyes flutter open and blaze with gold. She traps me in them, holding my soul prisoner. Pressing forward, my balls slap against her ass, and she arches her back, her neck pressing into the pillows. Her gaze never leaves mine and her hands stroke my horns as we begin to move together.

"More," she murmurs, her hips rising to meet mine. I do as my princess requests and pick up my pace. Her legs wrap around my waist, her feet locked over my ass, pressing me more firmly to her. "More," she says again, her voice sharp with demand.

Bracing my hands on the bed, I withdraw and then slam back into her, groaning as she clamps around me. "I want to mark you again," I pant out, the urge to rut her like an animal is strong. I want to roar and fill her with my seed. I want to bite her so all will know she is mine. I want to fill her belly with my babe.

The thought of her round and full with my child nearly undoes me. "Do it," Snow pants, gripping my horns harder. Slamming into her one last time, I come with a roar and bite into the base of her neck.

Snow's hips jerk under mine, and she shouts out, once more coming undone.

Mine, mine, mine, Aren growls as my seed pours into her. Carefully sliding out of her, I fall to the side, chest heaving, sparks of pleasure still igniting in me. I haul Snow into my arms, pressing a kiss against her sweat-dampened forehead. Tears leak from the corners of her eyes, and my heart freezes in my chest.

Pulling back, I ask, "Are you okay? Did I hurt you?"

She shakes her head and reaches up, sliding her hand into my hair. "Thank you," she murmurs. "I didn't know it could be like that."

Not knowing how to answer, I tuck her more firmly into my arms. I eye the bite mark on her neck, satisfaction pouring through me. I'll never let her go.

A knock on the bedroom door has Snow gasping in surprise. "I am sorry to disturb you, Your Highness, but we must leave within the hour," Merlin's muffled voice comes from the hall. "Oh, and Cassian, your horse is being extra finicky this morning. Perhaps you might find your way to the stables to prepare him for our journey?"

My mouth purses as I try to not laugh. "Yes, sir," I call back. Snow buries her head in my shoulder, her hand clamped over her mouth. I peek down at her, chuckling at her rosy cheeks and sparkling eyes.

"Do you think he heard us?" she whispers, part mortified, part amused.

"It matters not," I declare, running my hand down her side to where she's the most ticklish. A wicked smile stretches across my face. Snow peers back at me, her bottom lip caught in her teeth. She shrieks when I tickle her, her laughter ringing through the room.

"Stop," she gasps out, her eyes streaming with tears. I pull back, grinning down at her. She leaps out of the bed, racing for the bathing chamber. Chuckling evilly, I chase after her, scooping her into my arms. Pressing her against the wall, I claim her lips with mine, then rest my forehead against hers.

"I love you, Snow White."

Her arms wrap around my neck in a death grip. "And I, you, Cass."

Chapter 25

Snow White

Traveling is tedious. I came to this conclusion the third day after leaving the cottage. I may have been grumbling—okay, whining—around the campfire that evening, while gingerly trying to sit down on the logs Cassian hauled over for us to sit on. I rode enough as a child to understand the mechanics of it and had ridden a few times at the cottage—enough to be proficient. But an experienced horsewoman I am not, and that day, my legs and ass were on fire. Merlin, who must be the most patient person on the planet, finally had enough.

Bright stars light up the navy sky, the pregnant moon casting a silvery glow over the small meadow we chose to spend the night in. The sharp scent of pine and smoke permeates the air, and a bonfire roars happily, thanks to the logs Cassian cut.

Every bone in my body aches, muscles I didn't even know I had protesting against days of sitting in the saddle. Leaning against the trunk of a fir tree, I watch guiltily as Cassian hauls logs into a pile, his muscles straining under his tunic. He stops and reaches his arms into the air, stretching as sweat pours down his back. He rolls his shoulders and sighs, then scoops up our flasks, heading toward the river to fill them.

I should be helping. My shoulders sag in defeat. My head pounds with headache, and my arms feel as if hefty weights are attached to them. I start grumbling under my breath, knowing I sound like a spoiled little princess, but unable to muster up enough strength to care.

Pushing off the tree, I stumble over to the makeshift benches on wobbly legs. I bend and contort my body into alien positions, desperately trying to work out how I am going to lower myself onto it without further hurting myself or landing face down on the needle-covered ground. After several minutes, I finally manage it, my posterior complaining loudly over the rough bark it finds itself sitting on.

Dropping my head into my blistered hands, I press my thumbs into my skull, hoping for some kind of relief. The heat from the fire eases a little of the tension in my muscles, but only takes the edge off.

A shuffling on the other side of the fire makes me glance up to see Merlin taking a seat. "Can't you magic us to the palace as you did with the Valkyries? Why must we travel like this if we don't have to?"

Merlin settles his staff against the log, then braces his elbows on his knees. His face is serious as he gazes back at me with a raised brow. "Is that your plan, Princess Snow White? To turn up outside of the palace with just the three of us?"

I squirm under his scrutiny. "Well, no, but—"

"Have you forgotten how powerful Morana is? Or how she is destroying your kingdom? You have heard the stories. Your people are dying, fleeing, or have become the queen's puppets. They have no hope, Your Highness. They haven't seen you since she married your father. They believe you are dead and that nothing and no one will save them or the kingdom."

Tears well in my eyes, and emotion clogs my throat. Merlin leans back and raises his staff. "Perhaps you need to see for yourself. You have been outside of the real world for far too long." *He sweeps his staff in front of him in an arc, and the air shimmers before images begin to play. I cover my mouth with a trembling hand as I watch the black poison seep into the ground. The earth cries out as it crumbles and perishes. The picture fades into another, this time, hordes of ravens blacken the skies, terrifying the citizens. The dead are left to rot where they lie, while others, their eyes black and unseeing, wander like zombies. The pictures change, over and over, each worse than the last. Starving children attack travelers for food. Husbands, full of grief and despair, kill their families before the queen's magic can take hold of them. Plants, trees, and crops wither and die, the once verdant valleys and lush countryside nothing but a barren wasteland.*

Tears pour down my cheeks as the magic fades, taking the horrific pictures with it. "I didn't know," *I whisper shamefully. Cassian and the Valkyries had told me what was happening, but seeing it is different than hearing about it.* And you were whining about having a sore ass, *I admonish myself. Wiping the tears away, I feel determination settle on my shoulders. Straightening my back, I meet Merlin's eyes.* "What do I need to do?"

Merlin offers a small smile in return. "What your people need most is hope. They need to see you, to know you're on their side. We need word to spread of your return, and we need to reawaken their desire to fight for the kingdom." *He raises a brow and tilts his head.* "And we can't do that if I 'magic us to the palace.'"

Merlin's words have stayed with me, and I replay them often. Nothing worth having comes free. If I want to defeat Morana, restore order to my kingdom, and take the crown, I'll need to work for it.

It has been three weeks since that night, and we have yet to come across another living soul. Monarch Glen is hundreds of miles long and still untouched by Morana's magic. We passed the little village the Valkyries used to trade with a week and a half ago. It was abandoned.

Cassian's arm appears in my periphery, holding out a water flask. I take it gratefully and sip the cool liquid, my parched throat grateful for the relief. His fingers slide over mine when I hand it back, and my heart warms. Even though his shoulders are slightly bowed with weariness and lines carve his forehead, he still looks handsome. He rides Fire Heart with ease, one hand loosely holding the reins while the other rests on his thigh. His hair has grown down to his shoulders, and his beard needs a trim. I remind myself to offer to help with his grooming.

He glances over, catching me watching him, and winks. One day, my cheeks will stop flaming when he looks at me with heat in his eyes, but unfortunately, that day isn't today. We have been too tired each evening to do anything more but fall into bed in an exhausted heap, but now that my body has learned about pleasure and orgasms, it craves more. I have an excellent imagination, and during the long days of travel, I have found myself conjuring up all sorts of scandalous scenarios. Wondering what Cass might say if I asked him to bind my hands, or to take me up against a tree.

Or if, perhaps, he might chase me through the forest and claim me.

When these thoughts come, I wonder at myself. Surely, after what my father did to me, I should recoil from such ideas. Why, then, do they appeal to me so? Why does the thought of Cass claiming me make my core clench and stomach fill with heat? Many days I have pondered this in silence, ignoring Cassian's questioning looks as I ride beside him.

Perhaps my past does not define who I am now. Yes, my experiences have shaped me. Good ones, bad ones, terrifying ones, joyous ones. Each incident has carved itself into my soul, shaping me into the woman I have become and setting me on the path I now walk. But I do not need to cower before the memories of what was done to me. By accepting who I am, what I want, and giving in to my desires, I can take back the power they tried to steal from me.

No one but me can destroy my light. They might try. They might even dim it a little. But never will I give my enemies the power to destroy me through their evil acts.

Cassian reaches over and takes my hand, giving my fingers a squeeze. He knows me so well, always providing what I need. I squeeze back and return my attention to the path before us. Morana may know we are on our way to confront her—but she won't be expecting the two of us. We're not the same people that left the palace, we are so much more.

When the sun begins its decline, we decide to stop for the night in a tiny clearing at the edge of a brook. I've gotten better at riding over the weeks and my muscles have acclimated to the use. The blisters on my hands have disappeared, replaced by thickened skin that no longer feels the pain of either reins or bow. I once might have lamented over the loss of soft hands, but now there is satisfaction in knowing I might yield weapons and reins alike without fear of pain.

Cassian and I work together to unsaddle and brush down the horses. While he rides his black stallion, I've been riding his opposite—a gorgeous pure white mare by the name of Zohar. The two horses have an affinity for each other and travel well together. "Don't you let Fire Heart get you with foal," I murmur in her ear as I stroke the brush down her neck. "At least not until this is all over."

Cass chuckles and claps his horse on the rump. "Hear that, boy? No shenanigans from you." I meet his sparkling gaze over the back of the horse and grin at him. No shenanigans indeed.

After turning the horses out to graze as they will, we turn to find two tents set up. Both are forest green in color to blend into our surroundings. Merlin's tent is plainer, while ours sports a banner that snaps merrily in the breeze. It carries my family's crest on it, an ornately decorated shield behind a rearing unicorn.

The tents are the best thing about traveling. I'm not sure how I would have coped without Merlin along to provide this luxury. Inside the spacious tent, thick rugs line the floor, adding warmth underfoot. A large mattress rests upon the rugs, piled high with feather pillows and quilts. A dark wooden dresser holds a few changes of clothes, which go in dirty each night, and come out clean each morning. On top of the dresser sits a pitcher of water and a large bowl containing sudsy water that remains clean and warm no matter how many times we use it. It doesn't compensate for a bath, but we have rivers and lakes for that. I'm not sure what we'll do when it gets too cold to utilize them, but I'm sure Merlin will be able to magic up a tub.

After we've eaten and retired for the evening, I gesture for Cassian to sit on the floor next to the bed. He narrows his eyes playfully. "What are you doing?"

Grabbing the bowl off the dresser, I walk carefully over to him, setting it on the floor. "Sit," I command in my haughtiest voice, pointing to the rug. He heaves a long-suffering sigh, then sits while I get the comb, cloth, and scissors I readied earlier. Kneeling in front of him, I dip the cloth in the water and wring it out. He watches me quietly, one brow raised. "You always take care of me. It's my turn."

I gently wipe the cloth over his face, washing away the dirt of the day. His eyes search mine as I do, and he swallows thickly. Biting my lip, I concentrate on cleansing his face, then move the cloth around the back of his neck before washing the front. Dropping it back in the bowl, I pick up the scissors and trim his beard, smoothing my fingertips over his cheek.

The only sound is our breathing and the steady chirp of a cricket nearby. The candles placed around the tent give off a delicate glow, projecting flickering shadows on the thin walls. It feels intensely intimate, almost more so than when we had sex.

Bringing myself to my feet, I place a hand on his shoulder and sit on the edge of the bed behind him. Setting the bowl on my lap, I gently tug on his hair, making him tilt his head back. My fingers dig into his scalp as I wash his hair, and he groans deep in his chest. He closes his beautiful eyes, his thick lashes casting shadows on his cheeks.

I trace my gaze over his face, blinking back a sudden onslaught of tears. Lowering my head, I let them fall into the bowl, then dash them away. When I'm finished washing his hair, I squeeze it out and dry it with a towel, then work out the tangles with the comb until it's gleaming. I deftly pleat his hair into war braids, my breath catching in my throat at his good looks. Leaning forward, I wrap my arms around his chest, holding on to the one constant in my life.

This man undoes me. He never deserved the anger I threw at him, but he took it anyway. He shouldered that burden while also carrying his own guilt. He spent years training and learning, helping me in the only way he could. Since he's been back, he's done nothing but support me and cheer me on, was there for me even when I was horrid to him.

I'm not sure what I ever did to deserve him and I'm not entirely sure I do. But by the gods, I will love him with all that I am and hope it's enough.

Chapter 26

Snow White

Wake up, mate. The deep voice washes over me, pulling me from my dreams. I snuggle into the warm furry blankets with a sigh, determined to sleep five more minutes.

Snow.

The furry blanket presses against my side and consciousness comes roaring to the forefront. Shrieking, I throw myself to the left and promptly fall off the bed in a tangle of sheets and pillows.

Rumbly laughter echoes in my head. My eyes fly open, and I dash hair out of my eyes. Pushing up on my knees, I peer over the bed and come face-to-face with a grinning Aren. His emerald eyes are full of mirth, and he gives me a very feline smile.

Good morrow, mate.

Climbing back on the bed, I narrow my eyes at him. "I didn't know you could talk to me. Why haven't you spoken before?"

We couldn't until you and Cassian mated. I thought maybe you heard me that morning, but when you didn't answer, I worried you couldn't hear me.

Reaching out, I stroke his nose, and his tongue dashes out to lick my fingers. "When did you shift?"

Cassian was so exhausted, I decided to shift so he could sleep. And— His head tilts down. I'm not sure if manticores can look embarrassed, but Aren pulls it off.

"And?"

I wanted to cuddle with my mate.

It's not easy to hug an eight-foot-tall lion, but I manage it. "You can have cuddles whenever you like. Thank you for protecting me while I slept." His chest rumbles with a deafening purr, loud enough to wake the dead.

After Cassian shifts back and we're both dressed, he slings back the tent opening. Merlin sits by the fire, a pot of porridge bubbling merrily away over the fire. Bowls of mixed berries and nuts accompany the porridge, and we make quick work of our meal.

Once we saddle the horses, and the tents have disappeared, Merlin purses his lips and looks us over with a disparaging look. "This won't do." He thumps his staff on the ground and our clothing transforms.

Cassian spins around, glancing over his new attire. Tan hose covers his legs and dark brown boots laced up to just under his knees adorn his feet. A sleeveless navy doublet etched with gold cording sits atop a white tunic, coming to rest mid-thigh. Leather bands crisscross his chest, strapping his axes to his back. He's the perfect cross between a prince and a huntsman.

Glancing down at my clothing, I see Merlin has dressed us similarly. I wear matching hose and boots and the same doublet, but mine carries the family crest embroidered onto it. It has fancy cap sleeves with red material peeking through strategic slashes in the fabric. My tunic has a touch of femininity in its billowy sleeves and lace cuffs, and my quiver and bow rest on my back.

The horses, too, have had a makeover. Fire Heart wears an engraved silver chamfron and peytral—armor for his face and chest—and a navy caparison—a cloth that lies over his back—embroidered in silver peonies. The leather reins have been replaced with silver ones, made up of circular coins bearing my family's coat of arms. Zohar is dressed similarly, but her chamfron and peytral are black and the facial armor has a metal unicorn's horn attached to it.

"One more thing," Merlin states, walking toward me. He circles his hand in the air, and a small silver crown appears. It's dainty and delicate, nothing like the crown the queen wears. "This will do until you claim the rightful one."

Bowing my head, I allow him to place it on me. When I straighten my shoulders, a sense of peace and rightness comes over me. Destiny has come knocking, and it's time I answered.

Several hours later, we come to a sudden stop at the edge of Monarch Glen. Twenty-four dwarfs block the first road we've come to. Despite their small stature, they give off a menacing air. Their bronze skin stretches tightly over packed muscle and deep lines carve their foreheads and around their eyes. Each has a magnificent beard—some short, others nearly touching their feet, and all in a range of colors.

They stand with crossed arms and outspread legs, preventing us from reaching the road.

Their heads snap to me as one, their eyes widening. "Your Highness," they intone, sinking to one knee and pressing a fist to their heart.

I flap my hand helplessly, unused to this sort of attention. "Please rise," I beg. They do, and the one at the forefront steps forward.

"I am Randrith Blackfoot, Your Highness. The Valkyries informed us of your return. We wish to join you on your journey."

My gaze roams over the men, my chest tight with emotion. The corner of my mouth lifts, and I incline my head. "We would be honored to have you accompany us, but only if you do so freely. I cannot ask any of you to risk your life for my crown."

Randrith once more thumps his fist over his heart. "We fought once with your grandparents, and we will fight again with you. The evil queen must be vanquished and our country returned to us." The other dwarfs cheer, raising their arms in the air.

"I thank you for your loyalty and welcome you."

Merlin glances over at me. He travels not by horse, but by magic, hovering over the ground. "And so it begins," he tells me with a twinkle in his eye. He raises his staff, and six heraldic flags appear, carried by invisible standard-bearers. I blink. Surely, I have seen everything by now.

Clicking my tongue, I rein Zohar left, turning our little army toward the capital and Adarvan Palace. A flock of ravens screams above us, and a victorious smile breaks out across my face.

We're coming for you, Morana.

Two Months Later

My heart cries out in despair at the devastation. No amount of Merlin's magic pictures or my people's recountings could prepare me for it. The dry brown grass crunches under the horses' feet, not a single green plant in sight. Zohar and Fire Heart blow harshly out of their nostrils at the inedible plant life.

Orchards, once filled with our delicious apples, now lay barren, the trees petrified. Fields are nothing more than blackened wastelands, plows left abandoned mid-till. We've passed more than one abandoned village and have had to redirect around piles of dead bodies. Even the sky seems ready to give up; the once sapphire blue is now a pale imitation of itself, and the sun barely produces any warmth.

Our numbers have grown, but not by many. We are roughly fifty strong now, mostly farmers and peasants armed with pitchforks or whatever other weapons they had to hand. Most sentient citizens have chosen to flee instead, and I cannot blame them. They are starving, terrified, and will not risk their families on an eighteen-year-old princess with no magic. I do not fault them for this, indeed, I wish them well. Merlin gifts a basket full of food and water to each person that chooses not to join us and blesses them on their journey. It is my fervent hope that one day they may all return, their country restored to its former glory.

Morana's puppets are a different story. We have named them the Controlled, and the hope is they'll be freed when Morana is defeated—when, not if, I refuse to think otherwise—so we are careful to not harm them when they attack us with outstretched arms and clumsy legs. Sometimes they are alone but often are in large packs. Merlin magics them away to a fortified keep in the Principality of Kisfeld, where they can be held safely until this is over.

I don't know what we would do without him. It is a certainty this war could not be won otherwise. Each night we stop and set up camp as best we can. There is somehow always enough food to fill everyone's bellies, and as we meet and talk, friendships are formed.

One of the farmers, Elrich, carries a fiddle with him, one extravagance he couldn't bear to part with. His story is like so many others' we have met; his wife and children have fled to Granton while he stayed behind, praying to the gods his crops might be spared the devastation. Unfortunately, they have turned a deaf ear, and he narrowly escaped a horde of the Controlled.

Many nights, once we have eaten and the fires burn brightly, he brings out the fiddle, and we laugh and clap along. I am the only woman amongst us, and at first, the men were either too cowed by Cassian's presence or too nervous to ask a princess to dance. But Merlin swept me off the ground and flung me around, much to everyone's delight. I made sure to dance with each man that wished it, leaving the shyer ones blushing and tripping over their feet.

I may have tripped over my own feet once or twice when I caught Cassian leaning against the blackened bark of a petrified tree, heavily muscled arms folded, his eyes blazing with love and desire as he watched me dance.

Tangling my fingers in Cassian's hair, I arch my back, pressing myself more firmly to his mouth. My breath hitches as his tongue rolls over my clit, and a tiny moan escapes me when his fingers brush against that erogenous spot inside me.

"Shh, love. We can't have you waking up the entire camp," he whispers before sucking on the delicate skin of my upper thigh. I grab a pillow and bite on it, my eyes rolling to the back of my head when he puts his mouth over me, his tongue doing wicked, wicked things.

Sparks of pleasure dance through my body, igniting a larger fire that desperately wants to burn out of control. Tighter and tighter the heated coils compress, narrowing to a point before exploding outward, flinging me into the universe, letting me fly amongst the stars.

Glancing down the length of my body, I watch Cassian prowl up me like the animal he is. A devilish grin splits his face, smug satisfaction etched on his features. His lips come down on mine, encouraging me to open for him. I taste my desire on his tongue, the salty-sweet taste making me moan.

Moving to his side, he encourages me to face him. "I'm going to claim you now," he murmurs, stroking a finger down my cheek. He lifts my leg, draping it over his hip, then slides into me. His eyes lock on mine as he rocks into me, our souls greeting each other through the intensity of our gaze. "I want to try something. Do you trust me?"

"Always."

His lips curl, and I gasp when I feel something slide up my leg. Glancing over my shoulder, I realize Cassian has shifted his tail. It works its way up my leg and over my ass, then presses between my cheeks. Biting my lip, I stay silent when it leaves my body and dips into a jar of oil he left by the bed.

"You are mine, Snow. And I will have all of you." His lips come to mine again, kissing me deeply. His cock thrusts gently inside me, languid and slow. I lose myself in the feelings, in the pleasure and joy he brings out in my body. The tip of his tail moves between my cheeks, spreading the oil around me. "Let me in," he whispers, and I banish whatever reservations I might have. I know he won't hurt me.

The tip breaches the tight ring of muscles, and I suck in a deep breath, my eyes widening at the pinch of pain. Our gazes remain locked, and he watches me carefully for signs of discomfort. He presses farther in, and I stiffen at the foreign feeling. "It hurts."

He tucks my hair behind my ear and pulls me close. "It's okay, Snow. Give it a minute, I promise it will feel good." He continues to rock into me, his tail pressing deeper inside. "Such a good girl. Look at you taking my cock and tail." His eyes flutter closed, and his hips pick up speed. I preen under his praise, the elation on his face making me want to give him as much pleasure as he gives me.

The burn melts away into pleasure and I start rotating my hips, pulling him deeper inside me. "Cass." I hiss as bliss rockets through me.

He pulls my leg farther over him, using his other hand to grip my ass tightly. A growl pulls from his throat, exciting me. He moves faster, cock and tail pounding into me. "You're so beautiful," he murmurs. "You feel so good." He swells inside me and his arms tighten. "Yes, Snow. Come for me, love. I need you to come with me."

His hand slides down and pinches my clit, and I'm done. I bite into his shoulder, muffling my scream as my orgasm grips me in its hold. He explodes inside me, ropes of cum painting my insides.

Cassian gently pulls out and wraps his arms around me. Our labored breathing slowly returns to normal, and I bask in the afterglow of our lovemaking. When I previously thought about getting his tail involved, that wasn't quite what I imagined, but it was so worth it.

"What are you thinking about?"

Snuggling into his chest, I peek up at him, a mischievous smile tugging at my lips. "When we might do that again?"

His shoulders vibrate with suppressed laughter before he kisses my forehead. I love when he does that, and I sigh happily. "You're perfect, you know that?"

"Mm. So are you." I yawn and curl my fist under my chin before slipping back into dreams, most of which feature a gorgeous huntsman that rocks my world.

Chapter 27

Snow White

We bring our company to a stop in Thornleach, the first village we've come by in the past few days. As the sun has begun its descent, we quickly decide we'll stop here for the night. Zohar and Fire Heart touch noses, the jingling of the reins and stirrups loud in the surrounding silence. A ball lies abandoned on the ground outside of a tiny cottage, its door left wide open. Cassian cups his hands around his mouth. "Hallo the village!"

A shiver works over my shoulders. I should be accustomed to these sights by now, but each one wrecks me. The abandoned ball should be kicked by little feet or bounced by little hands. Not left behind, an extravagance unable to be carried while fleeing for their lives. A frigid breeze whistles through open doorways and windows, chilling me to the bone and making me grit my teeth. Morana will pay for what she has done.

Movement above one of the cottages catches my eye, and quicker than I can blink, my bow appears in my hand and I release an arrow. It smashes into the one aimed at Cassian's head, the two falling to the ground with a clatter. Zohar rears, neighing loudly, while Fire Heart stamps his feet, snorting. Cassian shouts out, wheeling the horse around to settle him.

I murmur softly to Zohar, my legs clamped tightly around her flanks. She snorts loudly, dropping back down on all fours. The whites of her eyes show and her ears are flattened, but she listens and eventually calms.

"Who's there?" Cassian shouts. "Show yourselves."

A man leaps from the thatch of a roof. He stands with his legs spread and arms on his hips. He's dressed similarly to Cassian but wears forest green rather than navy. A hood hides his features, but his air of cockiness and the fine cut of his cloth speak of his standing. Urging Zohar closer, I narrow my eyes and stare up at him. There is something eerily familiar . . .

"Robin of Loxley! Get yourself down here this instant."

The man throws his hood back and shades his eyes with a hand. "Snow White? Is that you?"

I roll my eyes. "No, it's Aoife, Queen of the Fae."

Cassian nudges Fire Heart closer to me and crosses his arms, mimicking Robin. "Why the hell did you shoot at me? Still sore over when I dunked you in the lake?"

Robin skates down the side of the roof and jumps off, landing as nimbly as a cat. He stalks toward us, a wide grin stretching across his face. Cassian dismounts, holding his hand out to me. I take it and slide gracelessly off Zohar, who helpfully prances to the side. Luckily, Cassian catches me before I land in the dirt in total humiliation.

Robin's parents had been friends with mine before their tragic passing many years ago. He was a regular visitor at the palace before my mother passed, although spent more time with Cassian, as they are of an age.

He grabs Cassian by the shoulder, planting an exaggerated kiss on his cheek before thumping him on the back. "Sorry, Cass. Didn't recognize you with all those muscles. Who knew your scrawny ass would grow up into this?" He gestures at him before turning to me. "Princess." He bows, then takes my hand, placing a kiss on the back of it. Cassian growls and moves closer to me, making Robin chuckle. He releases me and steps back, raising his hands in the air. "Now, now, I have my own lovely maiden, I have no need for yours. Although I'm happy to see the two of you together. Watching you moon over each other even as children was nauseating."

Snorting, I cross my arms over my chest. "Mmm. And just who would be crazy enough to take you on?"

"I'm hurt, Snow, truly. I thought we were friends."

Chuckling to myself, I glance around, then widen my eyes comically. "Oh, hello!" I say to the empty space to the left of Robin. "It's so very nice to meet you." I hold a hand out while Cassian guffaws.

Robin narrows his eyes. "Funny. Our scouts saw you coming three miles ago. The rest of my group are in the huts at the far end of the village."

"And you didn't know it was us?" Cassian asks incredulously. He tips his head toward the flags, still being carried by the invisible standard-bearers. "They didn't give it away?"

"Just because you carry the flags, doesn't mean it was the princess. It could have been the queen or the huntsmen. They've been plaguing the countryside for months."

"Is there enough room for us to stay here tonight?" I ask Robin. "Or maybe two?" The horses could use an extra day of rest, we've been riding them hard.

Robin shades his eyes, looking over our group. "There should be enough if we double up. There's a stable with a connecting paddock on the other side of the village for the horses. We've set up in the inn." He points to a pale-yellow building on the other side of the square. "Feel free to join us for a drink after you've settled in. The proprietors left several casks of ale behind."

The dwarfs cheer at this, and my lips curl into a smile. Merlin takes charge, doling out cottages and huts. After we freshen up and take a short nap, Cassian and I emerge from the little one-bedroom cottage Merlin assigned us. He pulls me close, scanning the area for any threats.

He makes me feel safe and protected, something I haven't felt for so long it's almost foreign. Leaning back on my heels, I pull him to a stop. A line creases his forehead when he peers down at me. "What is it?"

Pushing up on my toes, I place my free hand on his cheek. "Thank you."

"For what?" he asks, searching my face.

"For being patient with me. For protecting and caring for me."

Untangling our hands, he rests them on the side of my neck, rubbing his thumbs over my cheeks. A delicious shiver rolls down my body, and the love shining in his eyes both excites and humbles me. "Always," he murmurs before lightly pressing his lips to mine. "Now, come on, let's go see what Robin's up to." He tucks my arm into the crook of his elbow and pulls me after him.

Evening fell during our nap, blanketing the village it its dark embrace. Someone has been good enough to set torches into the ground, their glow creating a dim path to the inn. Thick shadows huddle like wraiths in the narrow spaces between cottages, and my overactive imagination creates danger where there is none. A shudder rolls over my shoulders, and I press myself more firmly into Cass's side.

We round the corner, the brightly lit inn coming into view. Laughter spills out of the open door, drawing us toward it like a beacon. As much as the sound brings me joy—there has been too much devastation of late—it also brings me sadness. This should be a common event, not a rare one. It makes me even more determined to destroy Morana and return my country to what it once was.

Someone has set up hay bales in the square, each one farther than the last, and each containing a target. A few have arrows embedded in them, while still more litter the ground. Robin laughs and jests with a group of his men, while a beautiful woman with waist-length auburn hair looks on with an amused smile as she watches him.

We come to a stop beside her, and she hastily curtsies. "Your Highness."

"Please, none of that. Snow is fine. I heard Robin has finally met his match. Would that be you?" The torchlight is bright enough to see the blush spread across her cheeks. I'm glad to see I'm not the only one that suffers from the affliction.

"It would. Maid Marian, Your Hi—sorry, Snow. And this is Little John." She gestures toward the man on her right. I blink up at the man that towers over everyone here. I doubt the man was little even in the cradle.

Cassian shakes his hand, and we're introduced to a few others standing around. A round, pleasant-looking man with an ale-flushed face by the name of Friar Tuck passes around pints of ale, which I gratefully take. "Is this all of your numbers?" I ask Marian once I've slaked my thirst.

She cranes her neck, glancing over the square. "No. There are a couple of families and elders traveling with us. They've remained in their dwellings for the evening." Robin bounces over and slings an arm over Marian's shoulder before tossing a mock glare at Cassian.

"You better not be filling my lady's head with stories about me," he warns, and Cassian chuckles in reply.

"If she asks, I will not lie."

Robin lets out a deep sigh. Placing a finger under her chin, he turns Marian's face toward him. "Just remember that I love you, and take whatever this scoundrel says with a grain of salt." He smacks a kiss on her lips before bounding away and jumping onto one of the casks of ale. Letting out a piercing whistle, he waits for everyone to quiet down before raising his bow over his head. "A competition!" he cries. "Who will shoot against me?"

We spend the next hour watching Robin defeat one competitor after another. The sound of cheers and good-natured groans echoes through the night. When no further opposition comes forward, he holds his arms out, spinning slowly. "Are there no others?"

Cassian elbows me. "Go for it," he says softly, mischief sparkling in his eyes.

"A kiss for luck?"

"The day I turn down such an offer is a day I may as well stop breathing," he murmurs, dipping his head to give me a brief kiss, one full of promise.

Merlin appears at my side, holding out my bow and quiver. Strapping it over my back I step forward, full of ale-induced confidence and Cassian's luck. "I, Snow White, Princess of Valderán, hereby challenge Robin of the hood!"

Robin throws his head back and gives a throaty laugh before sweeping his arms out to the side and bowing. "Your Highness, it will be a pleasure to defeat you." He points his bow at the targets. "Ladies first."

Shaking my head at the fool, I stalk up to the X marked on the ground. Instead of aiming at the closest one, I go for the farthest. Fixing my gaze on Robin—ignoring the hay bale—I draw the bowstring back and let the arrow fly. *Bullseye.*

The crowd hurrahs and I step back with a grin. Robin strokes his chin and moves to the mark. He raises his bow, pauses, releases. The people hold their breath, craning their necks. The arrow hits mine, splitting it down the center. The crowd begins to chant his name, but before he can taunt me with his win, I release another arrow, shattering his. Turning on my heel, I rapidly release several more, splintering each of his in all the other targets.

Robin freezes, blinking rapidly before turning toward me. "Where did you—"

Setting the bow on the ground, I rest my hands on the top, my face split in a wide grin. "The Valkyries taught me."

"Unfair advantage!" Robin calls out, folding his arms over his chest. "I declare Snow White eliminated."

Some boo while others cheer. Chuckling under my breath, I move over to him and grab his hand, raising it in the air. "A tie!" I call out, and this time, the crowd roars with approval.

"Hmm. A tie, huh? I suppose it will suffice." He ruffles my hair, then pushes me toward Cassian. "For now, anyway. You won't be so lucky next time."

"If you say so," I toss over my shoulder. "I wouldn't want to damage your fragile ego by losing to the girl you used to push into the mud."

Cassian bursts into laughter at the aggrieved look on Robin's face. Cassian hands me my glass while I ignore Robin's sputtering. I always did want to get him back for ruining my favorite dress.

Chapter 28

Cassian

"Come on, you two. Rest day is over," I say to the horses as I lead them out of the stables. We spent yesterday resting, but time is of the essence, and we need to keep moving.

Robin and most of his gang of merry men have opted to join us in the coming war. A few will stay behind in the village with the women, children, and elderly. Merlin agreed to stock one of the huts with food and water for them. The village is far enough away from the capital that they should be free from any interference from the queen, or from any fight that occurs.

Nodding hello to a couple of passing farmers, I turn the corner, casting my gaze over the square, looking for Snow. Time seems to slow, each second a heartbeat.

An elderly woman, frail and shaky, trips over her feet. She drops to the ground, crying out in dismay as the basket of apples she was holding spills across the cobblestones.

Tick.

Snow leans over, her brows drawing together with worry as she helps the woman up.

Tick.

After the apples have been gathered back into the basket, the woman smiles up at Snow. Her trembling hand offers up one of the apples, and Snow White accepts it, her eyes lighting at the treat.

Tick.

Dark gray clouds slide in front of the sun, casting shadows over the square.

Tick.

One of the dwarfs backs into me, then spins around, apologizing. When I glance back up, Snow is gone. I drop the reins as an icy finger of fear slides down my spine. "Snow!"

Tick.

The old woman catches my eye, the corner of her mouth lifted in a smirk. "Too late," she hisses, disappearing into thin air. I stare at Snow White lying in a heap on the ground.

Tick.

People gape, eyes wide with horror, their shrill screams blocked out by the steady thumping of my heart. Terror clogs my throat as I begin to move toward her, a roar of anguish ripping from my throat.

Tick.

Morana appears at the opposite side of the square, and my blood turns to ice. "Cassian," she shouts, throwing an object at me. I automatically reach out to catch it, and a skull lands in my hands. I stutter to a stop, staring dumbly at it, my uncomprehending mind a mass of confusion.

Tick.

"Daddy says hello!" Morana screams before throwing her arms out to the side, disappearing in a puff of raven feathers. Her vicious laughter remains behind, taunting me. Snow. Father. Denial fizzes in my veins, refusing to believe they are both gone. Time returns to normal, the sounds of women screaming and children crying slamming into me like a wall.

Panic sweeps the village. Men shout from the roofs, scanning the area for any further threats. Mothers clasp their children to their breasts, hurrying them into the cottages. Those that missed the action listen with slack-jawed curiosity as they are filled in, and still more gather around Snow's lifeless body.

I stand there stupidly, unable to move, almost in some kind of trance, until Aren roars at me to do something, anything, to save our mate.

Snow.

The skull drops from my trembling fingers, and I race across the square. Marian leans over her, her fingers at Snow's neck. *No.* She shakes her head at Robin, tears slipping down her face. *No.* Robin crashes to the ground beside her. *No.* "Don't touch her!" I bellow as my heart tries to regain its rhythm. Somehow I know it never will again.

I fall to my knees and scoop Snow's limp body into my arms. An apple rolls from her fingers, a single bite taken from it. Deep racking sobs shatter me as I tuck her against me, rocking back and forth. "Please don't leave me," I murmur over and over. "I cannot do this without you."

The ravens' caws mock me, laughing at my devastation. I ignore them, lost in my grief and insanity.

Sometime later—hours, days, I cannot say—Merlin drops a gentle hand on my shoulder. "Come, lad. Bring the princess with you." I stagger to my feet, swaying under the burden of my dual loss. Ahead of me sits a golden slab resting on a flat-topped boulder. I'm too weary to make out the symbols etched around the edges, but in the middle, "Snow White" has been engraved.

It's her coffin.

I rear back, shaking my head. She's not dead. She's not—she can't be. "Cassian, come. I need you to set her down." My nostrils flare and tears fill my eyes. Swallowing the despair, I gently lay her down, then position her so that her hands rest over her chest.

She looks peaceful, as if she's sleeping. Disbelief still blankets my mind, muddling my thoughts. Nothing seems real. When a crowd gathers and people lay flowers around her, it takes me several minutes to understand what they are doing.

She's gone.

They bow their heads, dabbing at their tears. Merlin raises his staff, and a glass cover settles over Snow, protecting her from the elements. Unable to continue standing, I once more slip to my knees, hanging my head.

My one job was to protect her, and I failed.

Chapter 29

Morana

Materializing in the tower, triumph blazes through me. It was so easy. The little whore took the poison herself, with very little prompting needed. And Cassian? Ha! The traitor's son deserved the dual blows I dealt him. Not only did I kill his love, but I literally threw his father's death in his face. I thought the skull was a nice touch.

In a month's time, all of Valderán will have fallen, and my revenge will be complete. Then I will sacrifice King Silas to the mirror and move on to Granton. Nothing will stop me from taking over the Restüra Continent, and all will bow before me.

Tossing my hair over my shoulder, I saunter over to the mirror, running my finger over the runes. "Mirror, mirror, on the wall, who is the fairest of them all?"

The disembodied mask appears in the glass, its sightless eyes staring back at me. "You are," it intones, then fades away until only my reflection remains.

Satisfaction curls my lips into a victorious smile. *Of course, I am.* Then my brows lower. The mirror isn't usually so abrupt, or lacking in rhyme. It's almost as if it's unhappy with the turn of events. Refusing to let its rudeness ruin my mood, I shrug a shoulder, then stalk over to one of the windows and peer down. Two huntsmen loiter in the otherwise empty courtyard.

"Bring me a comfortable chair!" I screech, and they glance up, startled. "Now!" They trip over themselves to do my bidding, and minutes later, they arrive in the tower, huffing and puffing, sweat lingering on their brows. They set it in front of the mirror, then back away, heads lowered.

Settling into the plush chair, I lean back, lifting my skirts and spreading my legs. "Momma's in the mood to celebrate," I announce to them, snickering under my breath as their shoulders hunch and they exchange wary glances. "You," I point to the one on the left. "Come here and please your queen." He scurries over and buries his head between my legs. Snow White's death deserves an orgasm or three. "Mmm," I moan, tilting my head back. "Yes, just like that."

I narrow my eyes at the other, who freezes when I catch him inching toward the door. Wetting my lips, I run my gaze over him. Momma doesn't only want to celebrate; she's fucking starving. My lips tip up and I crook my finger at him. His Adam's apple bobs as he shuffles forward, terror flashing in his eyes. Grabbing hold of his tunic, I yank him closer, then rip into his chest, removing his heart.

As his body drops to the floor, I greedily eye the blood trailing down my arm. My tongue darts out, lapping it up. The other huntsman pauses at the sight of his expired friend, but I reach down and thrust his head back where it belongs. "If you stop, you'll join him," I hiss, and he quickly resumes his task.

"Mirror, show me the village." A destroyed Cassian kneels at Snow White's coffin, his shoulders bowed in defeat. The sight rips an orgasm from me, leaving me panting at his despair. "Again," I demand, then bite into the heart, my eyes never leaving the view of the village and the fall of the so-called army Snow White thought she could defeat me with.

Chapter 30

Snow White

Awareness comes slowly, nudging gently at my consciousness. It beckons me out of the oblivion, its skeletal fingers tugging and pulling at me, whispering promises I can't make out or understand.

My fingers twitch and jerk, the darkness receding further. The absolute silence wraps around me, not so much as a breath of air or the wings of an insect to keep me company. My body is heavy, lethargic, refusing to obey commands, as if it is not under my control. It's too much like when I was lost inside myself, and I swore I would never surrender to that despair again.

Aged eyes, heavily lined with wrinkles, dance in my memory. A coy smirk, malicious laughter. An unpleasant taste sitting on my tongue, numbing my face. A sense of impending doom shattering my psyche as I collapsed onto the cobblestone street.

Morana.

I heave in a mighty breath, my body springing up into a seated position. Panting heavily, I bring a trembling hand to my throat, then slowly climb to my feet, my heart thumping erratically as my gaze bounces around. Taking a stumbling step forward, I brush my sand-covered hands down my hose, realizing the ground is made of black sand instead of soil.

Where am I, and how did I get here?

The last vestiges of daylight ring the deep-purple sky, leaving me with the barest of light to see by. Peculiar-looking trees surround me, the trunks appearing to be carved from smooth stone. Their barren branches, misshapen and ugly, twist and bend in unnatural ways. It's when I take a closer look that I gasp in dismay. Each tree has a face carved into it, all with different expressions. Some look to be caught in an eternal scream while others appear to be sleeping.

Come back to me, Princess, Cassian's voice whispers overhead, and my heart lurches painfully.

"Cassian!" I scream at the sky, but no response comes. Spinning around, I call out to him, again to no avail.

"Snow White," my mother's voice moans, the sound low as if in pain. A finger traces up my spine, and I stumble over my feet before glancing over my shoulder. *It was just a branch.* The tree it belongs to opens its eyes, coming to rest on mine. Its face contorts into one of pain. "Help us," it says, once again in a voice eerily similar to my mother's.

"Momma?" I whisper, my mouth going dry. I shake my head, backing away. What is this place?

The eyes narrow, its mouth opening wide. "Come back," it screams, no longer sounding like Momma, but instead my father's voice. Fingerlike twigs reach for me, grabbing at my doublet.

"Let me go!" I break away, waves of horror washing over me. It reaches for me again and I dodge to the left, then turn and sprint as if Morana herself were chasing me. The trees begin to blur as I race past, each of them waking as I do. A thousand voices howl my name, and I cover my ears as my feet pound into the soft sand.

I'm unsure how long I run, but eventually, I break out of the forest and fall to my knees, my lungs burning and desperate for air. As my muddled mind tries to make sense of what is going on, the evening darkens further, twilight surrendering as night wrests control. There's nowhere to take cover, nowhere to go. Peering up at the sky, I notice there is no moon, or even a single star to break the vast expanse of midnight blue. A sob tears from my chest before I choke it off.

I can't do this without you, comes Cassian's voice, and a tear leaks down my cheek.

"I need you too," I murmur back, my eyes fluttering closed.

Something soft tickles my face, and I swipe it away sleepily. It comes back, wrapping around my ankle. For a moment, I think it's Aren's tail, and the corner of my mouth lifts in a small smile, until reality bursts through the wall of sleep fog and shakes me awake.

I hold very still when I meet the azure blue gaze of a large black cat. She sits regally beside me, her tail firmly wrapped around my ankle. Around her neck rests a collar made of several gold chains intertwined together, while an empty clasp dangles from the longest one.

We stare at each other, neither of us moving. I don't want to assume her friendliness; she may look like a larger version of a housecat, but her claws look plenty sharp. "Hello," I murmur, careful not to startle her. She cocks her head and unwraps her tail, purring loudly. "Does this mean I'm allowed to move?" She butts her head against my chest, rattling the necklace the Valkyries gave me. "Yes, I have one like you." She settles back on her haunches and narrows her eyes. Her gaze bounces from the necklace back to mine, and it clicks. Reaching behind me, I undo the clasp and spill the disks into my hand. The cat eagerly nudges one of them, the one with the hieroglyph of a cat. One that looks suspiciously like the one in front of me, gold chains and all. "Is it okay if I put it on you?"

She straightens, lifting her head. Taking that as permission, I clip the disk onto her collar. The design shivers and clears, the name *Bastet* replacing it. I freeze. Bastet is the protector of royalty, the cat goddess of love, passion, joy, and pleasure. Unsure whether this is the goddess herself, or merely one of her agents, I bow my head and lower my eyes to the ground.

Sharp teeth prick the skin of my hand. Raising my head, I meet the cat's gaze. She backs away and I stand, brushing the black sand off of my hose and backside. Bastet prances away, tail high in the air, and then glances at me over her shoulder, with a very human *come on* look. I take a second to wonder if following a strange cat—goddess or otherwise—is the safest course of action, but as no other avenues have been afforded to me, I shrug and follow.

Once out of sight of the haunted forest, there is nothing as far as the eye can see—just miles upon miles of sand in every direction. We walk for hours. Although the clear sky offers no relief from the sun, I do not thirst. Nor do I need to relieve myself or desire food. My mind shies away from thinking about this too deeply. I'm not ready to hear that my life is over before I had a chance to live it.

When the silence becomes too oppressive, I begin to talk to Bastet. Haltingly at first, then with more gusto. She's an excellent listener, talking back to me with an occasional chirp or meow. I explain to her all about Morana and the plight of my kingdom. She brushes against my legs in support when I mention my mother. I speak of the Valkyries and how they saved me, and of my love for Cassian.

By the time the sun begins to set, the landscape begins to subtly change. Sand gives way to marshland, and I'm thankful for the knee-high boots I wear. The scent of fish and salt grows thicker the farther we travel, and I stop my mindless chatter, too busy watching where I place my feet.

It's quickly becoming darker by the second. "Where are you taking me?" I ask Bastet, who peers over her shoulder and hisses at me. "Wow, okay, sorry. But there's no place safe here to sleep, and it will be dark soon."

I swear she rolls her eyes at me.

Shutting my mouth, I obediently follow, and just as the sun dips below the horizon, we come to a swamp. Trees shoot into the sky, towering above us, pale-green moss swinging from their branches. The thick air, almost palpable in its humidity, tastes oily and fishy on my tongue.

Bastet leaps onto my shoulders, digging her claws into me for purchase. Hissing under my breath, I swallow down my trepidation and wade through the waist-high water inundated with fallen leaves and branches. Fireflies blink in and out of existence, hovering amongst the branches and over the water. It's oddly beautiful in a Gothic sort of way.

After several minutes, we come to a tiny derelict cabin built on stilts. A rocking chair creaks as it moves back and forth by an invisible presence. The hairs on the back of my neck stand on end, and I nervously gulp back a cry of fear. Bastet nudges my cheek reassuringly with her nose, but it doesn't stop my blood from running cold when a finger of air slides down my cheek in a caress. The urge to look behind me is strong, but I grit my teeth and carry on, refusing to give in to the temptation. I have a feeling I wouldn't like what I saw.

Chapter 31

Snow White

The trees eventually thin, opening into a river that must be at least a mile wide. Sharp cliffs tower above me, the tops lost in shadows. They preside over a sliver of rocky beach, barely wide enough to stand on. Bastet jumps off my shoulders and lands nimbly on the beach. I'm not so graceful, having to pull myself onto it. It doesn't gradually slope off into the river; like the cliffs above it, it ends sharply, plunging the unwary into watery depths.

I carefully lower myself onto the sharp rocks, hissing when one cuts into my backside. My sodden, heavy clothes stick to my skin, and a shiver runs over me. The humidity of the swamp has gone, replaced by an icy wind that howls over the cliffs and tugs on my clothes. Wrapping my arms around myself, I glance around me, taking in the little scenery I can make out.

There isn't much to see. The river, the beach, the cliffs . . . there is nothing else. Except for the sky. I stare at it in wonder, having never seen anything of the like. Three moons hang in the velvety darkness, one so close, I feel as if I could touch it if I tried hard enough.

Bastet shifts beside me, her neck craning as she stares over the river. I see nothing, but my ears pick up the sound of movement in the water. Moments later, a boat comes into view, and I'm oddly both at peace and terrified by the sight of the ferryman standing at the stern of a papyrus boat. Black robes adorn his tall, thin frame, and a deep cowl covers his face. His bony fingers grip the long wooden pole he uses to steer the twenty-foot-long boat through the murky water.

The bow and stern rise sharply from the edges, colorful ropes tied in circles around the ends. The vessel's name, Meseket, has been stitched into its side with thick red thread, and in the center sits a canopy resting on a raised dais. The ferryman smoothly turns the boat to the side, resting it against the bank. A plank materializes out of thin air, setting down on the rocky beach. Bastet arches her back, stretching her legs, then climbs aboard, settling herself on the top of the pillared bow, then meows at me plaintively.

Swallowing down my unease, I pull myself to my feet, cutting off the groan at my aching muscles. I gingerly climb aboard, settling into the seat placed below the canopy. The ferryman steps in close, pointing to my neck, then holds his hand out, palm up. Unclasping my necklace, I pull off the chain and find a disk with a picture of the ferryman. He clasps it tightly in his hand and lowers his head in thanks before returning to the stern. His pole slides into the dark water, pushing us away from the shore.

As we glide out into the river, the current catches us in its grasp. The rocking of the boat soothes my exhausted mind, and I find myself fighting to remain awake. My eyelids become too heavy and I succumb to the Sandman's magic, my last thought is wondering why I feel no hunger or thirst, but still need to sleep.

The boat rocking heavily wakes me some time later, and I sit up with a gasp. The midnight sky is now a blood-red color, a giant sun burning so hot I can barely catch my breath. I glance around, spotting

Bastet waiting on the wooden dock, her tail swinging back and forth in annoyance. Gulping, I bolt upright and flip toward the ferryman.

"Thank you."

He raises his head, his face still covered in the shadows of the cowl. "Aken, Your Highness," he says, his voice a deep rasp.

I dip my chin and murmur his name, then carefully make my way to the bow. My legs wobble beneath me, and it takes a moment or two to scramble out of the boat. Bastet gives me a feline grin, I'm sure she's laughing at me.

I trail behind her, moving my gaze in a curious arc and taking in the fertile earth. Thick green grass lines the edge of the river. Palm trees sway against the maroon sky, while sand-colored hills rise in the distance. A path made of solid gold stretches out for miles before me, leading to giant obelisks jutting from the earth.

An impending sense of finality runs over me. It's as if my soul knows what is about to happen, as if my entire life has been leading up to this moment. It is familiar in a way I am not consciously aware of, speaking to me in a language I feel I should know, but do not.

As we draw closer, the landscape becomes more defined, as if designed not by nature, but by man. Date palm trees, soaring over sixty feet tall, now line the lane leading me toward the obelisks.

Princess, Cassian's voice murmurs on the breeze rustling the branches above. My hand rests over my heart, a wrenching pain drawing me toward my love. But now is not the time for reminiscing, so I take the comfort of his voice but push down the feelings and carry on, sweat dripping down my back as the sun attempts to roast me alive.

Take off some clothes, my mind encourages, but even though I'd love nothing more than to do so, I hesitate. They are all I have left of my life before . . . well, before here. They are an armor of sorts, something left to cling to.

We hike for maybe an hour or so before we finally reach an entrance blocked by two silver gates, easily thirty feet tall. Two limestone statues, one of Anubis and one of Osiris, rise on either side. *Oh, gods.* There is no more pretending. No more trying to deny where I am. *I'm not ready. It's too soon.* Tears mist my eyes, but I blink them away. After taking a moment to compose myself, I bow deeply before each statue. Inhaling a shaky breath, I rise, then remove two more disks from my necklace. I place the one bearing the engraving of a jackal on Anubis's knee, then turn to Osiris and set down the disk with the Eye of Horus. The gates part silently, as if moved by invisible servants, then clang shut behind us with a finality that leaves me breathless.

The walkway continues forward, now lined with obelisks covered in hieroglyphs that call to me, inviting me to stop and read them. Promising me knowledge and power should I just take a moment to study them. My steps slow as my gaze captures on a carving that looks suspiciously like Cassian. I move closer, reaching toward it, my every thought consumed by the need to touch it.

Bastet's sharp canines puncturing the skin of my hand forces me out of the spell, and I stumble back. *That way lies madness,* an unfamiliar voice speaks in my mind. Gulping, I lower my head and follow the cat onward, refusing to look at anything besides the ground and my feet.

The path opens out into a courtyard lined with date palms and dwarf palmettos. I sweep my eyes to both sides, sighing in relief to see no further obelisks. I finally raise my head and gape at the blood-red sky that perfectly showcases the massive pyramid before me. It rests on an extensive platform, with a column in each corner topped with statues of various gods.

A beautiful fountain topped with an ankh sits in the center, its crystal-clear waters tinkling as they fall from the seven layers. Several peacocks, their bright tails fanned open, wander freely in search of food.

Bastet patiently waits for me at the bottom of the platform. Hundreds of stairs soar before me, and my eyes widen in consternation. I take a second to thank the Valkyries for whipping me into shape. The cat spins around and races up the steps, and blowing out a breath, I follow.

My limbs become heavier with every step I take, my calf muscles begging for relief. Sweat coats my body in a fine sheen, dripping annoyingly between my breasts. I keep my eyes trained at the top, willing myself to continue. *Almost there.*

When I eventually reach the top, I haul in air, fighting to fill my starving lungs. Bastet meows at me, urging me to hurry. Sighing, I drag myself to the two heavily engraved golden doors that guard the entrance to the pyramid. Pulling the chain from my neck, I unhook the final disk and press it into the indent made for it. Just like the gates earlier, they swing open on their own, a cool breeze rushing out to greet me.

I ignore the touch of fear that tugs at me, the aching thought of never seeing Cassian again. The Fates have led me here, and if this is where I meet my end, so be it. I will greet my destiny with honor, not cowardice.

Sucking in a deep breath, I square my shoulders and step over the threshold, the doors slamming shut behind me.

Chapter 32

Snow White

I startle at the sound of the doors closing behind me. The sparse anteroom I find myself in holds no decoration, nothing to soften the harsh edges of the stone walls and floor. The air, so much cooler than outside, has a mustiness to it that makes my nostrils twitch. My pulse races as I stare at the rectangular doorways hewn into each of the three walls. I flick my gaze between the three, unknowing which to choose. Bastet wandered off too quickly for me to take note of where she went.

Rubbing the back of my neck, I blow out a breath and make my choice. The moment I step through the middle doorway, torches flicker to life and the scent of spiced orange and clove incense invades my senses. The flickering glow of the fires reflect off the hammered gold ceiling, the light lovingly caressing the statues that line the left side of the corridor.

Carved from marble, pharaohs old and new stand at attention, interspersed with large black urns containing potted palms. I slowly make my way down the sloping hall, the statues' eyes seeming to follow me as if already passing judgment. I wonder if they find me lacking.

The corridor turns right sharply, and I follow the ramps farther and farther down. A chilly breeze comes out to play, tugging my hair and clothes, encouraging me to accompany it. A shiver runs over my shoulders, and I'm grateful I didn't remove and discard any of my clothes earlier.

Bastet waits for me at the bottom, watching me with solemn eyes. Running my hand over the soft fur on her head, I ask, "Where to now?"

She lifts her back and turns, her tail swishing in a hypnotizing sway as she leads me into a large room. Like the anteroom, the core of the pyramid is fully laid out in stone. The floor has been worn smooth by the thousands of travelers who have come this way. Hundreds of torches set the wall on the right ablaze, their light enough to send any shadows scampering to hide in the corners. To the left, platforms built out of the wall host dozens of seats, a railing separating each section, with steep stairs to the side providing access to each level. A small doorway sits to the left of the seating area, partially draped off by a burgundy curtain.

The one in front of me, however, holds double doors a good fifty feet high. Again, made of gold and carved with a number of designs. The doorway pulses with a glowing light, matching the steady rhythm of my heart.

In the center of the room, resting on top of a golden circle inlaid into the stone floor, sits a throne, the back of which must be at least eight feet tall. Made entirely of obsidian bone, the backrest consists of ribs while thigh bones have been melded together to form the legs and seat. Two golden human skulls adorn the very edge of the armrest, grinning obscenely at me as if eagerly awaiting my sentence.

A narrow podium stands in front of the throne, a silver scale resting on its surface. Bastet urges me toward the circle, and when I step into it, the edges flare with light. Inhaling a sharp breath, I unwittingly try to step back, but find myself frozen, some kind of magic holding me in place. Bastet disappears through the small doorway, and I'm left on my own, nervously plucking at the hem of my doublet.

Minutes pass, my anxiety ramping up with each ticking second. I startle when a booming gong shatters the silence, my head whipping to the side at the sound of rustling clothing and soft footsteps. I gulp audibly at the sight of dozens of black-robed figures taking their seats, my nerves begging me to run from the fate that will soon become me. I couldn't anyway, even if I wanted to—the holding spell is too strong. The levels fill up quickly until no seat is left empty.

Once they are seated, a figure strides in confidently. His bare chest gleams in the torchlight, while a short kilt swishes around his powerful thighs. He's tall and muscular with the body of a man and the head of a jackal. An ankh necklace adorns his neck, and elegantly curved gold armbands circle his biceps. I recognize him immediately from my studies as a youth, as all children are taught about the gods. *Anubis.*

He turns, placing his hands on each side of the podium as he regards me. The throne behind him seems to almost melt into the background as if being consumed by shadows that shouldn't exist due to the wall of torches. I can't focus on that mystery when my gaze locks with Anubis's. The amber orbs assess me, then he inclines his head. "Princess Snow White, welcome to the Hall of Final Judgment."

I bow my head, a sense of calm finality settling over me. "Thank you for receiving me, my lord."

Anubis throws an arm out, gesturing toward the forty-two cloaked figures in the stands. "You stand before me and the judges, and we are ready to hear your case. We shall now listen to your confessions."

Letting my eyes fall closed, I exhale a deep breath, allowing the forty-two negative confessions to run through my mind. I cannot, in good faith, claim all of them, but once I have them prepared, I lift my head, open my eyes, and speak clearly.

"My lords, I stand before you not as a picture of perfection, but one of imperfection. I do not come to offer false witness, but to lay at your feet the sins I have not committed, to be weighed against the ones I have." The evaluators sit quietly as they watch me from the depths of their hoods. "I have not told lies," I begin, a silent strength running through me. One of the judges leans forward as if determining the truth of my statement. "I have not cursed a god, nor struck terror. I have wronged none, and done no evil." My voice stays strong and true as I continue to list the sins I have not committed. When I am finished, my shoulders slump slightly, relieved to have spoken my truths.

The congregation murmurs amongst themselves, and I do my best to calm my nerves. It doesn't matter how woefully unprepared I am for this, how much I yearn to return to Cassian and save Valderán from Morana's clutches. All I can do is pray the gods might find mercy and help my kingdom and my people.

While the judges continue to debate, too quietly for me to hear, I allow myself to feel the loss of the man I wanted nothing more than to spend the rest of my life with. I hadn't been able to process it as I traveled through the underworld to arrive here, but now that I have nothing to do as I await my verdict, I feel his loss keenly, the grief burning through me while my heart twists painfully in my chest.

During our first separation, I at least knew he was out there in the world. Jealousy brought intrusive thoughts of other women, insisting he would forget about me and never return. As abhorrent as that thought was to me, knowing he was alive and happy somewhere offered me a little comfort, even if I pretended to hate him and wanted to tear at the fictitious women with claws.

And now, I have left him. Unwillingly, yes, but the result is the same. All because I didn't trust my instincts when they tried to warn me when I took the poisoned apple from Morana. Everything he went through to get back to me was for nothing, and everything I suffered was in vain. Not only have I lost my best friend and love, but my kingdom as well.

An agonizing pain tears through me, rending my soul in two. If I were able to move, I would be lying prostrate on the floor. Waves of devastation pound into me, over and over, closing off my throat as I scramble to breathe.

It's always been you, Snow.

I clamp my mouth shut on the keening wail that so desperately wants to breach my tightened lips. *I'm so sorry, Cassian. Forgive me.*

"Enough!" a deep voice demands. The room falls silent, the torches dim, and the spell that holds me in place shatters. My knees wobble from the onslaught of loss, and I collapse to the floor.

Shadows swirl around the throne and the torches blaze with the might of a thousand suns. Squinting against the harsh glare, I throw a hand over my eyes. Horror at my loss of dignity in front of the God of the Underworld consumes me, mixing with my grief until I'm nothing more than a puddle of raw emotion.

Osiris rises from his throne, and I quickly bow my head to the stone floor. "Rise," he commands. I scramble to my feet, keeping my head lowered. I can feel his eyes on me, and my cheeks flush with shame. All

I had to do was get past this with a little dignity, and I couldn't even manage that.

A finger lifts my chin, and I meet eyes eerily similar to my own—hazel with a gold ring around the edges, with flecks of gold throughout the iris. The god is handsome, his hair as black as mine. He wears a seven-tiered collar, each row made up of gleaming gold and precious jewels. A tall Atef crown graces his head, and a golden snake settles in the middle, watching me with slitted eyes. He is attired in royal robes and a sash instead of the short kilt his son, Anubis, wears.

"Please forgive my unseemly outburst, my lord," I murmur.

Osiris raises a brow. "You have endured much in your short life, and you are still very young. I can forgive such, especially when it comes from grieving the loss of the one you love. Your mother did much the same when she passed through here."

My eyes widen. "You have seen my mother?"

Osiris drops his hand from my chin and inclines his head. "Indeed." He gestures toward the large doors behind him. "She has passed through to Aaru and awaits the soul of your father. Your daughter is with her, along with Alaric."

I sway on my feet and my mouth goes dry. I cannot compute what he has just told me. "My . . . my daughter?" I whisper, tears misting my eyes.

"Yes, your mother cares for her in the afterlife. Alaric joined them when Morana killed him for his betrayal."

Osiris catches my elbow before I land on the floor in a heap. "Because of me. She killed him for helping me, didn't she?" He nods. Oh, gods. How will Cassian survive this?

He patiently waits for me to process, his gaze never leaving mine. It's as if he peers into my soul, which is not the most pleasant of sensations. "Due to the suffering you have been through, I would feel it within my power to offer you a choice. You must think this over carefully; I am not prone to doing such." I suck in a harsh breath, a flicker of hope lighting in my chest.

The room goes deathly silent as if this were some momentous occasion. Anubis shifts slightly, and I notice the scale is no longer empty. A feather sits on the right-side pan, which rests on the podium. The left-side pan appears empty, resting above the surface. Osiris clears his throat, and I bring my attention back to him.

"I will offer you two choices, Princess Snow White of Valderán. The first is this: you may enter through the doors into Aaru, be reunited with your mother and daughter, and live out eternity there. You will know happiness and peace, and your soul will be at rest, no longer forced to reincarnate. When Cassian's time comes, he will be free to join you." The glow around the doors brightens, rivaling the light from the torches. A yearning for peace envelopes me, a siren's call that entices me to choose it over the unknown second option.

"Your second choice is this: I and the other gods will intercede on your behalf. Morana will be destroyed and your country returned to its former glory. A new royal family will be appointed, and your people will live in harmony and prosperity. In payment for this, you will wander the underworld, from whence you have just traveled, for five thousand years. At the end of that time, your soul will be released, free to be reborn, where you can then find another life with Cassian, should your souls find each other once more."

I bow my head, the enormity of the two choices a heavy weight over my heart. But the minute he spoke, I knew there was only one choice I could make. My heart hurts at the thought of never meeting my daughter, but she is safe with her grandmother. I send out one last thought to Cassian, hoping somehow, his heart will hear my words and know the truth of them. My love for you is endless, Cassian. I will search the worlds for you, and one day, we will be together again.

I raise my head, running my gaze over the judges and Anubis before meeting Oriris's inquiring look. "I choose option two."

Chapter 33

Snow White

A blinding smile grows on Osiris's face, and behind him, the scale moves so that both sides are equally balanced. I watch in confusion as the judges leave the chamber as quietly as they came in. My brows furrow when Osiris takes my hand in his. "Well met, granddaughter."

Anubis comes to stand beside his father, and I look between them, not comprehending. "Granddaughter?"

He tilts his head, and I gasp, taking a step back when his eyes begin to glow as mine do. "I—I don't understand," I murmur.

"I rarely visit your world," Osiris begins, "as there is too much to be done here. I found myself one day yearning to walk amongst the mortals, and in doing so, came upon your grandmother. We entered into a brief affair, which your mother was a result of."

I blink at the realization. "But, she was married—"

"Yes. She was able to convince her husband the child was his. Luckily, your mother wasn't born with the god eyes, nor was she endowed with any powers. I have not had a mortal child before, but it seems to have skipped her generation and settled on you."

My mind whirls, overwhelmed by the knowledge being thrown at me. One thing stands out, though. "What do you mean, powers? I have none."

Can jackals smirk? Anubis does a very good impression of it. "You do, niece. Yours just haven't been awakened yet."

I stare at them both stupidly. The child I lost was a girl, who resides behind the doors opposite me along with my mother and Cassian's father. My grandfather is the god of the underworld and resurrection. My uncle is the God of the Dead. It's too much to wrap my mortal mind around.

But you're not so mortal now, are you?

"I suppose having powers will be useful during my stay in the underworld. Will I be allowed to have them, or would that be an unfair advantage?"

Anubis takes my hand and leads me over to the scales. "Your confessions and willingness to sacrifice yourself to save your people have balanced the scales. Usually, that would indicate a person's suitability to enter Aaru. But your case is a little different, due to you being a demigod. We are willing to offer you a different course of action."

Osiris crosses his arms over his wide chest, the collar around his neck flashing in the light of the torches. "As offered before, you can go through to Aaru and reunite with your family, living in peace and waiting for Cassian to join you. Or, I can awaken your powers and send you back to your world. As a demigod, your powers are limited. Should you use them sparingly, you will be able to live a very long life, one that spans several mortal lifetimes. But I must warn you; should you use them all, you will return to your mortal status and live out a normal lifespan."

"Will you and the other gods still intercede and destroy Morana?"

"You should be able to do that with the army you gathered and with the one that is coming. Some are more than what they seem."

I try to hide the sigh that desperately wants to escape. More cryptic messages. "I will return to my world."

The corner of Anubis's mouth lifts. "We thought you might. Take our hand." I reach out, taking their hands in mine. "Close your eyes," Anubis instructs, and I comply. The light before my eyelids dims, then blazes, a scorching heat beginning at my feet before traveling up my body. I throw my head back, mouth open in a silent scream as it races up my throat and shoots into the air.

Strong winds howl through the room, whipping my hair around me. Power thrums through my veins, and I snap my eyes open. Swirling shadows surround me like living creatures, writhing and slithering like demonic snakes. Lightning races through my veins, elevating my heart rate. The rush is heady and intoxicating, and for the space of a second, I understand how corruptive it could be in the wrong hands.

The winds die down, and the shadows withdraw. My hands tremble at my sides with the force of the retreat, and my mind spins with knowledge I previously did not have access to. As it settles into me, my lips curve. I know what must be done.

"Might I ask one more thing of you, Grandfather?" Osiris's eyes soften at the informal title. "My father . . ." His face darkens, and he lashes a hand out. He must know what Silas did to me. I try not to think of him, of what happened. But this is the right thing to do.

"What of him?" he grinds out. Anubis watches with wary eyes, swinging between the two of us.

"When his time comes to stand before you, I wish to offer my forgiveness to counter against his sins."

His brows lower. "You would do this for the man that hurt you?"

Swallowing thickly, I nod. "He was corrupted by Morana's evil and would not have done such a thing otherwise. That woman has taken too much from all of us. My mother deserves the opportunity to decide for herself if she can forgive him and whether she wants him by her side in the afterlife. She shouldn't have to suffer his loss. Morana would be delighted to know that she can still cause misery and havoc even after death." I dip my chin. "Please."

Osiris pulls me into an awkward hug, patting me gently on the back. "I am proud of you, Snow White. It shall be done." Anubis kisses my cheek, and they step away. "Until we meet again."

Raising my arms, my shadows pour from me, surrounding me in a storm. It's time for me to return to Valderán.

Chapter 34

Cassian

The square is a ghost town, much like most of the village. The silence blankets me, comforting me in my grief. Merlin has been clearing out the families and elderly from our ranks, sending them off to Alba or Granton, whichever will take them. I'm not sure where everyone else is, but I've spent the last day on my own, except for when Robin tries to shove food and water at me. I'm not ungrateful for his thoughtfulness, but I can't stomach the idea of it. I haven't eaten or slept in three days. I'm sure I look like hell—I most certainly feel like it.

Snow's gone. I still can't wrap my head around it. I can't remember my life before her. Even when we were separated, she was with me in every thought I had. I carried her in my heart when I couldn't in my arms. She was here one moment, gone the next. I should have been standing by her side, protecting her. I should have known that evil bitch would show up and ruin everything.

The sun shines but its warmth leaves me cold. Darkness envelops my world, draining my will to live. Everything I've done, the training, the education, the travel . . . all useless. All for nothing. I should have taken my chances and dragged her from the dungeons. I should have spirited her away somehow. Morana might have killed us both, or maybe we would have made it. Perhaps even now we would have been living in Granton or Alba in a tiny cottage surrounded by children. We could have been happy. We might have . . .

I suck in a shuddering breath, the remains of my heart just barely beating. What's the point? Nothing can be as I dreamed. What's worse is that I'm not only fighting my own grief but Aren's as well. He hasn't stopped raging inside me. He goes from wanting to burn the entire kingdom to the ground and tearing King Silas limb from limb to howling in anguish for hours, making me want to split my head open and tear him out. When I get especially desperate with the conjoined despair, he starts growling about his plans for Morana.

He cajoles and whispers to me, tempting me to eat and sleep so that we can keep our strength up. We have to avenge her, he insists. And once we're done, once the king and queen are nothing more than bloodstains coating the walls of the palace, we'll burn the kingdom to the ground and join her in the underworld.

A part of me wants nothing more than to raze the palace to the ground. They deserve to pay for what they did to Snow. But while she might be okay with the plans for Morana, she would never want the kingdom to suffer. So I hold back, doing everything in my power to keep Aren chained down, withstanding his rage as I do nothing more than keep vigil over her coffin.

I know I don't have much time left. Merlin will soon come to take Snow away. She can't be left here alone in an abandoned village. I don't know what his plans are, I haven't dared to ask. Not that I've been in any position to. The thought of her being buried in the cold dark ground, all alone, makes me want to rip my heart from my chest and just be done with it all.

There is no life without her.

The only positive thing is that the ravens finally left this morning. Morana must be bored watching us as we do nothing but mope around. I've only moved long enough to relieve myself before taking up my vigil once more. But at least I don't have to have my grieving interrupted by their constant mocking caws.

I swallow heavily when Merlin comes to stand by my side, resting a hand on my shoulder. I stiffen. No, I'm not ready yet. A low growl erupts from my chest, and I push myself to my feet, unsteady with hunger and thirst. Placing a hand on one of my axes, I narrow my eyes at him. "You can't take her," I say hoarsely.

"Cassian—"

I throw myself over the coffin, knocking the glass cover off. It clatters to the ground, shattering on the cobblestones. "I said no," I hiss. Hauling Snow's limp body into my arms, I wrap them protectively around her.

Merlin peers at me for a moment before his eyes flick to Snow. "Do you know what is more powerful than death?" he asks conversationally, making me blink at him.

"Pardon?"

He clears his throat. "Love is the only thing that transcends death. It is more powerful than any magic, more potent than any spell. It is the sole meaning of life."

My brows lower. "I don't understand."

Merlin sighs and reaches toward us. Fearful that he's going to take her from me, I press my lips to hers in a final goodbye. I know I must let her go, but I can't bring myself to.

"True love is the most powerful thing there is. It might sound ridiculous, like something out of a child's tale, but it is the truth, nevertheless."

Dark shadows begin to swirl around her body before dissipating as quickly as they appeared. My heart jumps into my throat when her fingers twitch. "Snow?" I breathe, my eyes wide with disbelief. I shift her body, leaning her back against my arm. Her lashes flutter, then her eyes blink open. A slow smile filters across her lips.

I help her sit up, my mind whirling with disbelief as I run my hand over her back. I slide my gaze to Merlin, who looks more than a little smug. I could hit the bastard right now. Knock him to the ground and pummel him over and over. Three days he left me to suffer when all I had to do was kiss her?

Aren growls, fully on board with the plan to demolish the wizard. His eyes twinkle at me, and he raises a brow. "I could not have told you sooner, young Cassian. Morana's spies were everywhere, and your reactions had to be believable. If I had told you from the start that your love could bring her back, Morana would have rained hell upon us. Now she sits in her palace, secure in the knowledge that Snow is dead, thinking she has won. We have the advantage. Plus, Snow had her own quest to complete before she could come back. She's more than what she was," he states before quickly hurrying off.

His words make sense, but the pain of her loss is still too soon, and it will take me a while to forgive him. *We could eat him*, Aren replies helpfully. *I've never tasted sorcerer before.*

If I have my way, you never will either. We don't eat people. He huffs back at me and settles down for the first time in days. Thanks be to the gods.

Returning my attention to the woman who means more to me than life, I fuss over her, still in shock that she's here, alive and breathing. I can't stop staring at her, fearful that she'll be taken away from me again any moment now. "Hi," she says shyly, searching my eyes. I crush her to me, my broken heart beginning to mend.

"Don't ever leave me again," I murmur brokenly into her hair. "Promise me, Snow. Promise we'll die together when we're old and gray, surrounded by our children and grandchildren, and not a moment sooner."

Snow wraps an arm around my neck and pulls my face down to hers. "I promise," she says, her eyes beginning to glow. Our lips meet, and I scoop her into my arms, carrying her into our cottage. I need her naked and under me, immediately. I need to reassure myself she is truly alive and that I'm not having some sort of hallucination brought about by a lack of food and water.

I shift her in my arms until she's facing me. She wraps her legs around me, clinging to me like a monkey as I crush my lips to hers, inhaling her as if I could take her inside me and keep her safe always. I mumble against her lips, "I need you now, Snow. I can't be gentle." She nods and I rip her hose down her legs before doing the same to mine, then back her into the wall. I thrust into her, unable to even make sure she's ready for me.

"Cass," she moans at the intrusion. "Please, I need you too."

I press my face into her neck, breathing her in. "I love you so much. You are my everything." I lean back, then press into her harder, making her arch her neck against the wall. Aren purrs contentedly as I thrust into her over and over. It's not pretty, it's not loving or gentle. I can't be, not now.

Tears stream down Snow's cheeks as she strokes my hair, holding me to her as she does her best to meet my strokes with her hips. "I'm sorry," she whispers. "I'll never leave you again."

I swear my heart practically leaps out of my chest, so desperate it is to be with hers. Reaching between us, I flick her clit, making her scream out her release. Her walls clench around me, and I follow suit, my breath labored and loud in the aftermath.

Gently withdrawing from her, I set her on the ground, then grab a cloth off the dresser and cleanse her. I pick her up, holding her tightly, and her arms come up around my neck. We stand there for an immeasurable amount of time, our souls calming with our nearness.

"I'm so sorry about Alaric," she whispers into my neck, and my arms tighten around her.

"You know?"

I can feel her nod against me. "I have much to tell you, but just know he's safe in Aaru with my mother." That knowledge brings me a measure of relief. At least his soul is at peace in the afterlife and not stuck here in some sort of hellish limbo. I'll grieve for him properly once this war is over. My heart cannot take any more at the moment.

Scooping her up, I toss her into the bed. She brushes her ebony hair off her face, grinning up at me with sparkling eyes. "Tomorrow, you can tell me everything," I inform her, ripping my tunic off and tossing it on the floor. "I haven't convinced myself yet that you're truly alive. I think by the morning you'll have made me a believer." Snow shrieks with laughter as I pounce on her, then moans deeply when my mouth finds her core.

I take her three more times throughout the night, my soul slowly stitching itself back together with each touch.

"Cass." A finger pokes me in my side, and I grunt. Grabbing on to it, I pull her into me.

"Go back to sleep," I mumble. "It's too early." Snow places a hand on my cheek, and energy flows into me, snapping my eyes open in shock. "What was that?" I feel my cheek, and a slight buzz zaps my fingers. The exhaustion vanished in the blink of an eye.

She tucks her lips in and shrugs a shoulder. "The Valkyries are on their way. We need to get up." She leans up and places a soft kiss on the tip of my nose, then pulls herself from my arms. My gaze traces over the line of her back as she sits up and stretches her arms into the air.

She turns and my mouth goes dry, my cock twitching under the covers. There's just enough light coming in through the tiny window to outline the sharp points of her nipples. I admire the curve of her hips and the length of her legs before meeting her eyes. Her brush with death hasn't cured her of her blushing curse. I'm glad—it's endearing.

"Stop," Snow whispers, covering her face with her hands.

I snort and pull myself out of bed. Grabbing her hands, I gently pull them away. "You're mine, Snow. We've already established that. Never be embarrassed or ashamed with me. I love every inch of you."

Her bottom lip trembles. "Even my scars?" she asks quietly, searching my face.

I pull her toward me, running my hands carefully down her back. "I hate that this happened to you, and I want to tear Morana apart for it. But yes, Snow, even your scars. You fought your way back, overcame the evil while still holding on to the incredible person you are. You're a fighter, a warrior, and all warriors have battle scars." I press a kiss to her forehead, then back away. "Let's get cleaned up before the whole village comes pounding on the door to see you. I'm sure Merlin has spread the word of your miraculous recovery."

Snow runs a hand over my chest and nods, blowing out a breath. "Let's hope they don't want to burn me at the stake for being a witch."

Chapter 35

Cassian

The sun has just crested the horizon when Snow and I arrive in the fields near the stables. A few determined stars still sparkle through the rose and turquoise sky, soon to be lost as the sun begins its climb. The village behind us still sleeps, and we made our way here without being accosted.

I keep sneaking glances at her. Her lips press tightly together while lines carve her forehead. I squeeze her hand and ask, "What is it?"

Snow blows out a breath. "What if they reject me?" She lowers her head and inspects her boots. "What if they are scared of me just as much as they are of Morana?"

I lift her chin and search her eyes. "Your people love you, Snow White. You are good and kind, everything Morana is not." I gesture toward the sky, pointing out the Valkyries in the distance. "Is your return more frightening than horses that walk on air? Or Morana's ability to take over people's minds? Or me turning into a manticore?"

She pulls her lips in and toes the grass. "But—"

"But nothing. Aye, some may find it scary or unnatural. But we live in a world of sorcerers and wizards, of oracles and gods. And you didn't come back just to be with me, you returned to save your kingdom and people from the malevolence that lives in the palace. You are a hero, someone to be celebrated, not feared."

And if anyone treats our mate poorly, we can always eat them, Aren states.

By the gods, what is your fascination with eating people all of a sudden? He does a mental equivalent of a shrug and settles back down.

Snow leans up and places a slight kiss on my lips. "Thank you for bringing me out of my head." I spin her around and pull her back to my chest, wrapping my arms around her. She rests against me as we watch the Valkyries approach.

"Thank you for being mine," I return.

"There was never any other option. My heart has belonged to you since before I can remember." I kiss the top of her head, grateful she doesn't witness the sheen in my eyes.

Moments later, the Valkyries land a few yards from us, and Snow White breaks free, running toward them with her arms out. I amble behind, but keep her in my sight. Once the women finish hugging and greeting, we make our way back toward the village. Snow wants to tell everyone her story at once so she doesn't have to repeat it. She may be worried about what the people think of her return, but as we walk, I notice she carries herself more confidently. Her back and shoulders are straighter, and there is an anticipatory flush to her cheeks. Her eyes sparkle as she laughs at something Hilda says, making my lips curl.

A mighty cheer goes up when we round the corner of a house. The narrow road, lined with cottages on both sides, is filled with people cheering and chanting Snow's name. She comes to a halt and grabs my hand, strangling my fingers with her grip. She peeks up at me, her bottom lip trembling.

"See?" I whisper. "Your people love you."

She swallows and gives a tremulous smile, looking out over the small crowd. She raises an arm to wave, and they cheer again. It takes us twenty minutes to walk thirty yards, as it seems everyone wants to touch Snow's sleeve or shake her hand. She makes time to have a quick word with everyone who wants one and nearly gets bowled over when Maid Marian throws her arms around her.

I quietly speak to Robin Hood, Randrith the dwarf, and Evrin, one of the farmers who appears to be the spokesperson of his group. I know Snow doesn't want to tell her story to everyone, but if we can get the leaders together, we can sit down and hash out our plans. They agree and follow me to the inn, where I catch up with Snow, the Valkyries, and Merlin.

Merlin places a silencing spell over the room so we may talk freely. Over the next hour, we partake in the breakfast Merlin arranged—thick slices of warm bread dripping with butter and honey, poached eggs, ham, spiced potatoes, and bowls of mixed fruit.

Time and again, I find my gaze locked on Snow, tracing over her features. Seeing her laugh with her friends has me thanking the gods for allowing her to return. Although the room rings with merriment, tension ripples in the air; a feeling of Fate holding its breath in anticipation, the calm before the storm.

Snow clears her throat, and everyone quietens. I am just as curious as they are to hear about her adventure, and we all eagerly listen as she begins to talk.

"Hilda, you and your sisters once taught me about listening to my intuition. To never ignore when the hairs stand up on the back of your neck or the sick feeling in your gut." Snow bites her lip. "Several days ago, outside in the square, an elderly woman carrying a basket of apples tripped and fell. My instincts were screaming at me that something was wrong, that there was danger. I ignored it, fully caught in the spell Morana weaved over me. When the woman offered me a poisoned apple, I took it."

Hilda leans over and places a hand over Snow's. "She's a powerful sorceress, Snow. Do not blame yourself."

Snow blows out a breath. "I have at least learned my lesson. I will never ignore those feelings again." She continues her story, telling us about the different levels of the underworld she traveled through to get to Osiris's temple and the entrance to the afterlife, Aaru.

All of us sit quietly, enraptured by her story. Evrin, who has had little experience with magic and other such matters, sits with his jaw agape. Except for the Valkyries, who are frequent visitors to both Valhalla and Fólkvangr, Snow White is one of very few to have traveled to the underworld and returned.

I reach for her hand, understanding now how she felt when I was gone all those years. At least I only had to wait three days—I'm not sure how she coped for all those years. "I wish I could have been there with you to keep you company."

She grins back at me before taking a sip of juice. "I had company." When I raise a brow, she winks at me. "The goddess Bastet accompanied me on my journey." She tells us of meeting the goddess in her cat form and how she helped Snow navigate the desert and swamps.

"Very fortuitous indeed," Merlin says, wiping his hands on a bit of cloth. "It is rare she takes an interest in matters like these."

"I was very grateful for her guidance and companionship. I'm not sure I would have made it without her," Snow replies, then glances at me. "I heard you calling to me, begging me to come back. Although it saddened me to hear the grief in your voice, it kept me going. When I might have let fear rule me, you gave me strength." I lift her hand to my lips, placing a kiss on her knuckles. She doesn't know she does the same for me. Her light is what makes me wake each day. I had a glimpse of what my life would be like without her in it, and I can only pray to never have to experience the like again.

She goes on, telling us of the ferryman and the entrance to the pyramid. "Confessing to Anubis and the judges was terrifying." She stops, squirming in her chair while she considers her words. My throat clogs up. I wish I could have taken it all from her, spared her having to go through such a thing. No one should have to do it twice and I can only hope when it's truly her time to pass into the afterlife, that she is spared doing it again.

"I was offered two choices . . ." I am sure she is leaving some things out, but I won't press her about it. If she wants to share it with me privately later, I'm sure she will. "I could travel on to Aaru and reunite with loved ones, or return to Valderán. But if I chose to return, I wouldn't be the same as I left."

The room, already silent, takes on an even deeper hush. Hilda leans back in her chair, a smile growing on her face. "I was right," she muses, watching Snow.

"Right about what?" I ask in confusion.

"Osiris is my grandfather. I'm a demigod." I blink at her, my jaw hitting the floor. Snow chuckles and places a finger under my chin, closing my mouth. "He and Anubis awakened my powers. And along with them has come . . . I'm unsure how to explain it exactly. But I know things now. I can envision moves and possible outcomes, use them to work out the best course of action." She swivels her head, meeting each person's eyes for a moment before moving on to the next. "We're going to defeat Morana, and I know how."

Just as she finishes speaking, the room lights up with a tremendous glow and thunder booms so loudly the inn trembles beneath its might. Linne jumps up, clapping her hands. "Father's here!"

Leaning back in my chair, I peer out into the hall when the entrance door crashes into the wall. My brow raises when the God of Thunder appears in the doorway. At nearly seven feet tall, he has to duck as he comes into the room. I have heard much of the legendary god's temper but he is also known to protect humanity from evil. Just what we need in a fight against Morana.

While he greets his daughters, I wonder at what my life has become. I spent most of my life as a huntsman and the princess's protector. Now I sit with a god and a wizard, the famed Valkyries, and the woman I love. Who is not only a princess but a demigod. It's enough to boggle the mind.

"I have not just brought myself," Thor tells us over a pint of ale. "You will find that the Princes Charming have sent an army, along with one from Granton. Beast was able to convince the king to aid us."

Snow goes very still. My heart skips a beat when she comes back to herself. A shiver runs over her, and her hands clench. "Morana's poison is moving faster. It has destroyed Monarch Glen and will reach Granton's and Alba's borders in three days. We must move out tomorrow."

We spend hours hashing over plans. Morana isn't just going to let us walk into the palace, lay down, and surrender. We have both Snow's and Merlin's magic, along with Thor. We have the Valkyries to help in the battle and the dwarfs, who are already fierce warriors. We have Robin and his men, who are extraordinary archers, and the two armies, which the farmers and villagers will incorporate into. And then there's me with the unmissable axes provided by the Valkyries and my ability to shift into a beast that magic can't touch.

"Can't Merlin just use his magic and kill her?" I ask in exasperation when we argue over some of the finer details. "Why do we have to go through all this?" I know it's selfish, but I don't want Snow to risk her life. I can't lose her again.

Merlin leans on his staff and side-eyes me. "All magic comes with a price, Cassian. Death magic is an insidious evil that permeates your soul, destroying it slowly over time. I will help however I can, but I will not use magic to call upon the Grim Reaper." I run a hand over my face and blow out a breath, nodding. I understand, but frustration rides me, urging me to look for the easiest solutions.

We continue talking, and as the sun arcs across the sky and begins its descent, we all sit back with a sigh. The plans have been finalized as much as they can be, and now it's up to each leader to prepare their men and women for tomorrow's battle. I've had enough of sharing Snow for one day. We don't know what tomorrow will bring, but until then, I'm going to spend every minute with her in my arms.

Everyone turns to me when I bring myself to my feet, the chair scraping loudly against the stone floor. "Excuse us." My face breaks into a grin, and I scoop Snow out of her chair. She shrieks in mock indignation, pounding on my back when I throw her over my shoulder. "Have a good night!" I call back, and their laughter follows us out.

"Cassian!" she hisses at me. I'm betting her cheeks are bright red right about now.

I smack her bottom. "Shush. I need you under me. Or over me. Whichever you prefer. But I'm not wasting another second without being inside you."

That shuts her up.

Chapter 36

Snow White

Cassian wakes me with his hands on my breasts and his tongue inside me. I've lost count of how many times he's loved me since I returned from the underworld. I need it as much as he does—the desperation, the need to verify by touch that we are alive, that we have another day to love each other.

Desire races through my veins, heady and intoxicating. My head presses firmly into the pillows, my eyes closing against the raw pleasure that is almost painful in its intensity. "Come for me, Princess," he demands. My body recognizes its master, obeying him as easily as it breathes. I splinter apart with a harsh cry, then arch my back when he enters me forcefully.

"Look at me." I obey, hazel clashing with green. He thrusts into me, hard and fast, his brow dripping with sweat. My hand reaches for him, but before it can touch him, his tail whips out, forcing my hands above my head. "You will not die on me today. Swear it. Promise me you will walk off the battlefield in one piece."

My eyes fill with tears, a tearing pain scorching through my chest. "You know I cannot promise that." His hand wraps around my throat, and his face hardens.

"I vow, if you do not, I will follow you. You will not leave me behind again. Do you understand?" I nod against his hand, and a little of the desperation leaks from his hardened expression. His mouth crashes against mine, hungry and pleading.

His tail releases me, and he hauls me up so we're facing each other. His gaze doesn't leave mine and in it, I see both his love and his fear. Threading my fingers into his thick hair, I lean into him, watching as the fear melts into pleasure. "I am yours, and you are mine, Cass. Always. Nothing that happens today will change that."

He lowers his lips to mine while his hands run up and down my back. I arch against him, taking him deeper, and he shudders against me, his cock throbbing as it empties itself deep inside.

Cass holds me for a few minutes, breathing harshly into my shoulder. "I don't want to let you go," he admits, and I tighten my arms around his neck.

"I know. Come, let's clean up, and I'll plait your hair for you."

After washing, we dress in the garments Merlin has provided for us. I can't help but watch Cassian with admiration as his muscular body flexes as he dresses. He is a work of art, and if we both survive today, I know I'll remember how my breath catches at the sight of him well into old age.

He dons simple hose and tunic, as he will spend most of the fight as Aren. He'll be more powerful that way, and since magic can't touch him, he'll be safer. It won't protect him from arrows or swords, but I have a plan for that. After he packs his axes and leather protective gear in a bag, I make him sit on the floor while I braid his hair. "That goes both ways, you know," I say, bringing back our earlier conversation.

"Don't you or Aren do anything foolish out there. I need you by my side for the rest of my life."

He tilts his head back, his lips tipping up into a teasing smile. "Is that a proposal?"

I push his head back down so I can finish tying off the braid. "What if it is?"

"I'll give you my answer when the battle is finished and you stand triumphantly over your fallen enemy."

My heart skips a beat, and I press a kiss on his head. "A fine reason to make sure we win, then."

Our little army occupies every inch of the square and spills out into the adjoining lanes. Although it's not so little anymore with the addition of the ones provided by Granton and Alba. Sitting on Zohar's back, I run my gaze over the company, which now numbers in the hundreds. The horses, decked out in metal armor, chew on their bits, calm even through the current of excitement humming through the air.

Half of our numbers ride horses while the others are on foot. Armor, shields, and weapons have been provided for everyone who needed them, and I know I will owe Merlin much when this is done. More than once I have wondered why he is exerting himself so. He has asked for nothing—not gold, nor land, not even so much as a title.

Without him, our cause would have failed at the start. Is there some motivation I am unaware of? I mentally shrug and turn my thoughts to other matters. Whatever his intentions are, he seems to be on our side, and I'll take every ounce of help I can get.

Cassian pulls Fire Heart to a stop beside me, checking that I've been allocated weapons. My trusty bow and quiver have been slung over my back, while a short sword rests in its scabbard attached to the saddle. Both sets of his axes are on display, the ones from the Valkyries on his back, the others at his waist. Zohar and Fire Heart press their noses together in greeting, the clinking of their bridles lost amongst the noise of the crowd.

"Ready?" Cassian asks, and I shake my head. I cast my gaze out over the troops. Robin and his men, the dwarfs, the Valkyries, the armies. My throat constricts at the sight of the villagers and farmers, guilt raging in my chest. They have chosen to be here, they want to fight. But they have no magic, no training, no real way to defend themselves. I know what I must do, what I must sacrifice to defeat Morana and wrest my kingdom from her control. I have made my peace with what lays ahead and have accepted my destiny. But they shouldn't have to risk their lives for me to do so, and I know not everyone standing here now will still be doing so at the end of the day.

Do I have the right to order them to stay behind? And if I do, am I just as bad as Morana by taking away their choice? Swallowing down the lump in my throat, I turn inward. I do not want to be the kind of monarch that asks others to give their lives for them. But I also don't want to spit on their loyalty. They may want to fight for a variety of reasons, but their allegiance is one of them. They want Morana dethroned, and for me to take my rightful place as queen. Do I have the right to take that away from them?

"Heavy is the head that wears the crown," Cassian murmurs just loudly enough for me to hear. The man knows me too well, I am an open book to him. He allows me to just sit, staring at him blankly as I make up my mind. He offers his support without demanding I tell him what's on my mind. He trusts me to ask if I need help or advice and doesn't talk over me or take the decision from me. I would love him for an eternity for that alone.

In his eyes, I find the answers and squeeze his fingers in thanks. Clicking my tongue, I move Zohar to the center of the square and raise a fist in the air. Cassian lets out a piercing whistle and it eventually goes quiet as people peer toward me.

"We go to fight Morana!" I shout, and they raise their weapons and cheer. "Each of you has chosen to be here today, and I know I am the most blessed of princesses to have your loyalty and support." I fist my hand and place it over my heart. "Know that your love and loyalty have been marked. Should you change your mind about wanting to join us, know that you will face no punishment or recrimination. I love my people, and would not now, or ever, force anyone to join in a fight for the crown." Zohar stamps her foot and snorts, causing laughter to spread across the square.

"We are with you, Princess!" a voice shouts from the far side. A wide grin grows across my face as more cheers go up amongst much thumping of weapons against shields.

"For Valderán!" Cassian shouts, and Merlin pounds his staff into the ground. In the course of a heartbeat, we materialize in the fields outside Ardavan Palace, cloaked by Merlin's magic. Everyone has been briefed on the plan. There's no turning back now.

Chapter 37

Morana

Strolling through the halls, I hum a happy little melody. I revel in the feeling as it is not something I am particularly familiar with. The few servants or huntsmen I come across stare at me in horror, their eyes wide with terror. I waggle my fingers at them and pass them by, ignoring their sighs of relief as they scurry away like the vermin they are.

Snow White is dead, Silas might as well be, and each day, my magic encroaches farther north. Impatience tugs at me but I toss it away, unwilling to entertain it. I have waited years, decades even, for my revenge, and I will have it.

A roar shatters the silence, echoing through the halls. I tilt my head, curiosity plucking at me. Rubbing a hand down the goose bumps that have sprouted on my arms, I listen intently but hear nothing further. Moving silently down the hallway, I peer around the corner. Nothing. Eyes narrowing, I move down the next, my gaze sweeping from side to side.

The torches extinguish simultaneously, small trails of smoke filtering up to the ceiling. "Huntsmen!" I shout, but no reply is forthcoming. "Where did they all go?" I grumble under my breath. They were here only moments ago. Another roar, closer this time, has the hairs rising on the back of my neck. Racing over to the balcony, I lean over, eyes flying wide when my gaze lands on a huge beast which appears to be part lion, part eagle, part ram.

It leaps into the air, its powerful wings carrying it toward me. I spin on my heel and race back the way I came, heading toward the tower. Peering over my shoulder, I suck in a breath when I see the creature stalking me, its head lowered, eyes fixed on me like I'm its last meal.

My magic begins to swirl, and I shoot it at the creature. It slides off it seamlessly. True fear, something I have not felt in decades, settles over me like a mantle. A myth I heard long ago filters into my mind, the story of an ancient beast that magic has no effect on. *Manticore.*

It snarls at me, saliva dripping from its ten-inch fangs. An explosion follows, shaking the foundations of the palace, causing me to nearly lose my footing. The manticore gains on me, one step of his equaling three of mine. Panic tightens my throat and when another blast comes, I teleport myself to the front doors of the palace. I slam the doors shut, barricading them with powerful spells which should keep the manticore from escaping and coming after me.

Pursing my lips, I wonder where it came from and how it got inside. The good-for-nothing servants must have left the gates open, or the huntsmen were too cowardly to stop it. A whimper snaps my head to the side, and I grit my teeth when I see several servants huddling behind a hay cart, Silas amongst them.

Just as I am about to rip into them for removing him from the castle, they shriek, ducking down. A bright light flashes and the curtain wall shatters in an explosion of stone and dust. My hands curl into fists as deep vicious anger begins to grow low in my belly. Three lightning bolts race across the sky, each one hitting the outer walls. The servants run for their lives, their faces filled with panic and dismay, dragging a stumbling Silas off with them.

Before I can do anything about that, thunder booms so deeply that I stagger on the steps. The scent of ozone makes my eyes water, blurring my vision just as another volley of lightning bolts strikes the grounds around the palace. There are only two people I can think of... but no, it can't be. No one has seen Thor or Zeus in years.

I storm down the stairs, skirting debris from the walls. Why would either of them attack me? Thor, I can understand, especially if he found out about his brother. But I refuse to believe he could have discovered my secret—the mask I wear is too perfect, my deceptions too strong.

Using my magic to elevate me, I soar upward until I'm above the tree line. Another lightning bolt whizzes past me, so close it singes my dress. I pat the flames out, growling, before throwing my arms out. "Come out and face me, you coward!" I scream at the heavens. "Your power is no match for mine!"

How dare the gods come for me. Do they not know who I am? I throw my head back, malicious laughter pouring from me as my shadows swirl like a tornado. They have no idea who they are dealing with.

Chapter 38

Snow White

The tower soars above me, its stone face blank and impassive as I stand in its shadow. Staring up at it, my mouth goes dry. The palace holds so many memories. A few good ones—my mother reading to me before bed, Cassian playing hide and seek with me, Alaric carrying me on his shoulders so I could pretend to be a giant. The corner of my mouth lifts as the memories play through my mind. But being here doesn't bring me peace. Yes, there are good memories, but those are heavily tainted by Morana's and Silas's sins. The palace no longer rings of happiness and laughter, but practically oozes malevolence and despair.

I may not love living in a tent, but I have done so quite successfully so far. I can happily continue to do so, and I might just have to—because after today, Adarvan Palace will cease to exist. It isn't something I have discussed with Cassian or anyone else, but it's been playing on my mind, and being here only confirms it. I could never live here again, not with any measure of happiness.

A loud boom makes me jump, bringing me back to the present. This isn't the time to dwell in the past. I'm going to ensure my country's future, no matter the cost.

Thor's distraction should work to get Morana out of the palace so we can get into the tower. The Oracle told Cassian we need to break the glass from the inside. My "knowing" had informed me the glass was none other than the mirror itself. The only way to do that is to go into it, although I can't say I'm not a little apprehensive. It sounds so simple . . . go in, break the glass, get out. But we don't know what's on the other side. Even Merlin, with his seemingly omniscient knowledge, was unable to tell us.

"Snow!" Cassian hisses, breaking me out of my reverie. "Come on, she's gone."

Unfortunately, he lacks hair long enough to use as a rope. Calling on my power, I bend my knees and jump, laughter ripping from my throat when I shoot into the air. His eyes grow big, and he throws himself over the ledge, arms outstretched to catch me. I reach out, grabbing his hands, and he hauls me into the tower.

Cassian steps back, running a hand over his face. "I'm not sure I'll ever get used to this." He shakes his head and pulls breeches from his bag, quickly pulling them on.

"It's only one day," I remind him.

He tugs his tunic over his head, his muscles rippling enticingly. I wet my lips, my gaze trained on his delicious body. Is it bad that I want to lick him?

"Are you sure it's the right decision?" He turns, catching me watching him. A cocky grin lights up his face. "If you keep looking at me like that, we won't make it through the mirror."

Giving myself a shake, I answer his question. "It's the only decision, Cass. There's no other choice."

He blows out a breath, then removes the mirror and sets it upright, leaning it against the wall. "I know. But I hate what you'll have to sacrifice for it."

I place a hand on his chest and press my lips to his cheek. "I would give up any number of lifetimes to have just one with you."

He crushes me to him, wrapping me tightly in his arms. Another boom sounds, rattling the foundations. He breathes a sigh and releases me. "Ready?" I nod, and my eyes begin to glow. Remembering how Morana activated the runes, I reach out, sweeping my hand over them. The surface shudders, wisps of smoke sailing across it. Cassian and I exchange glances, then step into it.

It grabs at us, simultaneously trying to keep us out and pull us in. It's thick and viscous, a humid, wet space we have to forcefully punch our way through. My lungs seize, unable to breathe, and I experience a moment of panic when our hands are torn away from each other. I reach for Cassian, my hand grabbing at the empty air, but before I can find him, the mirror spits me out.

I stumble out of a stone wall and crash into a hard chest. The man it belongs to steadies me by my shoulders, and I look up, then up some more, meeting the quizzical, icy blue gaze of the goliath before me. Cassian follows me out of the mirror, landing much more gracefully than I did. He tears me away from the man and thrusts me behind him with a snarl on his lips and a hand on his axe.

The blond-haired man takes a step back and raises his hands. "I meant no harm. But do not raise a weapon to me. I do not wish to hurt you." His eyes flash a warning, one I recognize immediately.

Placing a placating hand on Cassian's back, I say, "Please forgive us our intrusion, my lord." I allow my eyes to flash in return so that he recognizes me as one of his own. "My name is Snow White, Princess of Valderán, and this is Cassian." The tension slowly leaks from Cass's shoulders.

"Your Highness. Welcome to my humble abode." Humble indeed.

The small square room is perhaps twelve by twelve feet. Roughly hewn stone lines the walls, while the ceiling, made of dark walnut beams, soars above us, making the area feel bigger than it is. A lone window graces one wall, open to the elements without the benefit of glass or shutters, a bench of sorts resting beneath it. A narrow cot sits against one wall. There is no door, just a slight shimmer on the wall we came out of.

"Do you mind?" I ask, jerking my head toward the window. The man inclines his head. Clasping my hands behind my back, I wander over to it and lean against the wide sill, catching my breath at the sight before me. A lavender sky dotted with pink and gold clouds stretches out to the horizon. Dragons gracefully soar amongst them, their shadows lighting over the turquoise sea below. Waves pound against brilliant white sands, while farther afield, jagged mountains preside over rolling fields. Their snow-capped peaks glimmer in the light from the two suns, both tinging the world in a golden glow. It is one of the most magical, beautiful things I've ever seen.

Cassian joins me, placing his hand on my lower back. I turn to the god. "May I ask your name?"

"Forgive me, Princess. I have been alone here for some two hundred years, and I forget my manners. I am Baldr, son of Odin and Frigg."

"We are family, then, as I count your nieces, the Valkyries, as my kin."

Baldr's eyes go misty. "I have missed them greatly. Tell me, how do they fare?"

"They will be better now that we have found you. Your brother, Thor, is with them now at my palace." Baldr slides down onto the bench and places his trembling hands on his lap. I'm sure he has a million questions, but time is of the essence. If Morana figures out Thor is only a distraction, we may not have much time.

Cassian must read my mind. "We've come to destroy the mirror. We are just about to engage in battle and have little time. Will you come with us?"

Baldr runs a hand through his hair. "Time works differently here. An hour in your time is a week here. And there's no way out. Believe me, I have tried."

"The Oracle of the Forbidden Isles gifted me a weapon with which to break the glass. That is why we have come," Cassian explains.

Hope lights Baldr's eyes, and he goes still, his gaze swinging between us. "Truly?"

"Truly," I reply with a smile. I quickly fill him in about our situation, explaining the poisoning of the country, the control or deaths of the people, and the army we have waiting for us outside.

Baldr listens intently, his jaw ticking. When I finish, he stands and braces his hands at the sides of the window frame, looking out over the mystical scenery. "I have been here for over two hundred years," he says. "And that's two hundred years in your time. Math was never my strong suit, but I believe it works out to be over thirty thousand years that I have been trapped in this room." He turns and his eyes are bleak. I'm horrified by the thought—my mind broke much sooner. The fact he is still standing is a testament to his strength and willpower.

"And that," he continues, gesturing at the scenery outside, "is ever-changing. One day I might appear in the Fae realm, another—deep in space. One year I was underwater, laying at the base of King Triton's castle, drowning over and over again. No living being outside of this box seems able to see or hear me. But I am immortal, and cannot die, so I suffer eternally." He returns to the bench, collapsing onto it. "The only thing that saved me was the mirror. The being trapped inside it speaks to me on occasion."

Cassian takes a seat on the floor and pulls me into his lap. "How did you come to be here?" His arms tighten around me, and I lean back into him, still troubled over Baldr's incarceration.

Baldr blows out a breath. "You are from Valderán, do you know the story of Ravensly?"

"The Valkyries told me she was a powerful sorceress and that your father had sent you to deal with her. You vanished without a trace."

Baldr opens his mouth but hesitates when the wall we came through begins to shimmer. A masklike face appears, and I gasp, remembering seeing it once before when I was a child. "I believe I am best suited to tell this tale," the disembodied voice says. It shifts its empty eyes toward Baldr. "Hello, old friend. I am afraid I have not been fully honest with you over the years, and I beg your forgiveness. I worried you might hate me for my part in your circumstances."

Baldr sits back and crosses his arms over his chest. The mask watches him for a moment, then begins its story. "I am Prince Khallan of the Light Court, son of Queen Aoife. Ravensly was from a village at the base of Clawback Mountain. She was incredibly beautiful and had suitors from far and wide vying for her hand. Tales of her beauty and innocence spread throughout the lands, even making their way into the Fae realm. Curious to see if the stories were true, I traveled to Valderán. So enchanted was I by not only her looks, but by her apparent kindness and generosity, I lured her to a fairy circle and whisked her away.

"Like this room, time moves differently in Faery. I was fully caught in her spell and fancied myself in love with her within a few short weeks. For the first time in my immortal life, I was happy and working diligently to get my mother to agree to let her stay. But slowly, things began to change. Ravensly was never satisfied, nothing was good enough. She was insanely jealous of other women and began to sow seeds of discord throughout the court. Nothing I did was enough to satisfy her, and she would often lash out with her wickedly cruel tongue, her insults cutting like knives.

"My mother had enough and banished her from Faery, demanding I return her immediately to her world. By this time, I no longer loved her, but she was with child. I gifted her the mirror which would allow me to communicate with my daughter once she was born. It could also gift Ravensly with a small amount of power. Not much, but enough to ensure my daughter could be cared for without Ravensly worrying about poverty."

Khallan pauses, the mask turning downward. As interesting as the tale is, I cannot help but feel a smidgeon of impatience. Cassian's arms tighten around me when I fidget, and my cheeks blaze. I do not wish to seem rude, but there is a battle waiting for us, and I don't understand why we need to have this conversation now. These events took place hundreds of years ago—surely they have no relevance to today's proceedings?

"Just let them tell their story," Cassian breathes in my ear. "Remember what Baldr said about the time difference. Spending fifteen minutes here will make no difference." I give an almost imperceptible nod and give them my attention.

"I did not know that Ravensly's family already had a propensity for magic. Adding the little I gave her allowed her natural abilities to strengthen. She became stronger, and after our daughter, Kali, was born, she spent every free second learning everything she could. She found a witch willing to train her in dark and death magic, and when Kali was five, Ravensly was able to use the runes to trap me in the mirror, enslaving me."

"Why would she do such a thing?" Cassian asks.

"She was furious that I had taken away the immortality she could have gained by living in Faery. She felt entitled to have everything her heart desired and being denied it made her jealousy soar. Trapping me here was my punishment for leaving her and taking away the life she thought she deserved."

Baldr picks up the story. "She began rapidly gaining power, but the death magic she practiced required killing sprees. The earth cried out for help, drowning in the blood of her victims. Odin heeded the cries and because I am indestructible, sent me to stop her. Back then, she relied heavily on her raven spies, who caught wind of my impending arrival. She was waiting for me. The moment I arrived, I was sucked into the mirror, and have been trapped here ever since. As a god, I am extremely powerful. My magic warped the mirror, turning it into something it was never intended to be. She now has access to my powers—"

"Along with mine," Khallan interrupts. "Which makes her one of the most powerful sorceresses that have ever lived."

A line etches into my forehead as I mull over their words. "Wait, what did you mean when you said, 'back then,' Baldr?"

He tilts his head to the side. "I suppose that was a poor choice of words. She still uses the ravens, does she not?"

I lean my head back, exchanging glances with Cassian. "Ravensly died hundreds of years ago," I say slowly, wondering what I am missing. "Morana is her . . . great-great-granddaughter, I believe."

Baldr shakes his head and crosses his arms over his chest. "Morana *is* Ravensly."

My brows furrow at this. "How can this be? She's not immortal. She looks no older than thirty!"

"And how long has she looked that age?" Khallan asks. I open my mouth, then slam it shut. It's been several years since I've seen her—I'm not counting her disguise in the village—and I realize she did, indeed, look the same as she did when she married my father. I was a child at the time and not observant of such things. And when I was older, I was too busy being tortured by her to notice she didn't seem to age.

"The witch taught her how to obtain immortality . . . in a sense. She must offer sacrifices regularly to the mirror and feast on the flesh of humans."

"But wouldn't people notice she wasn't aging?" I ask.

"She wears a mask," Khallan explains. "Keeping it in place requires a tremendous amount of magic. She bathes in the blood of innocents to keep up the deception. As for not aging, she would simply use her magic to create a 'child' and then take over their lives once they reached a certain age. So she is her own great-great-granddaughter, in a sense."

My stomach roils at the thought. Creating fictitious children and reliving lifetimes over and over? She must have had a steady supply of new servants to be able to pull off such a thing. "What happened to the people she sacrificed?"

"Their souls became part of the mirror."

"I wonder what caused her to become so evil," I muse.

"She was never a good person," Khallan replies. "She never had much of a heart, always focusing on what others had. Jealousy ruled her more often than not. But she did love Kali. When the Valkyries came to find Baldr, a fierce battle ensued. My daughter, wanting to see the 'pretty horses,' raced onto the field and was killed instantly under the hooves of one of them. Ravensly, who was already a little touched, lost her mind. She rewrote our history and convinced herself I was some great love of hers. Reality became a mass of lies and confusion until she no longer remembered what was true and what wasn't. Everyone became an enemy, and everyone was out to get her."

I mull this over, thinking back on some of our interactions when I was growing up. The fact she accused me of voluntarily laying with my father, rather than seeing it for what it truly was, highlights her unhinged state of mind. Not to mention her insane desire to be the fairest of them all. But one thing I never understood.

"I can understand her anger toward the Valkyries, although, I know them well. They would never purposefully hurt a child. Her spite toward you can be chalked up to jealousy and pettiness. But why make the entire country suffer?"

Baldr sighs. "Your father's great-grandparents were traveling through the area at the time, as they were doing a tour of the kingdom. Just the simple fact that they were seen within five miles of her castle convinced her they were in league with the Valkyries, and therefore, responsible for Kali's death."

Leaning back into Cass's chest, I shake my head in sorrow. So much death, so much destruction. For nothing.

"She went on a killing spree the likes of which haven't been seen until now. For miles around Clawback Mountain, the rivers ran red with the blood of the innocent. She enslaved the horses by turning them into kelpies and punished the Valkyries by turning them into dwarfs and banishing them from their horses. Which not only took away their magic but relegated them to this realm and unable to return to Valhalla or their father," Khallan explains. "She then spent decades steeping herself in black magic and lore, strengthening her powers, and setting her plans in place for the kingdom."

She may be evil, but my heart still twists at her loss. I can't imagine a loss like that. Having her rip the babe from me nearly destroyed me, but having a child you have birthed, held, and loved for five years only to be killed? It must have been devastating. You would think a loss such as that would teach her some empathy toward all the children she has killed and families she has destroyed.

I suppose that is the difference between us. Horrific things happened to me in my eighteen years. The loss of my mother, my father's habitual rape and beatings, the loss of my child, the torture Morana subjected me to . . . and yet, my ability to extend compassion to others has not dimmed. I have not turned into a monster. But no amount of sympathy or goodness I have will prevent me from putting an end to her and her reign of terror. We need to return and end this.

I pull myself awkwardly out of Cassian's embrace and come to my feet. "I thank you both for your stories." I incline my head, first to Baldr, then to the mirror. "We have a field full of people waiting for us and must take our leave. Will you join us in our fight?"

Baldr pulls himself to his feet, a gleam in his eye. "I am with you. I have missed battle."

The mirror wavers, Khallan's mask blinking in and out before solidifying. "I will join you as well. The Fae normally stay out of human affairs, but since this all began with me, I will lend my aid."

"Thank you," I murmur. "Know that I will be in your debt."

Cassian comes up beside me, reaches into a hidden pocket inside his tunic, and pulls out a sheathed iron dagger. Its hilt is intricately detailed with runes and tiny gemstones. When Cassian slides it out of its scabbard, the room shudders violently under our feet. My knees threaten to give way, and I grab Cass's arm to remain upright. Small stones and grit fall from the ceiling as the earthquake grows stronger and several of the ceiling beams snap in half.

"Hurry, Cass," I urge, and he strides toward the shimmering portal in the wall, thrusting his knife into it. Cracks appear in the walls around us, brilliant white light leaking through. Stones begin to crumble in earnest, the noise nearly masking the sound of shattering glass.

The mask disappears, and a voice shouts from the other side, "Make haste!"

"Go!" Cassian shouts, pushing Baldr through the portal. He grabs my arm just as the back wall falls away with a thundering roar. Wind tears at my hair and clothing, and my heart leaps into my throat as I'm pulled toward the oblivion beyond.

"Cassian," I scream, as he loses his hold on me. His head whips around, eyes filled with horror. He reaches for me, his fingers just able to grasp onto mine. He yanks me toward him as the floor starts to crumble beneath us. We hastily scramble into the portal, falling through into Morana's tower room and landing heavily on the floor.

I shakily climb to my feet, my heart fluttering like a hummingbird's. "Are you okay?" Cassian seizes my shoulders with trembling hands, his wild eyes running over me, searching for injuries.

Placing a hand over one of his, I reassure him I am fine. When I can breathe again, I turn to Baldr and Khallan, who is no longer a faceless mask, but a very handsome Fae prince. He stands only a handful of inches taller than me, but he holds himself like royalty. His white-blond hair falls to his shoulders, showing off his pointed ears. He's dressed finely in rich materials, and a small crown rests on his head.

I bow my head. "Your Highness."

He gives me an elegant bow, then stands in front of the mirror. Although it's no longer a mirror—only the frame is left. Khallan raises a hand, blue sparks dancing along his fingertips, but I beg him to stop. "Please don't destroy it. I have a plan."

He turns to look at me, his face hardening. "I will not leave it whole to be used as a weapon again."

"On my honor, it will be destroyed before the sun sets on this day."

He searches my eyes, then tilts his head to the side. "Very well, Princess."

A loud boom rocks the foundations. A wide grin stretches across Baldr's face. He cracks his knuckles, practically bouncing with excitement. "Sounds like my brother has started without us. Shall we?"

Chapter 39

Morana

No one rises to my bait, and a prickling of unease skates over me. My gaze tracks over the barren forests and fields, then back to the palace. *Something is wrong.* A minuscule tug, so faint I almost miss it, pokes at my magic. My eyes narrow as I turn inward, focusing on the foreign feeling. It is as if a leech draws tiny amounts of power from me. Not enough to have any true effect, but enough to make me suspicious.

I whip my head up, nostrils flaring. It cannot be a coincidence that this happens right after a fabled creature chased me from my home. *Distraction.* My heart begins to race, pumping red-hot fury through me. Turning back toward the palace, I let out a scream of frustration.

Another bolt of lightning streaks past me. "Morana!" The deep voice booms across the landscape, and I spin around with a vicious snarl, my cape flying out around me. The sky cracks in half, reality shattering as a powerful cloaking spell breaks and crashes to the ground. The empty field is now filled with hundreds of people dressed in armor.

My jaw clenches at the sight, the fury ramping up as a red haze lowers over my vision. Rolls of thunder threaten to deafen me, and I glance up to see Thor sitting amongst the clouds. His daughters, fully restored to their former glory, surround him. My nails dig into my palms as I seethe. This is impossible. Those fucking horses were hidden too well to ever be found.

Forgetting about the palace, I send a call out to my ravens, but for the first time in two hundred years, they ignore me. I clench my fists, refusing to allow the tendrils of fear skating down my spine to turn into full-blown panic. I am still the most powerful being here.

Thunder rolls across the sky again, and I've had enough. "Missing your brother, Thor? I wonder where he could be?"

"Right behind you."

Before I can react, I'm knocked out of the sky, my heart plummeting with my fall. Whipping my magic out, I manage to land on my feet, hiding my trembling fists in my skirts. I glare up at Baldr, my mind a mass of confusion. It must be some trick, some magical illusion. Nothing can come out of the mirror.

Snow White's arrow shot through it, my mind unhelpfully reminds me. But she's dead, I killed her myself.

"Advance!" a voice calls out, followed by the bellow of horns. The army begins to march toward me with shouts of "Kill the queen!" and "Murderer!"

Don't these fools know I could wipe them all out with a single thought? Dropping to my knees, I dig my hands into the soil, ignoring the volley of flaming arrows that arcs overhead. I call upon the dead things, the rotting things, the forgotten and unloved things.

An earthquake rips through the earth, opening a chasm between my side of the field and theirs. I watch on with glee as a number of the army falls into it, their screams calming a little of the anger in me. From out of the fissure come the dead, skeletons of people and animals alike, crawling their way out of hell, beckoned by my call.

"Destroy them!" I scream, pointing toward the army. The dead turn, their empty eyes so like those of my puppets. That reminds me. Throwing an arm out to the side, I shoot magic out toward the palace, rounding up servants, huntsmen, and even the king, and draw them to the battlefield. They arrive in their dozens, their eyes blacked over, each with a sword in their hand.

Glancing over my shoulder, I spy Baldr joining his brother amongst the clouds. Straightening my shoulders, I lift my hand, resting it under my chin. I blow out a deep breath, a magical kiss that twists into a horizontal funnel. It shoots through the air, blasting them out of the sky.

The Valkyries scream, two of them diving to catch them. My right eye ticks when I spot the one responsible for my daughter's death. Cackling, I whip my arm around my head, and a lasso, charged with electricity, slithers out of my wrist. I thrust myself into the air and release the rope, which finds itself wrapped around my target. I yank, hard, tearing her off her horse, and watch with satisfaction as she tumbles toward the ground. Of course, one of her sisters rescues her. I bare my teeth at them, then duck when the blonde one throws a spear at me.

I hiss angrily, my eyes darting in too many directions. I can't keep up. Landing back on the ground, I storm into the forest, the dead trees surrounding me like sentinels. I rip several of them out of the soil, their roots dangling, reminding me of a sea witch's tentacles. My magic molds them together, their trunks forming into a long body. A lashing tail appears, and a monstrous head with red eyes lifts, staring down at me. Huge gleaming teeth snap in the dragon's jaws, waiting for my orders.

I place a kiss on its snout and murmur, "Go, my beautiful. Kill them all." Swirls of smoke pour from its nostrils as it spreads its wings, flapping furiously to get off the ground. With a smirk, I watch it soar through the sky, breathing fire on all it sees.

I take a moment to assess, my gaze wandering over the field. To the right, a group of archers has settled in the trees, raining volley after volley of arrows down on my army. A group of dwarfs battles several of my skeletons, while soldiers wearing Alba's insignia busily construct a bridge to gap the chasm my earthquake made.

A blast knocks me into the air, throwing me twenty feet back. I land heavily in the dirt, dazed. Breathing in deep breaths through my mouth, I pull myself to my feet, wiping crumbs of dirt from my face. Tilting my head back at the sound of cawing, my lips pull into a victorious smile when my ravens appear above in their hundreds. *Finally.*

"Attack them!" I shout, but they ignore me, continuing to circle above.

"They no longer answer to you," a voice says before an older man appears before me. My lips curl in a snarl, and I throw a blast of magic at him. It should have melted the flesh from his bones, but it instead deflects off a powerful shield. He pounds his staff into the ground and shoots up until he is as tall as a giant. His long beard melts away, replaced by a shorter one, along with the wizard's cloak he wears.

The god looks down at me with his one good eye, the other covered by an eye patch and crossed with a thick scar. Metal armor covers him, and two giant wolves stand snarling at his side. One of the ravens lands on his shoulder, its beady eyes glaring down at me as if I am beneath its notice. "Ravensly Tamasvi."

His thunderous voice brings the battle to an abrupt halt, and I wince both at the use of my former name and from the raw power radiating from him. Raising my chin, I meet his eye defiantly. I refuse to quiver in front of the All-Father. "Odin."

His face hardens at my familiarity. He can shove his staff up his ass, I will not bow before him. He takes a menacing step toward me, the earth trembling beneath him. "You imprisoned my son. You cursed my granddaughters. You stole my ravens. Beg me for my forgiveness, and I may yet let you live."

A hush comes over the field, all eyes trained on us. Various scenarios race through my mind, none working in my favor. The sour taste of bile rises in my throat at the thought of retreating, but it is better to live to fight another day than to die like a dog at the feet of the gods. I rose up once before, and I can do so again. Even if it takes another two hundred years.

I take a hesitant step back, then another. Odin watches me with a narrowed eye, his lips pressed in a fine line. The raven on his shoulder cocks its head when arms wrap around my waist from behind, startling me. A long-forgotten voice whispers, "Going so soon, love?"

Ripping myself out of his arms, I turn, shaking my head in disbelief. "No," I mutter. Prince Khallan glares at me in the same beautifully haughty way he used to so long ago. He fairly reeks of royalty and privilege, something I had always coveted for myself. I didn't want to be Ravensly Tamasvi, daughter of farmers—even as a young child I knew my destiny was meant for much greater things.

But for him to stand here means he was released from the mirror. I press my eyelids closed, then snap them open. This was a distraction. I should have listened to my instincts, a mistake I will not make again. Lowering my head, I feign submission while I draw as much power as I can into myself. My breaths come faster and faster, and my body begins to rock gently with the force.

"Nothing to say?" Khallan mocks.

I twist my shoulders, then crack my neck before throwing my arms out, releasing the magic in a tidal wave. But nothing happens. I freeze in disbelief, deep lines knitting my brow as my gaze runs over the hundreds of people behind Odin. They appear to be frozen in place, as if time has stopped. My death creatures explode in a shower of dust, and my magnificent dragon falls from the sky, landing harmlessly amongst the trees.

The gods and Valkyries watch me impassively, and Khallan's low chuckle scrapes against me like nails on a chalkboard. I clutch at the remaining dregs of magic, demanding they revive. But after expelling so much, there is almost nothing left. My mind spins, unable to accept defeat. Spotting my puppets in the distance, I use the last of my strength, pulling my magic out of them. It might just be enough.

King Silas

Ever so slowly, the blackness seeps from my vision. I blink rapidly, the blurry landscape slowly coming into focus.

I swallow against the dryness of my mouth and run a hand over my eyes. A pounding headache fuzzes my thoughts, as if I have partaken in too much wine. I take one stumbling step, then two, walking much as a new-born colt does, shaky and unsure. People stand frozen around me, some with swords in their hands. My brows lower. Where am I?

Although I have a vague sense of home, nothing looks like it should. I stare at the black barren trees and the dried-out earth. Wheeling around, I search for something, anything familiar. A thick fog seeps out of the trees surrounding me, forcing me to back away as panic gnaws at my insides.

As it begins to swirl around my legs, a barrage of disjointed memories slams into me. I clutch my head, my eyes nearly popping out of my skull. Falling to my hands and knees, I begin to retch, bringing up a foul bile.

What have I done?

Chapter 40

Snow White

Pressing my back into a tree, I cover my eyes with my hands. Agony rips through me at the sounds of the wounded and dying. Cries ring out amongst the clash of weapons, a deadly cacophony that scrapes my nerves raw.

The scent of scorched flesh and blood turns my stomach, and I rage anew at what Morana's greed and misplaced anger has wrought. So much death, so much anguish, so much suffering for nothing. I knew this day would not pass without casualties, but knowing it and seeing it are two very different things.

Hanging my head, I breathe in and out, forcefully shoving down my feelings. I cannot afford to feel the grief, I must keep my wits about me. Tomorrow will be for mourning.

It is cowardly of me to stand here amongst the trees, shielded from view by an invisibility shield. But it and the promise to "not move one muscle" was the only way Cass would leave my side. He has trained and prepared for this day for years. He has hungered for it, dreamed of it, yearned to exact a measure of revenge for the both of us.

Before we left the village, he had forced the names of the huntsmen that aided Morana in my torture from me. Although my conscience vehemently objected, I gave them to him. He needs this, both him and Aren. The years of separation and the pain I suffered still weigh heavily on him, and if bringing me their heads is what soothes the primal need to protect me, then I will gag my conscience and lock her away somewhere her disapproval can be ignored.

I track Cassian as he charges into the field with no hesitation, no second-guessing. He clutches the axes the Valkyries gave him and heads straight for the line of huntsmen, a feral yell ripping from his throat. The axes glint in the sunlight, slashing and slaying. Blood arcs through the air in a crimson rainbow as he dispatches them one by one. He is magnificent.

I tear my eyes away, placing a hand over my racing heart and squeezing my thighs together to assuage my aching core. I'm a little disturbed by how much my body responds to the sight of him avenging me. My conscience tries to pipe up again, but this time, I shove it into a dark box and cover it in locks for good measure.

Casting my gaze around the field, I quickly tally everyone's movements. Thor, Baldr, and the Valkyries battle the dragon, while the army, dwarfs, and Robin's men keep Morana's company busy.

After promising Khallan I would destroy the mirror, I had filled him and Baldr in on my plan. I needed Morana to be overwhelmed, attacked from all sides. She wouldn't be able to fight everyone at once, and with attacks from land and air, by humans and gods, her attention would be so divided that she'd be unable to keep track of everything and everyone.

I needed her to expel as much power as possible, to weaken her enough so that when I eradicate what is left of the mirror, she will be powerless to stop me. I'm not surprised when Merlin transforms into Odin. The "knowing" that came when my powers were awakened informed me of his true identity.

Now that she is cornered, I can finish this. I throw out my magic, suspending the battle but leaving Cass unaffected. He strides toward me, gazing at me with hooded eyes. He clutches a severed head in each hand, sinew and tendons dragging on the ground, leaving a bloody trail behind. He tosses them at my feet, then grabs me by the throat, pulling me into his chest. My heart flutters, my core growing damp as he smashes his lips to mine.

I wind my fingers into the soft hair at the base of his neck, my breath catching in my throat at his tongue's invasion. He plunders my mouth as if it gives him life, and I cling to him desperately, dizzy with lack of air and lust.

I wish I could suspend time truly, to hit pause on everything around us. I would give in to that secret wish of mine and allow Cassian to hunt me through the forest. My body hungers for his, an electric desire thrumming through my veins, demanding to be sated. But as desperate as I am, I refuse to put on a show for the gods. I can only imagine what Hilda might have to say.

Placing a hand on his chest, I push him back, both of us dragging in deep lungfuls of air. "Later," I promise, and he nods jerkily, his erection thick against his breeches. "It's time. Are you ready?"

Cassian slides a hand over my cheek. "Remember your promise, Princess. You will walk off this field whole."

"I promised I would try."

"There is no 'try.' You *will*."

He steps back and pulls off his clothing, dumping them in a pile on the ground. The transformation into Aren takes only a moment before I stare into his emerald eyes. *I do not like this, mate,* he says with a rumbly growl.

"I know." I run my fingers down his chest, his eyes narrowing with pleasure. "But Morana is weak, and I have to finish this. For us, for my people. And remember, I'm no longer quite so easy to kill."

He stares down at me, then a giant sigh echoes in my mind. *Just don't accept any apples from strangers.*

A strangled laugh works its way from my throat, and I swear Aren winks at me. Shaking my head at him, I call upon the elements and a thick fog forms around us. I draw it out of the trees surrounding the field, encouraging it to slither around the frozen fighters. I pull it up, raising it high enough to obscure us from view, then run a hand over my body, changing my clothing. I plan on making an entrance.

Reality freezes for just a heartbeat, a gasp of air indrawn, a sense of knowing that you are stepping onto the path you were always meant to be on. I was born for this, this second, this minute, this hour. It has all led up to this. All I have to do is reach out and grab it.

It is time for me to take the crown and become the queen I was always destined to be.

Morana

Khallan grabs me, my back against his chest, and wraps his arms around mine to hold me still. "Get off me!" I hiss, squirming against him.

"Have a little dignity, Ravensly."

I growl, stomping on his foot. He laughs in my ear, infuriating me even more. I will not allow this to be the end of me, I will find a way. I just need to delay them while I come up with a plan.

"I never loved you," I spit. "You were nothing more than a means to an end." He remains silent but spins me around, forcing me to face the palace.

Although the forest lines the perimeter of the field, the trees blocking the view of the palace were removed long ago. I eye the blanket of fog seeping out of the trees, growing taller and thicker with each passing second. I can use this. If I can get away from Khallan, I can disappear into it, perhaps escaping in the confusion. There are hidden tunnels in the bowels of the palace, and amongst them, a hidden room with supplies I readied long ago.

Khallan's hand comes under my chin. "Look, my love. See who comes to bring your destruction." I cease my squirming, the blood freezing in my veins.

Snow White emerges from the fog, her head held high, eyes flashing with victory. Her gold skirts flare around her legs as she moves, the navy bodice decorated with gilded embroidery fitting her like a glove. A white collar circles the back of her neck, and blue and red puffed sleeves embrace her arms like lovers while a navy cape flows behind her. At her back rises the manticore, pacing behind her like a guardian, its eyes locked hungrily on mine.

"I killed you," I snarl, smashing my head back into Khallan's nose. His arms loosen, and I break free. Odin's wolves immediately circle me as I try to step away, their lips pulled back, teeth bared in vicious snarls. My soul shrivels, realizing I have not one ally. I swing my gaze around frantically, but there is nowhere left to go. Throwing my cape over my shoulder, I straighten my shoulders, pretending to be more confident than I am.

This is my last chance.

Throwing my arms out, I fire the last of my reserves at the princess. But it never reaches her. Silas appears out of nowhere, diving in front of his daughter. The death magic strikes him in the chest and bursts into blue flames, quickly engulfing him. He stands stock-still for a second, staring at me, then jerkily turns. "For. . . give me," he groans, crashing to the ground. Silas raises his arm toward Snow White, an eerie scream ripping from deep within. The flesh burns from his body before reducing his bones to ash, his burned crown all that remains of him.

Tossing my head back, I smirk at Snow. If I have to die today, at least I have taken one final thing from her.

The king is dead. Long live the queen.

Chapter 41

Snow White

A barrage of emotions swell inside me, more than I can handle at this moment. I can't afford to feel them now. Tomorrow. Tomorrow I will mourn for all that was lost, for all that could have been. My grief is not for Morana's eyes. I will not give her the satisfaction of knowing how deeply I feel, how easily she can cut me.

Lifting my gaze from my father's ashes, I school my expression into one of haughty disdain. I say nothing, just glare at her as if she is nothing more than an insect. She bares her teeth, all but daring me to do my worst.

If it wasn't for the fact that he's currently standing about fifteen feet tall, I would have almost forgotten Odin's presence, he's been so quiet. "I can take care of this," he offers, but I shake my head.

I haven't told anyone of my plan, not even Cassian. Not wanting anyone to try to talk me out of it, I've kept it to myself. Morana has been the cause of more heartache, more evil, and more destruction than anyone I know. Killing her is too kind. She deserves to suffer for what she's done. And I refuse to have the stain of her death on my soul. Killing her means she wins.

"Like you could do anything," she spits with narrowed eyes. "Who are you? Nothing but a cowering little princess, whose own father defiled her." Lifting my chin, I allow my eyes to glow. She steps back with a gasp, coming to a halt when the wolves grab her dress in their teeth and snarl at her. "What are you?"

I ignore her. I'll speak when I'm ready. Snapping my fingers, the wall of fog dissipates, leaving the palace in full view. I lift my arm, palm up, fingers flat. The earth shudders under our feet, and the palace breaks free of its foundations. "Mirror," I chant, my voice carrying over the field. Morana's eyes widen, her head shaking back and forth. "Mirror." The palace rises into the air. Ten feet, twenty, thirty. "On the wall."

"No!" Morana screams, her face twisting with a mix of hatred and fear.

I bring my fingers to my palm, my nails biting into the flesh. The castle explodes, a cloud of dust and fire shooting into the sky before imploding back in on itself and disappearing with a wink. A smirk flits across my lips as I stare into Morana's eyes. "*I* will be the fairest of them all."

Tiny puffs of magic leak from her, vanishing instantly. Her resulting wail grates on my nerves, and she sways against the hold the wolves have on her. Her hands come to her face, the trembling fingers patting it as it seems to melt away, revealing the woman behind the mask. *Ravensly.*

"Just do it," she hisses. "Kill me. If you don't, I will come back, again and again. I will destroy you and your children and their children after them."

"I'm not going to kill you." She freezes, staring at me as if I'm crazy. Maybe I am. "You wanted to be the most powerful woman alive. You wanted to live forever, to be the paragon of beauty."

I flick my wrist. Ravensly shrieks as she shrinks by several inches. Her back bows slightly and her chin lengthens, becoming more pronounced. Heavy eyebrows replace delicately arched ones and her nose grows large and bulbous. Her hair whitens and her teeth grow crooked. The fine clothes vanish, replaced by a tatty dress, worn boots, and a hooded cloak. She now resembles the old woman from the village.

A round bronze disk forms under her feet, trapping her in place. Liquid metal rises from the disk, sliding over her boots. It takes her a moment to realize what's happening, and when she does, she curses me. "You will pay for this, Snow White!"

"You wanted eternal life," I reply calmly as the bronze moves up her legs and over her hips. "And now you shall. Your punishment for your evil is to become a living statue. You shall tire but never sleep. Hunger but never eat. Thirst but never drink. Yearn but never be loved. You shall watch as I become queen and marry Cassian, see our children at play. You will witness the kingdom heal from your atrocities. You will be forever, and ever more, unwanted, unloved, undesired. Forgotten." The bronze encases her arms and chest, then works its way up her neck. "Goodbye, stepmother." Her face freezes in an ugly snarl, now an embodiment of her wicked heart.

Swallowing, I turn my back on her, withdrawing the rest of the fog and unfreezing the battle. When Morana sent out her blast of magic, it killed all of her creatures—the dragon, skeletons, and the controlled servants. There is no one left for our people to fight. They mill about in confusion, murmuring to themselves.

Aren nudges me, and I quickly scramble onto his back and pull myself to my feet, bracing my legs for balance. Raising my voice so all can hear, I shout, "Morana is defeated!"

A loud cry raises as what is left of our army celebrates the end of her reign of terror. Sliding off Aren's back, wrap my arms around his neck. "Can you shift back?" He licks my cheek, making me giggle, and rushes off into the trees to retrieve his clothes.

I roll my shoulders, pushing back the exhaustion. There are two more things I need to do today, then I can rest.

Hundreds of eyes stare at me as I stand solemnly with Cassian by my side. Odin, at my left, has returned to his normal height. Even the horses are quiet, sensing the somber mood.

I take a deep breath and blow it out slowly. Cassian takes my hand, lending me courage. I search for the right words, but in the end, allow my heart to speak for me. "Today is one of both loss and celebration." Some of the soldiers nod, one or two with a tear in their eye. "We have lost many, and although Morana has been defeated, it is a bittersweet victory. All of us have suffered in some way since she became queen, and I hope her punishment eases a little of your pain."

Many cast their eyes over the statue, then return their attention to me. "I cannot undo the pain she wrought, but I can, at least, do this." I drop Cass's hand, and he steps back. Slowly lowering to my knees, I dig my fingers deep into the soil, my eyes glowing like torches. Osiris warned me that using all my power would relegate me to being a mortal. This is my sacrifice for the kingdom; my demigod status for my country.

This is what Cassian had objected to. His need to protect me outweighs sense—I could never put something as trivial as a longer lifespan over the good of my country. My people deserve a flourishing kingdom. They deserve peace, prosperity, and continuity.

And what I had to force Cass to understand was that I did not wish to live without him. What is a life of hundreds of years, if most of those are without him? I would rather have one lifetime full of love, than a hundred without. When it is our time, we can be together in the afterlife, or perhaps reincarnate so that our souls might find each other again.

My magic beckons the poison deep in the soil. It seeps into my body, invading every cell. It is vile, disgusting, an oily substance that whispers of death and decay. It fills my senses, tasting of mold and smelling of bile.

I clamp my mouth shut, willing myself to not vomit. More and more of the toxin slithers into me, turning my blood thick and sluggish. My heart pounds frantically, working overtime trying to force the sludge through my veins. *Almost there.* I grow dizzy, swaying, unable to breathe as the poison invades my lungs.

Cassian places his hands on my shoulders, steadying me when I begin to panic. Just when my vision begins to blur and I'm about to pass out, the last dregs leak out of the soil. I rock back, sweat dotting my brow. Cassian's eyes fly wide, and he hauls me to my feet, my knees quivering under my weight. Throwing my head back, I open my mouth wide. The poison pours out of me, a thick roiling black gas, which streams into the air in a black cloud.

I need oxygen. It becomes the sole focus that I cling to. But the poison keeps coming. And coming. Finally, after what seems like eons, the last of it escapes and I haul in jagged breaths, greedily sucking in the cool air. The light in my eyes dims and extinguishes, and my head flops back onto Cass's chest. I wearily tilt it so I can see what's happening. The gas sits above me like a dark cloud, floating silently as if waiting for something.

"Look," Cass remarks, pointing to the ground. A lone tuff of brown grass quivers in the dirt, its base slowly turning green. A gentle breeze picks up and the cloud slowly disperses, disintegrating into nothing. My lips curve into a smile, just as everything goes black.

Chapter 42

Snow White

A lone candle burns on top of the dresser in the corner, providing the barest of light. The deep silence around me suggests the lateness of the hour as I quietly edge myself out of the bed. I stand for a moment, my heart warming as I look down on the man whose very existence brings mine meaning.

After slipping on my shoes and tossing a cloak over my shoulders, I sneak out of the tent. Stars twinkle overhead, and I shiver as a cold breeze ruffles my hair. Pulling my cloak tighter around me, I wander slowly across the field. A string of torches lines the way, and I follow the path they make, a deep sense of melancholy weighing over me. I was going to do this tomorrow, but I don't want an audience.

Tents have been set up across the perimeter of the field, the remains of our army sleeping within. After the burials tomorrow, each group will go their separate ways. After spending months with these people, getting to know them, eating, drinking, and dancing together, I find myself already feeling lonely. A deep sigh works from me as my shoulders slump.

The Valkyries will return to Valhalla, along with Odin, Baldr, and Thor. The dwarfs will return to their mountain and the villagers and farmers to their respective homes. The army will depart for Alba and Prince Khallan to the Fae.

Emotion clogs my throat, and I blink away the mist in my eyes. I am foolish to mourn over such things. I am the queen now and have a country to rule, there won't be time for drinking in inns and dancing beside bonfires. And it's not as if I won't still have Cassian. If he agrees, that is.

Coming to the end of the path, I pull to a stop, counting the bodies lined up before me. Ninety-two. I know it could have been so much worse; we could have lost everyone. Someone has mercifully covered them, and I am grateful for that. I slide around to the first one, laying two fingers on their head.

I spend a moment with each person, head bowed, thanking them and wishing their souls peace in the next life. Tears stream down my face and my breath shudders, but I don't stop, not until I come to the end. My father's crown sits on top of a large rock, burned and warped from the fire. Alaric's skull rests at the base, ever protecting his king, even in death.

Sinking to my knees, I wrap my arms tightly around my middle, low keening sobs racking my chest. I cry for the father I wish I could have had, the one Silas never was. I weep for the little girl desperate for her father's approval and for the pain and suffering she was forced to endure at his hands. I sob for the man who, at the very end, sacrificed himself for me.

An immeasurable amount of time passes and when the well runs dry, I wipe my eyes on my sleeves. "I forgive you, Father. I pray Osiris has mercy on you and you can join Momma in Aaru." Pulling myself to my feet, I sigh and run my fingertips over the edge of the crown. "Goodbye, Papa."

A weight lifts from my shoulders, and with one last look, I turn back to my tent. There is still one more thing I need to do today.

Cassian sleeps sprawled out like a starfish, his thick thigh on top of the blanket. My lips spread into a smile at the sight. I quietly remove my cloak and dress, laying them over the back of a chair before kicking off my shoes. Clad only in my chemise, I crawl into bed, snuggling into Cass. He pulls me into his arms, murmuring, "Where did you go?"

Tucking myself firmly under his chin, I wrap my arms around his waist, craving his warmth. "To say goodbye."

"Are you okay?"

I let out a breath and nod against him. "I've made my peace."

"Good." He runs an absentminded hand over my back, making me shiver. "We won today."

"Yes."

"And you kept your promise."

I pull back and peer up at him, the corner of my mouth lifting. "I did."

"Mmph."

I snort. Looks like it's going to be up to me. "Cassian of Valderán, son of Alaric, Prince of Granton. I have loved you every second of my life. You have been my protector, my best friend, my confidant, and my lover. There is no me without you. Will you tie your life to mine, become my king consort, and stand forever by my side?"

Cass brushes his fingers over my cheek, his eyes searching mine before he dips his head and softly kisses my lips. The gesture has my eyes tearing again, but this time with happiness. "You know there is only you, Snow. I could never have another. Yes, I will marry you. I can think of no higher honor."

Long into the night we worship each other, celebrating life and our love. Each touch a promise and a vow.

Tomorrow we will bury our dead and mourn, but then we will look to the future. An endless supply of tomorrows, where our country will rebuild and heal, crops will flourish, and joy and laughter will once more ring out across the kingdom.

"I'll always catch you," Cass whispers in my ear. I wind my hands in his hair, arching against him.

"Always," I agree.

Epilogue

And so the kingdom of Valderán began to heal, faster than anyone could have predicted. By the spring, the land grew green again, and the wildflowers once more danced amongst the tall grasses.

Snow White and Cassian decided against an elaborate coronation and wedding and instead held a small, intimate dual ceremony beneath the blossoms of the apple trees. Osiris himself officiated, and the people agreed that to have a god bless their monarchs' union was fortunate indeed.

For a wedding gift, and in thanks for their aid in freeing her son, Queen Aoife of the Fae gifted them a stunning new palace at the edge of the sea. Rising from the cliffs, the white castle sports a multitude of towers, a perfect warren of halls and corridors for children to play. Some say, on just the right kind of day, the castle appears to be floating in the clouds.

And of children, there were many. Three boys and three girls, each born with their parents' fair looks and Snow White's hazel-gold eyes. The palace rang with laughter and love, and every few years, the family made the long journey to visit the Beast, for he had a soft spot for the children.

As for Morana, her statue was moved to the new palace and set in a walled garden tended to by the nature fairies. It remains there until this very day, forced to watch over the happy family. Legends say that if you dare to get close enough, you can make out her screams.

The king and queen could often be found, much to the amusement of the servants and the consternation of their children, chasing each other gleefully through the meadows surrounding the palace. The people of Valderán rejoiced in their happiness, and a golden age of peace and prosperity followed their reign, beloved by all.

And they, of course, lived happily ever after.

The End

Dear Reader

Thank you so much for reading Shattered Glass! I hope you enjoyed my first foray into paranormal/fantasy. If so, would you please consider leaving an Amazon review? It's the best way to support authors. Thank you!

Acknowledgments

To my beta readers, ARC team, and street teams: Each and every one of you is amazing. I absolutely could not do this without you, and your support and help mean the world to me. Thank you so much!

To Anita: There is not way I would have finished this book without you. Thank you for all the time you spent, the emotional support, and dealing with me. You're a saint!

To Jay: Thank you for another beautiful cover! And the gorgeous map. And the stunning interior paperback design. Your work is incredible, and I'm so lucky you put up with my indecisiveness.

And to my readers, without who I would not be able to do this.

About the Author

A former Californian, Michaella now lives in bonny Scotland. When she isn't discreetly checking out men in kilts or chasing the wild haggis through the glens, you can find her skulking around the online bookish community. A cat mom and avid reader, she spends her days reading, writing, reviewing, promoting, and supporting authors. In fact, if it's not book related, she's probably not doing it.

She has an unhealthy attachment to Mexican food and margaritas (which lamentably are in short supply in Scotland), regularly has to tell her characters to keep their voices down, and even has to spank them into submission on occasion. Since most of them enjoy that anyway, she feels no guilt whatsoever.

She loves hearing from her readers, and would love for your to join her on Instagram or her Facebook reader's group.

Instagram: a_bookish_lass
Facebook Group: Michaella Dieter's Dark Demons Reader's Group
Email: author.michaella.dieter@gmail.com

Printed in Great Britain
by Amazon